UNSCRUPULOUS

MORGAN LEE WYLIE

First Sisu Publishing Edition, 2018
Print ISBN: 978-1-7324853-0-3
eBook ISBN: 978-1-7324853-1-0

Book cover design by www.ebooklaunch.com
Golden Whiskey licensed from OlegVoznyy
Sell Your Soul used with permission from Christopher Hansen

Published in the United States of America

For my heroes:
The loners, losers, outcasts, and underdogs

1

Maybe it was his daddy's blue eyes…

The bordello was not an establishment for lengthy propositions or discriminating tastes. Josiah Wyland entered with a swirl of red Arizona dust and the scent of manure through a doorway where the batwings had been ripped off and never replaced. He scanned the interior even as his eyes adjusted to the relative dark of the oil lamps. The dimness was populated with cowboys and gamblers, honest men and outlaws, some up on their luck and some down. They came to drink and they came for companionship—each other's and that of the painted ladies. The bar to his left stretched as long as Josiah's shadow across worn wooden planks. It was marred mahogany scavenged from a derelict saloon and polished by a row of men's elbows. At the tables to his right, cards were shuffled night and day as the games moved more legal tender than Wells Fargo. The second level curved like a horseshoe over the bar and tables. A charred oaken banister, rescued from the fire-ravaged remains of some grandiose hotel, lined the balcony that gave access to a half-dozen rooms. Up and down the staircase, prostitutes led a continuous parade.

Most men didn't glance up at the newcomer. Those that did quickly looked away. Josiah Wyland was known. When he had surveyed the crowd and was satisfied no man meant him any immediate trouble, Josiah turned his attention to the women. His scrutiny discovered one who looked as though she couldn't afford to refuse him. He approached her, gave a nod toward the stairs, and followed her up.

The small room barely fit the bed and was muggy from frequent use. Only a gauzy curtain guarded against the desert sun, and everything in the place appeared faded, including the whore. She wasn't so very old, yet the freshness of youth had dried up, leaving a tired, vanquished look about her. She stripped, lay on the bed, opened her legs, and waited. He undressed with little more enthusiasm than she, piling his garments in a chair in the corner, hanging his six-guns on the back. When he crawled atop her, she turned her head toward the wallpaper peeling in brittle curls and shadowed with the ghosts of purple flowers.

Josiah positioned himself between her spread thighs, moistened his tip along her ready slit and with a glance at her profile, shoved into her. An involuntary garble sounded in her throat as her body strained to accommodate his swell. Though he was deep inside her, she wouldn't look at him. Maybe it was the smell of miles in the saddle, being sweated by the sun. Or the scars that pocked and puckered his face. Perhaps the size of his cock was offensive or its crooked curvature. Or his reputation—maybe she had scruples, this harlot. All he knew was that she wasn't the first woman to be repulsed by Josiah Wyland, and she wouldn't be the last.

That precedent had been set by his mother who had, after one look at her newborn son, refused anything to do with him. Josiah couldn't recall who had told him or when—it was just one of the things he knew. So it was a whore who had nursed him, a whore he paid to take his virginity at fifteen, and a whore he went to whenever he came into town.

This whore wasn't handsome. Her appeal was her willingness to take his money and allow him to exhaust the need that had built over solitary weeks in the wilderness. He sought to temper it quickly, as they were both sinking into the mushy mattress and the space only grew hotter. She gripped a brass spindle of the headboard with one hand and with the other, clutched soggy and threadbare sheets. He angled above her with elbows locked and fists buried in the dilapidated cushion. An arid breeze stirred the curtain but didn't breach the confines of the room. Perspiration trickled between his shoulder blades and ran in rivulets along his spine. It dripped off his nose to splash upon freckled breasts. Wet skin slipped along wet skin and slapped with each thrust. Her scent was a sticky sweetness on the back of his tongue. He turned his head and spat at the floor to be rid of it. He tried to concentrate on the dusty-rose nipples floating on pink flesh, on his retreat and plunge into russet curls. But his focus kept coming back to her averted face.

Josiah drove her harder, until his entire body was intent on culmination, chasing that primal promise. Each muscle tensed down his back, up through his belly and chest. His body craved physical release. His soul starved for something more. He didn't know how to persuade her to look at him, so he closed his eyes and let go. His rhythm broke into a punishing pace impossible to rein in, like a full-out downhill gallop. He heard her breath hiss through gritted teeth, heard the bed shriek and the floor groan, and heard his own rasping pant.

With one final, desperately savage thrust, he pinned her to the mattress. A glimpse of life and a touch of death—Josiah never knew if it was victory or defeat, it felt like neither and it felt like both. What filled him drained away, flooding her. He kept his eyes shut a moment longer, wanting to leech some lasting satisfaction from the fleeting sensations, capture some sense of fulfillment that would not fade to obscurity in the time it took him to dress. Choppily, he exhaled. His chin dipped to his sternum and damp, dirty hair fell about his face.

Josiah backed off her, his three dollars and her service spent. She stayed sprawled over the twisted linens, her expression pinched, still watching the wallpaper. He wiped his face then his cock on a dry corner of sheet and swallowed the urge to spit again. He fitted himself back into dusty trousers, tugged on boots, and fastened belt with twin .45 short-barrels around pointed hips. When he reached for his shirt, he caught a glimpse of himself in the mirror. The man was as dingy as the glass, except for startling blue eyes that were hard and cold. He knew they were the eyes of a scoundrel who'd swung for rape twenty-some years past. The villain had forfeited his life for a minute's pleasure stolen on a drunken whim, his seed nary a consideration. From a father he'd never met, who'd known naught of him, Josiah inherited a name, a vile reputation, and those piercing, impenetrable eyes. Avoiding the gaze, he shrugged into his shirt, not bothering with buttons as the cotton plastered to him. He dropped a few creased and soiled bills upon the stained sheets, snatched up his hat, and left without a backward glance.

***

Each time Aimee came into Prospect, it seemed a different town. The sprawling settlement grew daily, fed by the mineral wealth being harvested from the surrounding hills. There was always a new cantina or boarding house springing up and an influx of people to fill it. Only time would tell townsfolk from transients, and the boom attracted as many bad bodies as good. A woman walking alone might fret to meet any number of disreputable men and yearn to see a familiar face. Aimee preferred the strangers, and the man she most dreaded to encounter was not a ruffian, desperado, or tramp, but the sheriff — her husband.

She kept off the plank walkways that lined the main thoroughfare, taking instead a parallel street that ran behind a long stretch of businesses, all anonymous from the back. The red dirt rouged the hem of her skirt, and the desert heat radiated off the splintered boards in prickling waves. Her pace was brisk and her posture rigid. With each step, she came up on her toes in an unconscious and fruitless effort to counter her diminutive size. She wore the practical, everyday dress of a farmer's daughter — calico, straight-skirted, and long-sleeved. Wheat-colored with fine apricot striping and matching buttons, it was her best. The pinkish-yellow bonnet did as much to conceal her features from recognition as to shield them from the sun.

Aimee dared to make her errand once a fortnight. After the constancy and seclusion of home, her usual route always made a rudely spectacular gauntlet for the senses. The stench of urine marked the alley between a brothel and one of the ever-increasing number of saloons. Above her, mismatched curtains fluttered in the windows of the rooms where fallen women entertained lonely men. Aimee kept her face forward and her eyes focused ahead. Though there was nothing to see, it wouldn't do to be caught looking. Yet, traitorously curious ears strained to catch a sound — a breathless endearment, an involuntary grunt, the squeak of a bed spring. A decent woman would never have occasion to set foot in such a place, and Aimee was appropriately shocked by the thought of what transpired within, of intimacy betwixt strangers and wife's duty turned to enterprise.

But still she wondered — it was a childhood trait, innocent in a girl, not quite proper in a lady, that she had failed to outgrow. She'd seen the prostitutes about town — how some slunk and others strutted, how some wore rags and others Parisian-inspired designs of silk no woman Aimee knew could afford, how some seemed caged by destitution and others boldly independent. Aimee once pondered whether her husband partook of bought women. But she'd come to understand that stimulation and gratification for Rook Kelly were found in a different arena than the boudoir, achieved through means other than the sensual. He seemed immune to the temptations that weakened other men, oblivious to the baser drives of the male gender. To her relief and shame, he hadn't even deigned to consummate their marriage.

Any indication of human mating within the bordello was drowned out by a commotion of an equine nature across the street at the livery. A huge black stallion stamped around the corral, flaunting his virility and unsettling the mares in an adjacent pen. His rippling coat was sleek and shiny like wet ink, and when he tossed his head, the flies scattered like droplets flung wide. His eyes gleamed and his nostrils flared. Not wild but not tame—unbroken. Aimee imagined it would take a fearsome man to sit him, one of kindred spirit. She shivered and was unsure if she felt admiration or aversion.

She had almost reached her destination. Another, cleaner alley separated the doctor's office and general store. Motes of dust twinkled in the sunlit corridor. Aimee turned into it just as a man's form filled the gap at the other end. She spun back around but not before glimpsing the deputy sheriff's badge pinned to his vest. She side-stepped out of his line-of-sight and flattened herself against the store's rear wall. The wood seared through the back of her dress and was scratchy against her palms. The bonnet's brim blocked her peripheral vision, so Aimee stared down at the dust-powdered toes of her shoes. The man was whistling. She heard his steps come to the end of the alley, pivot, and move away. When she dared tilt her head, she saw him strolling toward the stables, flourishing a branding iron like a sabre. Aimee escaped between the buildings. When she stepped out onto the boardwalk, into the main street bustle, her knees still quivered. Before she could duck into the storefront, a familiar voice accosted her. "Mrs. Kelly, is that you?"

Manners dictated Aimee force a smile and turn to face the doctor's wife. "Mrs. Finch, how do you do?" She suppressed the impulse to fidget as the older woman stepped close, looking her over. She knew the shrewd perception those kindly eyes could wield. She strived to not let her pleasant expression falter under the astute assessment.

"Dear, are you all right?" The genuine concern in Mrs. Finch's voice portended a delay Aimee couldn't afford. Bouts of childhood illness had well-acquainted her with the persistence of the matron's generous intentions. "Have you come to see the doctor?"

"I'm quite well," Aimee assured her, pushing the words up a parched throat. The other woman squinted at her. Aimee explained she had only a small errand to run.

"With your disposition? In this heat?" Mrs. Finch glanced uncertainly at the alley from whence Aimee came. "Without an escort?" Aimee realized her concern had shifted from health to propriety. "I have a mind to chide our good sheriff for not taking better care with his young wife."

Aimee clasped her hands together. "Oh, please do not mention it," she said. "I only wanted to get something extra for supper."

The other woman's lips curved in a knowing and sympathetic smile. "Do not worry so, dear." Mrs. Finch placed a hand over hers. "A mistake in the kitchen will happen occasionally, and for a new wife, such a forgivable offense."

Aimee said, "And Rook has so much on his mind with the coming election."

"You can tell Sheriff Kelly to rest easy about his appointment. He's proven himself an able lawman despite his youthful hell-raising. We've seen far less trouble than the surrounding counties, and his choosing to settle down proves long-term dedication."

"That's good to hear," said Aimee, half-listening as she searched for some excuse to get away. Mrs. Finch finally relinquished Aimee's hand with a gentle pat.

"And if it's a treat you're after, Mr. Brown has just gotten a shipment of apples," she said. "They'd make a lovely pie."

Aimee was thanking her when a trio of riders halted in the street beside them. "Howdy, ladies." They wore the biggest hats Aimee had ever seen and chaps made of some shaggy hide. The youngest of the three winked at her. They said that they were looking for a place called The Old Mare but having no luck since most of the shanties had no signs to tell one from another. Beside her, Mrs. Finch scowled at them. Aimee didn't know if it was the interruption, the interlopers, or the inquiry that irritated her. She told Aimee to go on into the store, out of the sun. Aimee didn't dally.

With wits and nerves frayed, she moved through the store, directly to the post desk at the rear. She carefully removed an envelope from her pocket and smoothed it with small, damp hands. She'd lost track of how many letters she'd sent over the past six months. All her hopes went with each and as of yet, each had gone unanswered. Aimee said a silent prayer, paid the ten cents she'd snuck from her husband, and sent it on its way.

****

Tyler Malloy pulled the brim of his hat lower, slouched in his seat, and watched the gunslinger trudge downstairs to the bar. He had a heavy tread for a thin man, but Tyler knew it would be a mistake to assume Josiah Wyland the least bit slow. But for an uncommon height and the shooting irons perched on each hip, his appearance was that of a regular saddle bum. His clothing was sweat-stained and rumpled from slumbering among snakes. Exposure had turned his skin to gritty leather, and his mangy brown hair looked like he used a Bowie knife rather than visit a barber. The sight of him made Tyler itch. There was a slight hunch to his shoulders that belied the nature of his profession—the man was a renowned predator. Patrons gave him a wide berth and eyed him warily. Wyland hooked a thumb in his belt, draped long fingers over the ivory grip of one scroll-engraved Peacemaker, and eyed them back. Tyler wanted to evade coming under that icy gaze. He'd be no help to his brother if he got himself recognized and hauled into the jailhouse or recognized and shot on sight.

***

Josiah slapped a quarter onto the counter and ordered whiskey to wash away the last of the sweetness cloying the back of his throat. Finding it as mediocre as the woman, he pocketed his short-bit in change. There was a painting behind the bar of an unclad beauty with lithe and milky limbs astride a horse. Josiah's eyes passed over it and settled on the inscription above: *An old mare rides as well as a young filly*. He took a moment to decipher each word. Josiah had spent a year inside Yuma Prison and learned two things. One was the value of freedom. The other was to read and write.

Though he had only come into Prospect that morning, Josiah was keen to be on his way. He'd already stocked up on ammunition and air-tights, as well as feed for his horse. Had he received payment for his latest bounty, he would already be cutting a path out of town. Instead he was delayed at the convenience of his employer, the sheriff Rook Kelly. Josiah claimed the seat at the end of the bar, rotated his back to the wall, and set to waiting.

***

Three strangers entered the brothel. All wore tall-crowned hats on their heads and six-guns at their sides. They shouldered their way through the crowd, up to the bar. One took the stool beside Tyler, and the others huddled around the first. Tyler reckoned by their hair pants that they came from farther north—down out of Colorado, perhaps. One man had a mustache and dark, close-set eyes. Another was portly, with a rash of orange freckles. The man seated next to Tyler was young, about the age Tyler had been when he and Trace left home—two farm boys hungry for adventure, eager to prove themselves men, and unable to imagine the changes to come whilst they were away.

The ten-gallon trio ordered three drinks and a fourth for Tyler. He nodded his thanks for the courtesy then nearly choked on his whiskey when the youth offered to show Tyler his hardware. Without awaiting his answer, the kid pulled the Schofield from its place along his thigh and proceeded to explain how he had sweetened the revolver by filing a notch in the hammer. "It about fires with a thought," the kid said. Tyler noticed he carried the gun fully-loaded. In a hushed voice, the younger man imparted the secret that he put talcum powder in the holster to quicken his draw. "Slicker than a whore's cunt," he insisted with a wink.

His rotund confederate told the bartender they were all "shootists," come to advance their reputations by laying down some of the territory's crack gunmen. They were on the lookout for Silas and Jerrod Kelly, and for Josiah Wyland. Tyler and the old bar dog shared an uneasy look.

"Say, ain't that him?" said Mustache, lifting his chin to peer over the sea of Stetsons afloat in a haze of cigar smoke. "Ain't that

Wyland?" Porky leaned out over the counter and the kid sat taller on his stool.

"That yonder scarecrow?" The kid guffawed. "Feller's ugly as a mud fence."

"Looks a bit mellow," said Porky. "He been irrigating long?"

The bartender ignored the question. Wyland and the Kelly gang might be the scourge of the territory, but they still belonged to the territory, as legendary in Arizona as the O.K. Corral. Tyler reckoned the old man wasn't about to disown a local hero—even a villainous one—to outsiders. He also reckoned the gunfighter didn't need the help. In Wyland's profession, survival meant you didn't let your guard down. The threesome was far too conspicuous to have escaped those striking blue eyes. Under his breath, the barkeep warned, "Raise that devil and you'll find he's not so easy to bed down."

The kid smirked. "Them devils are never so black as they're painted."

"Wyland's the exception." The bartender moved away, having the excuse of seeing to other customers. Tyler wished he too were at a greater distance.

"Old croaker," the kid said with a snicker.

***

There was a reason why Josiah preferred not to linger too long in any particular town or tarry in a place prone to barroom brawls: he didn't want to have to shoot his way out. His reputation deterred most men from crossing him. But some it attracted, like a challenge, daring them to test their mettle against his. Josiah recognized the three strangers as subscribing to that stripe. He didn't know the reason for their interest. Maybe they figured they had a score to settle with him. Maybe they wanted to make names for themselves. He didn't much care for the reason, only the result—if they wanted to have a fight, he would meet them. But their timing bothered him. It was nigh unto suppertime and Josiah had an invitation—more of a summons—to dine with the sheriff. He reckoned he'd better not be tardy if he wanted his payment.

***

"What's your thought, friend?" said Porky, turning to Tyler. "He as curly as they say?"

Mustache said, "Do you know, does he use his left or his right?"

Tyler said, "Both."

"Which is his better?"

"Both." Truth was Tyler hadn't seen him shoot since Wyland, the Kelly brothers, and the Malloy boys had been kids together. They'd all grown up in the vicinity of a small agricultural community called Promise. The Kellys' father had been town marshal. The Malloy family had owned a small farm. And Wyland was just there, left to survive by hook or crook.

The boys would often get together and make a contest of shooting at cans. Wyland had been the fastest of them, and the most accurate. They were all between hay and grass then, before the Gila overflowed and washed out Promise, before the silver mine and Prospect boomed, before Wyland shot and killed a man. The orphan had earned his board guarding sheep and cattle against coyotes and wolves, learning to shoot a rifle by his fifth year. When his repertoire extended to pistols, most figured it was only a matter of time until he advanced to rustlers or joined them. Wyland left the area three years ahead of him and Trace. In the time since, Tyler hadn't seen a man quicker on the draw. And to hear it told, the wiry crack-shot had only gotten deadlier.

The kid said, "Is it true that crows follow him wherever he goes?"

"Crows, jackals, the occasional boar," said the barkeep with a smile for Tyler.

***

Josiah couldn't recall ever being asked to share a meal with anyone. As a small child, he'd gotten scraps at back doors like other strays. A little later, food came as part of his pay, given to him to eat in the outbuildings where he'd slept. Most days he ate out of a can. Beyond the lure of hot chow and the bounty he was owed, supper with Rook Kelly didn't hold much appeal. He'd bet his guns Rook had some task to assign him the sheriff's office couldn't officially condone. But why gussy it up with the pretext of a social rendezvous, much less make good with the fixings, Josiah couldn't answer. He didn't feel obligated to clean up any, and left the brothel stinking of whiskey, sex, and a whore's perfume.

***

Tyler resisted the urge to turn and get a better look at the gunslinger when Wyland passed behind him. The three pistoleers didn't exercise the same caution. Porky said, "By the looks of his face, someone mistook him for a buzzard."

The kid laughed. "By the smell of him, I'd say he's buzzard bait and just don't know it yet." They ordered another round then the trio bid Tyler so long.

***

14

Aimee's letter, though mere paper, was such a burden to carry with the weight of all her hope within and the threat of discovery without, that by the time she entrusted it to the post master, she was exhausted. She would wait two weeks, then undergo the task again. For the present, she had other labors to test her. First, she must return home.

She left the store with a bundle of apples cradled in her arms, charged to her husband's account, to make good her excuse for coming to town. She retraced her steps, back down the alley and along the blank backs of buildings across from the livery where the black horse pricked up his ears and watched her go by.

She began to fret she had been away too long, that Mrs. Finch would let slip their encounter, that Rook already suspected, already knew. And in the back of her mind, she worried who her husband had invited to their home. He hadn't divulged a name. He'd only given the secretive, tight-lipped smile she found charming in courtship but had learned was strictly a sign of his own amusement.

Aimee discerned much about Rook Kelly in the year since they'd wed. The ambitious new county sheriff had been an attentive suitor, a distraction from the sorrow of her parents passing and a reassurance in the resulting isolation. But his demeanor was revealed as one of contained volatility, such that his wife could neither predict nor avert his displeasure. He had a simmering temper, meticulous cunning, and patient cruelty. Aimee found his calm moods the most dangerous. It was his watchful, calculating disposition at breakfast that had her dreading the evening to come.

As Aimee approached the alley between brothel and saloon, she noticed, out of the corner of her eye, that it was occupied. She heard a prolonged splatter and realized a man was relieving his bladder in the shade. She quickened her pace.

***

Josiah caught her scent. After leaving the bordello, he'd rounded the corner to take a piss. Amidst the pungent stench of the alley and the earthy odor of the livery, came the fresh and subtle scent of clean woman. He swiveled his head around in time to glimpse the cream of her skirt before she was eclipsed by the building. Then the hint of her was gone and Josiah was left standing with dripping appendage in hand. He shook and stuffed it away.

He buttoned and tucked his shirt. Then he slid out a revolver, opened the loading gate, and added a cartridge to the empty chamber. He returned gun to holster, leaving the six-shooter half-cocked. He did the same with the other. He looked back toward the street along which the woman had walked. His horse waited in the corral catty-corner to the gap between buildings. Josiah debated the wisdom of engaging in a gunfight in Rook Kelly's town. But he'd rather face a threat than leave it to dog his heels or shoot him in the back. He decided if he had to beef a man—or three—and disrupt the peace in Prospect, it was on Kelly for not having ponied up earlier when Josiah turned over his prisoner.

2

Trace Malloy had seen the inside of a few jailhouses. He had cooled his heels in a cell after a bender a time or two. A night in the pokey might even have spared him and his brother real trouble in at least one town. Trace had never taken umbrage at a stay—but he resented being locked in Rook Kelly's calaboose like all get-out.

He sat on the edge of a lumpy cot with his boots planted wide, elbows on his knees, and hands together. He skimmed one rough palm over the other then reversed the motion. "You can't keep me here," Trace said to the man standing on the other side of the bars, thinking by good rights their positions ought to be opposed. "I've broken no law."

Rook carefully refolded the letter he'd twice perused. He slipped it into his vest pocket and slanted his gaze down upon his prisoner. "You came to steal my wife from me."

Trace's hazel eyes narrowed. "Might be I just wanted to see her," he said. "Talk to her."

Rook shook his head and patted his pocket. Aimee sent a damsel's plea for rescue, and the ever-valiant Trace had heeded the call. The cowboy was trying hard to keep his dander down, to reason with Rook. He was out of his element. Subterfuge was Rook's game, and the eldest Malloy was too righteous for cunning.

Trace always thought the middle Kelly—shrewder and slighter than his brothers—cut to be a cardsharp. He imagined him as the mastermind behind the Kelly band's criminal escapades. It cocked Trace's hat to hear tell that Rook had gone straight, become a lawman—until he considered the wealth to be gained collecting taxes, the power Rook would enjoy over the general populace, and the distinction from his brothers the lesser known Kelly would covet.

When Trace and Tyler crossed the county line into Sheriff Kelly's bailiwick, they'd found his bloodhound waiting. Trace reckoned Rook had expected the brothers to resist and give him an excuse to detain them. Trace was certain Wyland had been dumbfounded when he promptly surrendered. Rook had no legitimate cause to arrest him and would inevitably have to let him go. According to plan, Tyler would be hiding out in Prospect, keeping tabs on Wyland and awaiting Trace's release.

"Where'd you get your horse?"

Trace blinked at the question. Rook's eyes glinted like obsidian. Trace felt them dissecting him. "I bought him in Texas."

"Have you a bill of sale?"

Trace scowled. "In my saddle bag."

Rook shook his head. "Your bag was inventoried." Trace's scowl deepened. Rook shrugged. "But I can confirm the sale when I inquire into the brand."

"He ain't branded."

Whistling accompanied the knock of footsteps out front of the jailhouse. The door opened and a deputy poked his head in. Rook glanced at him over his shoulder. The deputy nodded and closed the door again. Rook turned back to Trace and smiled slowly. "He is now."

The implication struck like a kick from a bangtail. Trace saw red. He bounded to his feet and seized an iron bar in each fist as if he could tear his way out of the cage. "You snake." His eyes radiated indignation. Rook didn't flinch. "Is that how you got Aimee to marry you?" Trace's voice went husky with rage. "Courted her with lies?"

Rook's smile slipped. One eyebrow arched in irritation. "Gratitude," he said, softly. "She was all alone but for me." He actually stepped closer, within Trace's reach. "How long since you'd been back, sent word?" He raised his chin. "How much longer would it have been had her letter not found you?"

Trace's jaw remained clenched, but some of the fire faded from his eyes. "False evidence won't fool Judge Cooper."

"Cooper retired. Three years ago. Judge Foster makes the circuit now," said Rook. "And my marriage to Aimee has nothing to do with you."

Trace said, "Her divorcing you won't have a thing to do with me either."

"Foster ought to be through Prospect in about four months. You'll get your day in court then." Rook saw the golden flicker in Trace Malloy's eyes. He couldn't resist stoking it once more. "Of course, if your brother tries to break you out of here in the meantime, then I'll have him too."

***

Tyler anticipated lying low in a brothel would be far more comfortable than confinement in a louse-infested cell. He assumed tailing a former outlaw would be easier than trying to match wits with a lawman. He changed his opinion on both counts. While the coffin varnish he'd been drinking was beginning to give him a bellyache, he suspected his brother was enjoying a nice cozy nap. He decided Rook Kelly's duplicity couldn't be more dangerous than Wyland's duel cannons and the only woman The Mare could boast worth a feller's notice was the nude on the wall. With Wyland taking his leave and the trio trailing out in his wake, Tyler took a moment to appreciate that he might've been a bystander, casualty, or reluctant participant to a shoot-in. Next time, he'd opt for the lice.

Since he still had a task to see to, Tyler pushed to his feet. He reckoned the safest way to confirm that Wyland left town was to check the livery for the black behemoth the gunslinger rode in on. He could steal back the paint Rook's deputies confiscated from Trace while he was at it. Tyler had imagined it would be great fun to orchestrate a jailbreak should his brother not be able to talk his way out from behind bars, especially since Trace was usually the one getting Tyler out a fix. But he changed his thinking about that too. Tyler was ready to collect Aimee and high-tail it out of Prospect. He tipped the bartender and exited through the always-open doorway onto the boardwalk. Turning, he came face-to-face with Josiah Wyland.

Tyler watched recognition flash like blue lightning in the gunfighter's eyes. He reckoned he could reach for the sky and join Trace in jail or make a play for his revolver and hope he was the one left standing. It occurred to him though he'd practiced on countless cans and shot plenty of varmints, he'd never truly expected to test his skill against another man. Wyland, on the other hand, was a seasoned man-killer. Tyler also realized he would have to reach across his body to draw his gun, since he wore it butt-forward on his left side for easier access while on horseback. Wyland would shoot from the hip, plucking gun from holster with a flick of his wrist and thumbing hammer on the rise, all in an instant. Tyler had the grim thought he wasn't fast enough to survive Wyland. He didn't doubt his soon-to-be opponent could put a bullet neatly through his heart from a much greater distance than they now stood. But surrender wasn't an option — Trace was counting on him. Tyler had just made the dismal decision to go for his piece when his attention was captured by a queer sight: something resembling a tombstone, sun-bleached bone-white, hovered over Wyland's shoulder. It was one of the ten-gallon hats sticking up out of the crowd.

***

Josiah watched Tyler Malloy's gaze shift. He slid his guns free and was already turning when, from behind him, came the challenge: "Wyland!"

For a span of seconds, there was gunfire. Then three men lay dead on the ground, and the twin Colts were smoking. The kid already had the Schofield loose, ere he hollered. But he wanted Wyland to see his demise coming. Unfortunately for him, Josiah wasn't one to hesitate, especially when facing death. The kid got the shot through the heart that might otherwise have gone to Tyler. Josiah didn't pause long enough for his first enemy to fall before seeking the second and catching him in his peripheral vision, advancing from the street. Mustache took the time to aim, which had likely served him well in other gunfights against other gunfighters, where a steady hand and steely eye typically trumps a trick draw and itchy trigger finger. Only Wyland wasn't another gunfighter and time taken was time wasted in a fight with him. Mustache got the first shot from the second Peacemaker, right between his close-set eyes. Instinct and momentum put the third man in Josiah's line-of-fire as soon as he too, was spotted. The lubber had the advantage of a Bridgeport, except the swivel-rig gave no advantage at all when one didn't have a chance to utilize it. The last of the threesome got two shots, one from each pistol, increasing the likelihood something more than fat was penetrated.

As the crack of gunfire echoed off buildings, bystanders belatedly rushed for the cover of doorways. As the haze of black powder dissipated, Josiah was left standing alone at the edge of the street. Tyler Malloy was nowhere to be seen. Josiah shook out the spent cartridges and reloaded his weapons, five in the wheel. He still didn't know the trio's motive and still didn't much care. He holstered his irons and went to get his horse.

***

"You want to lock up somebody's brother, look to your own."

Trace Malloy had three inches and thirty pounds on Rook Kelly. The blood in his eye might have made a bigger man cower even with the bars between them. Rook only chuckled. He rather relished having Trace imprisoned in his jail, growling with frustration. By Rook's estimation, it was past time the eldest Malloy be cut down a notch.

Even when they were kids, Trace considered himself and Tyler superior to the other boys—to the Kelly boys in particular.

22

Farm work made them stronger, and their bronzed and brawny physiques made them favorites among the Angelicas. Both had light hair bleached fairer by long days under the sun. Rook and his brothers all had black hair, which made it a matter of widespread—albeit discreet—contention as to whether the Kelly line was mixed-blood. Discreet because the eldest, Silas, who possessed a savagery all his own, had once lambasted a man for suggesting he was a half-breed. Raised without a mother, the Kelly brood was considered a bit wild by town standards, whilst the well-mannered Malloy boys had been received as country gentlemen. Peers in school, their differences led to a natural rivalry—first friendly, then less so.

Rook knew when he married Aimee, he'd eventually have to contend with Trace, though he'd hoped to win his reelection before the cowboy rode in on his high horse. Though the Malloy brothers had been away a long time, there were still many who would remember Trace and Tyler as Promise's golden boys, and some who might favor Trace for sheriff. But Prospect was Rook's town. And Aimee was his wife. Presently, he had no intention of giving up either. Past resentments aside, if Tyler attempted to spring his big brother and both Malloys were gunned down in the effort, it would be all the more convenient for Rook Kelly.

As the two men eyed one another with adolescent animosity hardened with maturity, the blast of close gunfire broke into the charged silence. Four shots, by Trace's count, though the last two came so close together as to be almost simultaneous. Both men listened, but there were no more. The deputy poked his head in again and asked if Rook wanted him to investigate. Rook said no, that he'd look into it on his way home. "If you'll excuse me," he said, meeting Trace's hazel glare with a mild, contemptuous smile. "My wife's got supper waiting for me."

Outside, Rook crossed his arms over his chest and surveyed the aftermath of the incident as a ripple of pandemonium swept through the town. Children cried. A spooked horse escaped a hitching post and barreled down the main drag. Some folk barricaded themselves behind flimsy walls and rickety shutters. Others armed and posted themselves in doorways, ready to defend their own. A few minutes passed, and in the absence of any additional excitement, the current of confused chaos gradually dissipated. A newspaper man scurried toward the scene of his next story, down the street to where a small crowd congregated to gawk at the casualties. The rest of Prospect resumed affairs per usual.

For Rook, the event meant paperwork and that he'd be late to supper. He didn't mind the requisite report and normally wouldn't give a damn about the delay in getting home. However, tonight it meant he would miss the initiation of the experiment he had planned between Aimee and Wyland. Rook wanted to gauge their reactions to one another. But a shootout in the middle of the county seat, though not infrequent, was too critical to entrust to a deputy, even if the victims turned out to be no counts. Rook needed to be seen personally handling the investigation. His reputation as sheriff was forged by public perception—it was why he'd taken a wife and why he chose Aimee.

His proposal came only after careful deliberation of the pros and cons associated with the match—that it irked Trace was merely a perk. Aimee hailed from an established family in the area. She had a meek, prairie mouse disposition that endeared her to the townspeople and gave Rook little trouble, excepting the recent discrepancy of her secret correspondence. Perhaps most appealing to him was her fragile physiology and its history that ensured no one would expect Rook to burden his wife with bearing his children. Aimee's only flaw was her naivety, the byproduct of a sheltered upbringing. Rook reasoned that his little wife would never have dared discontentment had she even a slight acquaintance with the evils of the world from which her husband and his station protected her. Rook reckoned an encounter with a man with a reputation like Wyland's should be sufficient to put Aimee securely in her place.

Rook glanced over at his deputy who was clumsily trying to roll a cigarette with too much tobacco, tearing the paper and peppering his suit in the process. Thurman Dawes was a fine brand artist but otherwise lacking in prowess. Rook asked if there'd been any word from the men he had out scouting for Tyler Malloy.

"Jerrod sent Lucas around earlier. All's well at the old Malloy homestead. No sign of little brother," said Dawes. "Silas ain't reported in."

Rook instructed his deputy to shoot first if Tyler showed his face at the jailhouse and to guard Trace but stay out of his reach. "If there's a fire, that cell stays locked," he said. Then Rook strolled off to do his duty.

***

In a two-room cabin on the edge of town, Aimee also heard the shots. Though a common occurrence, the sharp and sudden sound always made her pause. Her marriage had brought her within closer proximity to Prospect than she had lived with her parents, and Aimee was not yet accustomed to the nightly heralding of disputes being settled by way of the gun. She couldn't suppress questioning thoughts—who had fired, who had died, and did she know either? She considered that had she been delayed by Mrs. Finch a few minutes longer, she might have witnessed what the morning paper would dramatize. Had it been a drunken disagreement amongst gamblers? Or a jealous contest to win a woman's favor? Had some outlaw made his final stand against Rook's force, and had her husband dealt with the offender personally or delegated the matter to one of his deputies—men with black pasts, of questionable morals and deadly skills?

Aimee never knew whether it was relief or despair she felt in returning to the safety of her married home. Out of loneliness and fear, she had attached herself to a stranger without knowing what was in his heart, ignoring the warning in her own. Aimee expected she would come to know her husband, come to love him. Instead, she discovered that safety exacted a price. She thought of the prostitutes in town and wondered how she might have fared had she not exchanged freedom for protection.

Aimee tugged at the ribbon securing her bonnet, then tore the garment from her head, releasing a braid that uncoiled down her back. Damp tendrils of flaxen hair curled at her temples and the nape of her neck. Feeling choked, she plucked at the tiny buttons of her dress's high collar.

She'd started a stew simmering before she went to town. The aroma of salt pork, sweet potatoes, and corn hung in the air, along with the bite of the sourdough she'd set to rise, that now ballooned over the rim of the bowl. Aimee told herself it was the heat of the cast iron stove suffocating her, the confines of the small cabin making her feel caged, and the recent gunfire provoking her anxiety. She arranged the apples in a basket—there wasn't time to make a pie—and set them on a white-painted table.

It was a quaint piece intended for tea, a wedding gift from the mayor, catalogue-ordered. Touted to seat four, it barely supported a meal for two. The table in the home where she grew up seated eight and had been built by Aimee's grandfather. Its sturdy surface was utilized for everything from cleaning father's rifle to mother's canning. It had been made for families.

Outside the window, the horizon reddened with the setting sun. Aimee rolled dough into biscuits with small, nervous hands and sprinkled them with crumbs of cheese. The hour grew later and her apprehension grew with it. She slid the pans into the stove. While the bread baked, she set the table with plates and cutlery for three and swept the floor. As she paced the kitchen with a large carving knife in hand and nothing left to slice, she continued to wonder who her husband had invited to supper.

A breath of wind through the window lifted the curtain and whispered along her flushed skin. Though warm, it sent chills down her spine. When a flyaway strand brushed her cheek, Aimee remembered she'd had all her hair hid up under her bonnet. She left the knife on the table and hurried into the bedroom to tidy it. Her fingers raced to braid the hair anew, threading long locks over and under one another. She had just pulled the golden mass over her shoulder to finish when she smelled the bread burning.

***

The desert breeze increased to a hot wind by the time Josiah hitched his horse to a fence outside the Kelly home. There was a heaviness to the air that suggested rain and an energy that promised it wouldn't come gently. Dusk had fallen, and the cabin was bright beyond the white curtain. He watched a shadow move across it.

Josiah made his way around to the front porch. The wooden planks creaked under his tread. He struck the door with the heel of his hand and distant thunder rumbled like an echo. He thought about striking out ahead of the storm, skipping town and supper both. A glance over his shoulder showed the squall coming fast, swallowing up stars as it devoured the night sky. Josiah could already smell the hot meal the summons had promised. As his mouth watered, he wondered who cooked for the sheriff. Then he recalled that Rook Kelly was married.

***

Aimee held her breath, listening to the plodding steps, knowing they didn't belong to her husband. She was on her knees in front of the blazing stove, snatching the better biscuits from the heat, dropping them into the net made by her apron, and shaking her smarting fingers after each save. At the knock, she bobbled one and it hit the floor. She rose, resigning the rest to the cast iron inferno. She shook the buns into a second basket on the table and brushed crumbs from her apron. When she turned toward the door, she swayed as the room seemed to shrink and swirl around her. She sucked in a steadying breath and swiped perspiring hands over her skirt. Then she crept across the room. Aimee reached for the latch, hesitating when the knock boomed once more. She bent her head, closed her eyes, said a silent prayer, and opened the door.

3

Josiah heard the latch being drawn back. The door cracked open and a finger of light reached out. He looked down at the top of a woman's head crowned with sun-gold hair swept forward over one shoulder.

Aimee peered through the parted doorway, seeing only a wall of man's chest framed by a canvas duster. She had to tip her head way back to view his face. It was shadowed beneath the wide brim of a dark hat, but she could still discern stubbly jaw, rough complexion, and narrowed eyes like shards of sapphire. In a kinder countenance, those eyes might have been mesmerizing. But there was no kindness in this man's face.

Josiah remembered hearing Rook Kelly had got himself a pretty little wife, but he hadn't given the news a thought until the moment he found himself gazing down at her. He supposed she appeared exactly the type of woman a sheriff or a preacher or a shopkeeper would want for a spouse. She lacked the poise of a confident beauty, the kind a well-to-do man liked to drape in finery and put on his arm. She didn't seem hearty enough to weather the toils of a farmer's mate. Neither did she have the endowments a bought woman advertises. But Josiah didn't doubt that small, soft, and demure could inspire equally lustful sensations, not when one gander at Mrs. Rook Kelly in her concealing frock and apron was stirring in him what the bordello's painted lady in garters could not. He was accustomed to being met with dismay like that which shone dominant in her large gray eyes. He didn't expect to see a tentative curiosity there as well. He didn't expect for her to continue to examine him, to hold the blue gaze even he avoided.

Aimee saw the long-healed abrasions that made a knurled line high across his throat. She decided if this man had survived a lynching, the men who'd strung him up hadn't survived his escape. Lightning lit the night around him and she beheld in the flash a wolfish visage—gaunt face with long nose, protruding cheekbones, and hard-lined mouth. His skin was not bristled as she'd first perceived, rather the beard grew sparse and uneven around scars that marbled his flesh. Unfortunate as they were, the mutilations could inspire no compassion, not with those eyes studying her so shrewdly. The imperfections seemed to characterize his face rather than mar it, declaring both the kind of life he led and its history. It was them that gave him away. Though she'd never seen the man in person, she knew with one storm-lit glimpse who her husband had invited to supper. Josiah Wyland's description and reputation went hand-in-glove, and both were terrible. When the thunder cracked, Aimee shuddered.

With the thunder came rain. A prelude of heavy droplets smacked the earth with a dissonant spatter. Then the deluge roared down. Josiah realized she mustn't have known him at first. It was just like Rook to not warn her, to not warn either of them. Quivering before him, she resembled some gentle spring blossom, the sort that wouldn't hold up to a light shower. Wisps of gold about her face curled in the humidity and he imagined they'd be soft around his fingers. He knew her shivering wasn't owing to the storm. He wanted to dispel the fright that clouded her dove-gray eyes. Even as he began, he knew it was the wrong thing to say. "My name is—"

Aimee squeezed her eyes shut and pressed her lips together to stop them trembling. When he spoke, his voice was gruff as from disuse and so low she was surprised she could hear him over the downpour. She interrupted before he could finish, sparing them both. "I know who you are." Aimee took a breath, squared her shoulders, and opened her eyes. "You aren't welcome here," she said.

"I was invited." Josiah noticed a ring of silver lined each fog-filled iris.

"My husband isn't home yet." Aimee lifted her chin, though her courage crumbled under his frigid stare. "You can seek him in town," she said, "or you can wait on the porch." She made to close the door.

Josiah knew he should let her. He should step back and keep company with the storm, let it cool him. Instead, the toe of his boot wedged in the gap. "I'll wait inside."

Aimee deduced she could throw all her weight against the door and not dislodge him. She could make a fool of herself or let a notorious cutthroat into her home. Either way, she was alone with a man who could overpower her with minimum effort. Those blue eyes told her he was capable of anything. The scars proved not much would deter him. Then Aimee remembered the knife. She backed away, allowing the gunslinger to enter the cabin.

Josiah hesitated on the threshold, knowing he ought to remain outside but drawn to watch her some more. She hurried from him, snatching a knife off the table as she retreated to the stove and placing it within easy reach. Somehow, he felt better that she was armed. He entered the Kelly home, closing the door Rook's missus had abandoned. A quick glance around confirmed they were alone. The lantern that lit the kitchen was not as bright as it had seemed from without. Its intimate glow glinted upon the dark red skins of apples in a basket on the table's center and upon the gilded hair she hastily finished weaving into a long braid before tossing over her shoulder. She stood with her back to him, her spine taut as a lariat laced to a bronc. He took one step toward her and she shot up even straighter. He took another step and watched her hand hover over the knife. With the third, her fingers closed on the handle. He wondered if he reached out to touch that sunshine hair, if she would turn and stab him. He was mightily tempted to stake his fate against her resolve.

Even as she clutched the knife so tightly her hand cramped and her knuckles blanched, Aimee doubted her ability to fight him off. She held her breath again, striving to listen over the precipitation pummeling the rooftop, over the blood pounding in her head. She heard the scuff of boots shifting on the floor and the jingle of spurs as his steps moved away from her. She released her breath and the knife, and circulation returned to her hand.

Josiah took a seat at the far side of the table in accordance with his profession's propensity for always seeking a chair from which to keep an eye on the door. Except he found himself

watching only her. He observed she kept the large blade close—
in her hand if possible—and used it to cut the smallest
ingredients. The golden rope of hair swayed as she moved and he
envisioned it wrapped around his fist, gliding silkily through his
grasp. Restless fingers plucked an apple from the wicker dish and
squeezed to test its hardness. He slipped it into his coat pocket
and fished out a flask to keep from fondling his guns next.

Aimee went about preparing supper, feeling his eyes follow
her every motion. Her exertions were all pretense as the meal only
wanted eating. She busied herself with stirring the stew,
sprinkling in spices it didn't need, chopping additional vegetables
she didn't plan to use. There was a killer sitting at her kitchen
table, but she refused to give him the satisfaction of her fear. For
the sake of having something more to do, she began to slice the
biscuits into halves. As she worked, indignation and disgust rose
to fortify her nerves. She fed it with every complaint she could
think of—the man was filthy, rank with an overbearing
compilation of foul smells, he was armed, pistols plainly
proclaiming his nefarious nature, and he'd all but forced his way
into a lawman's house.

Except Rook had invited him. That singular thought
undermined all her anger and prompted a sense of misgiving
more chilling than the bead of those blue eyes. Rook had known
he was coming. Rook wasn't home. She had feared word of her
errands would get back to her husband, that he might intercept
her letters. But she hadn't considered what he would do, what
form his retaliation might take. She was wary of his temper but
couldn't anticipate how it might be manifested. Now, he'd sent
this man to her doorstep. To scare her or to punish her, what had

look given Wyland instruction or permission to do to his wife? Aimee's courage slipped, as did the knife. She gave a small cry, and it clattered to the floor.

Aimee watched blood stream from a cut in her thumb. It pooled in her palm and circled her wrist to run down her arm, soaking into the sleeve of her dress. She didn't hear Josiah approach, having momentarily forgotten his presence in her kitchen. When he reached for her, she recoiled, but with the speed of a striking snake, he caught her. Long fingers locked around her wrist.

She went rigid at his touch, and he also tensed, prepared for her to screech and scratch. But she swooned. The color drained from her face as the strength drained from her body. The slick grip on her wrist made a precarious hold. As she sagged, Josiah looped a lanky arm around her middle. She slumped against it. Her free hand flailed against his front, too impotent to ward him off. A whimpered *please* was all she said, though he didn't know if it was a plea for help or against it. She sank toward the floor and he lowered himself with her, down onto one knee.

Aimee found herself seated on the top of his thigh as though it were a bench. Her head drooped to rest upon his knobby shoulder. His open hand curved around the back of hers, the pad of his thumb pressing into her palm. She knew he looked down at her—his breath was warm against her scalp. He asked her name. Aimee's head snapped up. She tried to pull away, but his hold tightened like a trap and steely eyes glared a warning. He twisted her wrist, rotating their hands until hers faced up. Scowling blue eyes inspected the wound. He lifted something in his other hand—a flask—and offered it to her. She shook her head. He took a long pull, swished it around in his mouth, swallowed, and swigged another. When he bent his head and sucked her thumb into his mouth, she squeaked in protest. Josiah didn't know if it was for the burn of the whiskey or the touch of his tongue. He set the flask on the floor and once again slipped his arm around to secure her, trying to ignore her hip against his crotch. It occurred to him she could go for one of his revolvers and occupied as he was, he might not be able to stop her shooting him. But there was no awareness of it in her eyes, and her fingers only curled over the top of his belt. Josiah reckoned it wouldn't be the worst way to go.

He slid her thumb from between his lips and in a series of movements she was too stupefied to follow, nimble fingers wound and tied a length of cloth around it. Looking down, she recognized the bandage as the string of her apron. She watched him pick the knife up off the floor and use it to sever string from apron. He set the blade atop the stove and picked up the whiskey. He gave her a considering look and held it out to her once more. Since she only gaped at it, he returned the container to his pocket.

He knew he ought to put some distance between them before her sense of self-preservation returned. Instead, he took advantage of the moment she continued to sit docilely on his knee to breathe in her scent, to memorize, so long as her eyes were fixed on him, the swirling hues of gray. Up close, Aimee saw there were other scars, a coarse series of pits and bumps along the right side of his face from his temple down under the grimy bandana low about his neck. She imagined his cheek would feel gravelly beneath her fingertips. The thought prompted her to move both hands to the safety of her lap. He let his hang at his sides. Josiah noticed the pearl-shaped buttons—four at each wrist and a broken column of color dividing her bodice. His eyes followed the apricot trail from petite waist to dainty chin. Though a few at the top were unfastened, he couldn't glimpse so much as a line of her throat. His fingers itched to fiddle with a few more, but when he touched her, it was to slide his hands beneath her elbows and lift her as he stood.

Josiah stepped back a pace, ensuring she was steady before his arms fell away. The rain had stopped, and the cabin was quiet as an underground cavern. She answered his question, speaking to break the spell of silence. Her own voice sounded strange in the hollow space. She whispered, "Aimee."

He turned his head. This time, Aimee recognized the steps on the front porch. Josiah skirted the table to his seat. The door swung open, and Aimee yanked her injured hand behind her back. Rook Kelly entered, dripping from the storm. His eyes shot first to Josiah, then her.

4

On the trek from town to cabin, Rook had come into a churlish mood, the result of varying annoyances, frustrations, and suspicions working in accumulation. Most recent was the shootout which would reflect less than favorably upon Rook once word spread that the man who'd loosed his guns was in Sheriff Kelly's employ. Prior to that incident was Wyland's failure to catch the Malloy brothers together. Trace coming quietly and Tyler still on the dodge suggested the two had anticipated or been tipped off to Rook's trap. Even with Trace under lock and key, the cowboys were a threat to his plans, a danger to his position in Prospect.

The boldness of Aimee's betrayal was likewise vexing. Rook had underestimated his blushing bride. He counted her as an attribute in the upcoming election. If she became a liability, he would be forced to give her up and risk losing the support of those constituents who doted on their sheriff's darling wife.

As the clouds began to rumble and flicker, Rook began to brood. His concern wasn't for the impending shower but that Wyland may not prove as effective as his notoriety promised. He pondered whether the gunslinger might be in cahoots with the

Malloy brothers and was even infected with the idea that Aimee might charm the whoremonger into helping her fly from Rook's reach. He told himself the former was improbable and the latter was absurd.

If prior convictions held true, Trace Malloy despised Wyland more than all the Kelly brothers combined. Even if he were desperate enough to forego his lofty principles and conspire with the killer, Rook held the ace that ensured his pet gunfighter's loyalty. And Aimee, though perhaps not as guileless as she seemed, lacked the feminine wiles required for seduction. Neither was she so simple as to seek mercy from a man who had none. A woman would expect ample compensation to suffer the company of Josiah Wyland. Aimee would never be imprudent enough to sully her reputation with his.

Rook's reservations rankled all during the walk home, until the moment he stepped through the door and took in the scene he had set. With one glance, all dubiety evaporated. The casting of the gun-toting mongrel-of-a-man and saucer-eyed woman-child in the same small kitchen was farcical. Stooped in his seat at the decorative table, Wyland looked as awkward as tits on a bull. Across the room, Aimee stood by the stove, hands behind her back, nervous like she'd found an angry rattlesnake in her cookpot. Rook shed his wet coat and hat, utilizing the time it took to hang them to conceal his amusement. He crossed the room to his wife, his mood improving with each step.

Aimee was still reeling from her accident and from the unsolicited and unconventional aid rendered by Rook's guest. As her husband strode toward her with mirth in his dark eyes, she struggled to decide who was the greater threat—the blue-eyed stranger renowned as the very worst of men or the man who'd schemed to send such a villain to frighten his wife. The trials of the day seemed unending, with Rook's homecoming bringing no reprieve. Aimee didn't think she could be more affected, until her husband kissed her.

Rook seized her and hauled her against him, claiming her mouth with a thoroughness he'd never exerted previous. Aimee was stunned yet not so buffaloed that she forgot there was a third person in the room. She felt the spear of his gaze and remembered too, the touch of *his* mouth. By the time Rook released her, Aimee's cheeks were rosy with humiliation. When her husband's eyes slid sideways and his lips curved into a sly smile, she realized the kiss with all its ardor had been an exhibition—for the man at the table.

Rook met Aimee's stormy, accusing eyes without an ounce of contrition to dim the shine in his own. He turned to his guest and said, "You fail to live up to your reputation, Wyland."

Rook strolled over to take the seat opposite the gunslinger. He'd wanted to test Wyland and Aimee both. But the bounty hunter's response was less than conclusive. Blue eyes remained cool in a face stoic as that of a gargoyle. By all appearances, Wyland's blood ran as cold as his reputation foretold. But he always had been a tough one for Rook to read. Aimee, on the other hand, was expressive to a fault. Rook could gauge her reaction with his back turned. He said, "You brought in Trace Malloy alive."

Mrs. Rook Kelly uttered a faint cry. Josiah didn't have to shift his gaze to see her over the lawman's shoulder. His critical cobalt stare took in the response her husband couldn't see, and he understood it was the name and not the subsequent thunderclap that caused her to start, the name and not the pain of her cut finger that distorted her delicate features. Wounded gray eyes fell on him. Josiah said, "He gave himself up."

Rook said, "Why do you suppose he'd do that?"

Josiah reckoned Rook already suspected his wife and Trace Malloy were acquainted—intimately, judging from her expression. He reckoned it was the reason he'd been assigned to intercept the brothers' return. It was plain Rook was using the news of Trace's arrest to torment her and he'd had Malloy's captor to supper to serve that end.

"He didn't want to die," Josiah mumbled. He wondered whether Rook would still have invited him had he shot and killed Trace.

"Then maybe you live up to your reputation too well," said Rook.

Aimee sat with her hands in her lap, staring at her plate while the two men ate. She'd managed to serve the meal, though she couldn't recall whether her arm shook when she'd ladled the stew or if she'd spilled a drop. She couldn't remember if the gunslinger had manners enough to thank her when she'd filled his plate, forced to step so near him that the skirt of her dress brushed the leg of his trousers. She didn't know whether she'd succeeded in hiding her bandaged thumb and stained sleeve from her husband's notice or if her jittery evasion had attracted his scrutiny.

Aimee had no appetite. Wyland bolted his food as though it were his first meal in days. Rook savored his as though it would be his last. If there was conversation, Aimee hadn't the wherewithal to follow it. Only when Wyland put down his fork, did she stir, roused by the dim hope that he would soon be leaving. It was dashed when her husband made the offer of a second helping. Dagger-sharp blues detoured toward her on their way to Rook.

"I reckon I've had my fill," Josiah said. He reckoned too, he'd fulfilled whatever purpose Kelly had intended in inviting him and rose to leave. He'd made the door and was reaching for the handle when Rook said, "Hold up a minute, Wyland."

Rook thought it peculiar the bounty hunter had forgotten his pay. But it allowed him one final test. He drew the amount from his pocket and placed the crisp currency in front of Aimee. "Give that to Wyland. It's his fee for bringing in Trace." He watched the play of emotion on her pixie's face, saw trepidation morph into petulance. When the gunslinger moved to collect the fee himself, Rook stopped him with one finger raised.

All was still in the cabin as husband and wife faced off — supreme confidence and infinite patience against desperate pride and brittle dignity. Each knew it was only a matter of time before she relented. Josiah Wyland figured it too, but it roped his attention, the way she rose regally to her feet, swiped the bills from the table, and flounced around back of the sheriff to meet him toe-to-toe. He waited to see if she would offer the payment or fling it at him. Instead, she lifted her pretty chin and her eyes met his yet again. The fear was still there, but disgust took precedence. Josiah didn't know if it were for him or for Rook. She said, "How many men have you killed, Mr. Wyland?"

Aimee infused her tone with all the disdain she could muster. She didn't really expect *him* to quail at her confrontation.

Her bravado was entirely for her husband. She didn't know why it was imperative she stand up to Rook, that she show him she wasn't afraid of the man he'd sent to scare her. Aimee was prepared for a number—whether it was ten or a hundred. When Wyland didn't answer, she felt her pulse stumble. She said, "I thought men like you kept track of such things. Perhaps you can't count." As his blue eyes looked straight through her, Aimee fought to keep hers from pleading. He stood before her, seemingly devoid of feeling and impervious to hers about to break upon him. She prayed he would answer. She prayed he would leave.

"Women and children would be an easier number." Rook suggested, and two pairs of eyes drifted his way. He didn't turn to meet them but concentrated on buttering a bite of bread.

It was a dare from which Aimee couldn't back down. Rook was calling her bluff. She turned back to Wyland. It took all her fortitude to meet his blue gaze. She had none left for his answer.

Gray eyes awaited his reply. Josiah reckoned he could hold his tongue, omit what he'd done, but he couldn't deny what he was—that she'd seen from the start. His whisper rasped like wind through dead leaves. "No women." Again, he said the wrong thing. This time it was he who was responsible for the spark of anguish in ashen eyes. He saw it as she turned her head.

Aimee's arms hung limp at her sides, the money forgotten in her hand. She didn't notice when Josiah reached out and extracted it from her fingers. The warm touch lingered a heartbeat, but she didn't feel it. Josiah watched a tear run its course down her cheek to veer and vanish beneath her jaw. He wet his lips then realized it was her name on his tongue. He stopped himself, knowing what a violation it would be for him to utter it. There was nothing he could say, nothing he could do but leave.

The storm outside had all but passed by the time Josiah unhitched his horse. He couldn't account for the one brewing inside him. Back behind the white curtain, Mrs. Kelly stood where he'd left her. He wondered if she and Trace Malloy were lovers, and why then had she married Rook? His horse nipped at his pocket and Josiah gave up the apple. He looked on as the sheriff's silhouette joined that of his wife.

***

"What happened here?" Her husband took her injured hand in his, eyed it from several angles, then lifted her bandaged thumb to his lips. "You must be more careful," Rook said. "I hate to see you hurt."

Aimee scoffed. "You invited a murderer to supper."

"A novelty for him, I'm sure."

"Where are Trace and Tyler?"

"I'll bet he takes his money and gets himself a fair-haired whore." Rook watched her flinch at the insinuation. His wife was afraid of Wyland but not enough to satisfy Rook. Aimee had revealed an intriguing streak of bravery. Even now, he wasn't certain she was cowed. "He doesn't quite live up to his reputation, does he?"

"What have you done with them?"

Rook slid a folded piece of paper from his vest pocket and handed it to her. Aimee didn't need to unfold it—she recognized her own handwriting. "Trace is in a jail cell. Tyler will be joining him soon." Rook raised a hand to her throat. "You're mine now."

43

He touched a finger to each empty button hole. "Don't make me remind you again."

***

From atop his horse, Josiah watched the two shadows meld. It had been a long time since he'd contemplated what it meant for a man to have a woman of his own—his to admire, to shield from a storm or cover on a cold night, to return to, wherever he went. He pictured the slight, sweet, and sad flower that Trace and Rook were both vying for and wondered which man would come to keep her. In a fair contest, Trace had every advantage. But Rook was never one to fight fair. Josiah rode slowly back toward Prospect, oblivious to the residual drizzle, all urgency to leave the town forgotten.

***

Josiah got a bottle of whiskey from The Old Mare and a room at Prospect's cheapest inn. He sat on the end of the bed having removed nothing but the cork. He wasn't typically a drinking man but could think of no other cure for the stew of feeling roiling within him. He took one long swallow after another.

He sought to calm fingers that still ached to thread through sunshine hair, still itched to toy with tiny buttons. He strove to drug into a stupor the rigid cock he feared no whore could now appease, that throbbed at the remembrance of her hip snug against it while her fingers fluttered only inches north. He tried to purge the memory of her springtime scent, banish the vision of her gray eyes. Wide with fear, sparkling with temper, soft with curiosity—he was sure those eyes would haunt him. Mostly, he wanted to undo the single tear gliding like dew over petal-smooth skin.

44

Aimee—her name waited on his tongue like a forbidden wish. She belonged to Rook Kelly if not Trace Malloy. Josiah couldn't fault either man's taste. Like a soothing wave, she'd washed over him, making him feel he'd been thirsting all his life, wandering so long under the desert sun as to be dried up inside. He wanted more, to drown in her. Instead, he took another pull from the bottle.

***

Aimee felt empty, as though all feeling had been wrung from her. She was alone. Rook had departed not long after Wyland. It was an aspect of everyday life for Aimee since her marriage, and tonight an unintended kindness, that her husband left her after supper and returned to Prospect, back to the jail and the labors of his career for which he reserved all his energy and from which he derived all his contentment. By the time Aimee learned she'd have to contend with his ambitions for attention, she'd also learned there was nothing of his attentions she wanted. He didn't look to her for comfort, pleasure, or companionship, and he gave none.

The kitchen needed cleaning. Instead, Aimee drifted into the bedroom and collapsed atop the quilt, blanketed by the quiet dark. Her tears didn't come violently but bled from her eyes, until her cheeks and pillow were wet.

The events of the evening were so discordant with what was familiar to her that she might have questioned whether they'd transpired at all. But the bit of cloth binding her finger was confirmation. She'd been made to bear the presence of one of the West's most detestable bad men. And the worst he'd done was bandage her thumb. Idly, Aimee wondered if he would have touched her at all but for her clumsiness with the knife. Had Rook prohibited him, or had he simply lacked the inclination? She doubted Wyland would defer to any man lest it suit him. Sadly, she also doubted her husband would decree she be spared if her sacrifice better served his goals. Aimee had the ominous feeling her worth to Rook Kelly was waning.

Tonight, more than when her parents had passed, Aimee needed all those things of which her marriage was barren. She needed to be held, comforted, and reassured. It occurred to Aimee that the closest she'd had in over a year was the unwelcome embrace of a complete stranger with impartial touch, immunity of feeling, and soulless blue eyes.

5

Rook Kelly returned to Prospect by a route similar to that Aimee had traveled, taking side streets where he could wander undisturbed and undistracted in his thoughts. It was early night, his favorite time, when day succumbed to dark's slow seduction and like the surrounding desert, the town took on an alternate life.

By day, the frontier settlement was driven by diligence and desperation as folk slaved under a merciless sun to eke existence out of dry desolation. It was dominated by the clip-clop of horses and rattle of wagons up and down the dusty streets, and by the distant boom of explosives from the hills beyond. Nocturnal life was fueled by vice as workers crowded into saloons and brothels to gamble and drink and fuck their earnings away. While some pioneers of progress slept the sleep of good and weary souls, others sought only the fortitude to survive another dawn. Ladies of the line emerged from shaded windows and shut doors to advertise and sometimes perform their services shamelessly in the open. The veil of darkness enticed better than any garment, the cooler air thrilled more than any perfume. Cats and cutthroats prowled the widening shadows, weeding out the weaker species.

It didn't bother Rook that his badge shone less brightly by the glow of the moon. Where the authority of his office held sway in the light of day, the power of the name Kelly sufficed after the sun had set. The rogues about Prospect were well aware that any violence visited upon Rook would be met with the retaliation of two avenging brothers.

Whether he worked with the law or against it, Jerrod Kelly had made a reputation for himself as one of the best gunfighters around, as respected for the code he fought by as the skill he fought with. As much as Jerrod was revered for his resoluteness, Silas Kelly was feared for his unpredictability. He commanded a band of unsavory characters but was by himself as formidable as when he had them backing him up. Silas was a wild card with a devil-may-care stance and a confidence not many sane men could muster. Both brothers were loyal to blood above all else.

The rain brought emphasis to the night's vitality. The air cleared of dust and was crisp as if it retained the electricity of the storm. Smells were brought into sharp distinction—Rook could even detect the desert sage. The clouds were blown away leaving the stars to sparkle like silver flake sprinkled across a basalt sky. As he walked, Rook recounted the events of the evening and surmised the supper to have been a success.

Preceded by his reputation and looking especially unwholesome, coming directly from a gunfight if not a whore's bed, Wyland satisfied his role simply by showing up. And poor, sweet Aimee, striving to feign unaffectedness, had gone and struck herself a blow more crippling than any Rook could have strategized. He had little idea when he made the suggestion that the bounty hunter would actually admit to slaying children. It wasn't his wife's pain that amused Rook—Silas was the sadistic brother—but the delightful irony that brought it about. He chuckled to recall he'd dreamed it possible for unworldly Aimee to so much as consider enlisting the killer's aid. A rabid badger would inspire more cordiality from her. Admittedly, Aimee had revealed more backbone than he'd given her credit for, but Rook determined his wife subdued, for the present. Though he would continue to monitor her activities and behavior, the risk of woman's disobedience moved from the forefront of his mind. Rook decided he need only to secure Tyler Malloy for the large of his worries to be managed.

As if his subconscious were already treading along that line, Rook found himself standing in the soft ruby glow at the base of the steps of a quaint little parlor house. Located at the very edge of Prospect's red light district as to disassociate itself with the bawdy brothels that flaunted their faces to the masses, it was a small building with elegant architecture worlds apart from the mean shanties that characterized a frontier town. Thus, it was regarded as a jewel in the rough, where men of wealth and pedigree bought their company and the women fancied themselves courtesans. It was true the place presented all the appearance of as much respectability as could be contributed to such an organization, with the ladies wearing corsets and stockings under silk gowns. But a whore by any other name is still a whore. Only here, some men paid for the illusion and others to see it undone. The apt epitaph suggested precious commodity and guaranteed expense—it was The Treasure Room.

***

From without, The Treasure Room presented a picture of elegance and sophistication, as charming as it was displaced in the drab frontier town. Only the rosy gleam of the porch lamps and the heavy burgundy drapes shrouding the lower windows hinted at its less than proper purpose. Inside, the house had all the pristine order and lavish furnishings of a royal court. Crystal decanters of fine wine and bourbon awaited preferred patrons who would be invited to rest on velvet upholstery and enjoy a cigar and snifter before their scheduled pleasure with a select lady from the madam's cache of rare beauties. At such an early hour, only one room was occupied and only because an available girl had consented to accommodate a man who'd shown without appointment but offered too generous compensation to be turned away. The parlor was empty but for the night's hostess.

Evelyn Deveraux stood before a full-length, gilded mirror, looking to the young woman reflected in the glass for something she had yet to see. The name she'd chosen was far grander than the one given her at birth, her dress of silk and lace much finer than the coarse canvas and cotton sewn by her mother's weary hand, and the plush rug beneath her feet easier on her heels than the hard-packed dirt floor of the home she'd sworn to forget. She'd traded the sudsy waters of a leaky wash-bucket for a frame of gold, but the image within still engendered precarious satisfaction. She had changed but not transformed.

She recognized the truth of it in a subtle but growing dimness in the depths of her eyes, where shadows of an impoverished past threatened the bright splendor of a plentiful future. Evelyn still had the sweet face that had won her a position at The Treasure Room, but she knew now, more than she'd known then, that it was a limited opportunity—a chance for a pretty but penniless girl to recommend herself to an otherwise unreachable society, to attract a man of wealth and stature who might become so enamored as to provide her a secure and comfortable home, elevating her from a lady of the line to a respectable woman. It was a girl's dream, but no mere fantasy as the profession lost many choice women to marriage.

Yet Evelyn looked long and often enough to see another, likelier reality in the immaculate glass. As desirable as she was, she was a novelty whose shine would wear off, leaving her to wither under the thankless labors of those professions not so apt to lose workers to marriage. Single, she would be subject to less and less glamorous standards of living—hands calloused from the kitchen or laundry, or back bent from needlework—until she became the broken woman who haunted her memories.

A ring of the bell brought her back to the present. Evelyn crossed the parlor with the posture and grace of a status her origins denied her. She opened the door and felt for a moment the flare of a dormant hope. It faded the longer she studied the man. His suit and stylish bowler marked him as a professional, with the starched white collar and cuffs testimony to his success. Of medium stature, he was well-looking with barbered hair and mustache that gleamed black. It was apparent to Evelyn that he had the wealth and influence to rescue her, just as it was obvious he would not be the man to do so. There was an unsympathetic shrewdness in his dark-as-night eyes, a cool insincerity in his smile, and a restlessness to his manner that showed him being more a man of ambition than pedigree, with more love of self than any woman might hope to claim. She asked if he had an appointment, though she knew he did not.

He showed her his star. If she hadn't already detected his disinterest, she would have been disappointed—the only thing she knew and had cared to remember about the sheriff was that he was married. Evelyn found she did not envy his wife. He said, "Harboring any outlaws?"

"I don't know what you mean." Evelyn did not know his political stance regarding a house of sin, if he were tolerant of The Treasure Room's vices. She knew only that he wasn't known to partake. He seemed a man more attuned to business than pleasure, more inclined toward scheming than rutting. But business in a town with a name like Prospect did not guarantee honesty and laws were not synonymous with morals.

"Then tell me this," he said. "I wouldn't be the prettiest man to step through this door tonight, would I?"

"Him." If every room upstairs had been in use and the parlor crowded with waiting gentlemen, Evelyn still would have known which man the sheriff sought. That he was an outlaw did not surprise her in the slightest. He had the practiced charisma of a scoundrel, and the flashy six-shooter at his thigh befitted a bandit prince. He had the money to indulge in rich tastes—clothing and women among them—and was far handsomer than the lawman with fine black hair loose and long, an almost effeminate grace, and eyes like polished emeralds. But he wore wealth and beauty both with an air of indifference which suggested to Evelyn that he came by the latter naturally and the former less than honesty. The lovely glimmer in his eyes—cold like the sheriff's but with an added malice—hinted at hidden danger. She'd seen it as surely as he'd seen through her.

The sheriff asked which room and Evelyn told him.

***

The upstairs rooms were numbered as in a hotel, with Roman numerals engraved into brass plaques on the doors. Rook made his way down a low-lit hall where thick carpet silenced the fall of his heels, to the one the hostess directed him. He entered without knocking. As the heavy oak glided inward on well-oiled hinges, the only sound was the metallic click of a single-action being primed to shoot.

On a chair directly across from the door, a man sat naked with a nude girl on his lap. His wrist rested upon her shoulder, and the six-gun in his hand was leveled at Rook. His stern expression slithered into a broadening smile as he slowly tilted the barrel skyward.

"Sheriff, to what do I owe the pleasure?" The man eased the hammer forward and lowered the revolver, returning it to a small table beside him. The table, chair, and a kingly bed were the only furniture in the richly—yet sparsely—decorated room.

Candles in ornate sconces filled the space with golden light that glinted upon a mirror on the wall, upon the pistol's polished plating, and upon the sheen on the young whore's skin. She had small breasts, large eyes, and an abundance of dark curls. Her legs were spread wide, draped over the man's thighs so that her toes didn't touch the ground. Rook glanced at her, then fixed his gaze upon the man. "What do you think you're doing?"

Green eyes sparkled with devilry. "This is what a man does when his cock gets hard."

Rook glowered at him then crossed over to the table and picked up the pocketbook that lay next to the gun. He removed two five-dollar bills and held them out to the girl. When she pouted, he told her to take it and be glad. "By the time he finished with you, you'd be sorry to have met him." Whether she believed his warning or not, she took the money and scooted off the man's lap, collecting her dress and undergarments from the unused bed.

Silas Kelly watched her bare buttocks wiggle as she padded across the room. Before the door closed behind her, she looked at him over her shoulder and batted long lashes. He'd intended to see them wet with tears before she left. He turned to his brother and said, "You're no fun."

"You're supposed to be on the lookout for Tyler Malloy."

"I got bored." Silas stood, taking himself in hand as he rose from the cushioned chair. Clothed or not, he never seemed self-conscious. In the Old World, his willowy figure might be mistaken for that of an elf. In the West, he seemed a pale savage. He cultivated the image even as he rejected it, letting his black hair grow long and keeping his face shaved smooth. He wandered the room, absent-mindedly stroking his shaft. "You have Trace. Little brother won't move without him. But if you're impatient, have your deputies or Wyland hunt him down."

Rook told him that Dawes was guarding Trace and that Lucas was keeping watch out at the Malloy farm with Jerrod. "Waste of time," muttered Silas.

"And I had Wyland to supper." His brother stilled, giving Rook his full attention. "It was your idea, remember?"

"And how did the delectable Aimee find our odious long rider?" Silas spoke softly, and his green eyes glittered with a hunger Rook would never understand. "Was she frightened?"

Rook's gaze fell to where his brother's hand fisted and pulled. "Stop that," he said. "She's my wife."

Silas grunted in protest but began to dress. As he picked pants from the pile of clothing, Rook studied the scars that spanned his backside—some carved by rawhide whip, others by thick belt. Most of the time, Rook could forget he bore similar marks.

"I don't know why you wanted Sir's job." Rook thought Silas had caught him watching, except he spoke without turning around.

Rook tore his thoughts from the past and his sight from its reminders. "He was town marshal. I'm sheriff." He knew Silas wouldn't see the difference. "It doesn't change anything. We're brothers first. We help each other."

Silas shook out his shirt with a snap. "I don't need help from any lawman."

"Well, I need yours." Rook waited while Silas adjusted his suit, pulling his hair out from under his collar and tucking his trousers into his boots. He fastened his cartridge belt and tied the holster string about his thigh. He straightened with a sigh.

"I want Wyland. His talents are wasted outside of the gang."

Rook shook his head. "His reasons for going straight are his own." And Rook wasn't about to encourage the hired gun to change his allegiance, though he didn't tell that to Silas. "If he crosses the line, Cooper might come out of retirement, which would mean trouble for us all."

Silas moved in front of the mirror, but it was his brother's reflection he eyed. "You could let me have Aimee." He watched Rook's brow furrow and his shoulders shift. "I'd only want her once."

"You wouldn't ask that of Jerrod if he were married."

"Jerrod knows what to do with a woman. But don't think I wouldn't ask." Silas moved to the table. "To risk everything is the only freedom there is," he said. "You can't keep Wyland on that leash forever." As he hefted his gun, there was a knock on the door.

Rook said, "Go away." Silas said, "Come in." Through the door came their brother Jerrod's voice. "There's been a jailbreak."

6

The dream began one of a hundred different ways but always ended with a click of the hammer meeting an empty chamber. Josiah opened his eyes to the uniform dark of a windowless room, the stagnant air and absence of stars reminding him where he slept.

He'd become accustomed to the dream, to its awakening him and to the unease that followed him back into consciousness. He couldn't control it but could usually dismiss it—push the sense of inevitability to the back of his mind, roll over, and go back to sleep.

That night, his eyelids were still heavy from the whiskey, the blood in his veins like warm molasses. From another room came the repetitive squeaking of bedsprings. Josiah let the rhythm lull him back into oblivion.

***

When the world afforded her no other comfort, Aimee turned to a memory so faded it might only have been a dream. The vision had its origins in her childhood, but whether the product of fact or fever, she no longer knew. It came to her in times of utmost distress, when absolute exhaustion brought her to the precipice of sleep.

Aimee remembered sunshine warm enough to chase the chill from her bones and so bright that she saw everything through a lens of watery eyes. She remembered a white horse, the soft velvet of its muzzle beneath her fingertips and the scratch of coarser hide against her bare ankles when she sat astride it, the heat and power of its body when she rode it. The wind on her face was a breath of heaven, special and rare for a girl whose frequent illness kept her indoors. There'd been someone with her—a boy, whose identity was obscured by time, distilled to a protective presence but real enough for her to recall lean arms reaching around her to grip the animal's mane and the sure poise of a practiced rider as she rested her back against his chest.

There were times she was certain the boy had been Trace, but he never spoke of it and neither did she. She'd held it in her heart like a secret, all her life, as if to divulge it would shatter its power and forfeit something she had need of at some future point.

Aimee was still thinking of the white horse and imagined for a moment that the galloping of hooves was an echo of her memory. But the memory only ever faded while the sound grew louder. She sat up and listened to its approach, like the return of thunder. The clamor circled the cabin and seemed to ride up to her front door. Aimee stood in the bedroom, wondering whether to hide and unsure where she could. She heard a commanding voice give an impatient shout and thought she recognized the bark. Then he called out her name.

Aimee rushed to the door and flung it open. She was swept off her feet, into the embrace of Trace Malloy.

***

Josiah Wyland awoke to a violent splash as a bucket of water broke over him. He grabbed for his guns and sprang to sit up, all in one motion. Awareness penetrated, as cold and clear as the water seeping into his clothes. His wrists and ankles were manacled, his guns were gone, and he was looking at the inside wall of a jail cell. A stabbing ache at the back of his skull reminded him that he'd been hauled out of bed by no fewer than three men, seized from sleep only to feel the sharp strike of a rifle butt splitting his scalp and thrusting him back into darkness. He rotated his sore jaw, wondering what, if anything, he'd hit on the fall to the floor. He didn't bother to swipe at the moisture dripping off his face. He swung his legs off the cot and dropped heavy, shackled boots to the ground. He raised his eyes to the sheriff who stood with bucket in hand.

Rook said, "Where's my wife?"

Josiah slowly surveyed the jailhouse. Jerrod Kelly stood on the other side of the bars with two fidgety deputies. One had a crushed nose, half his face colored purple, and red slits for eyes. Josiah remembered his own encounter with the force of those fists. He said, "Where's Trace Malloy?"

The bucket hit the wall and clattered to the floor. Josiah's gaze drifted back to the sheriff. Rook's breath heaved and his eyes flared. Josiah couldn't recall ever seeing Rook so riled.

"Tyler sprang his brother," said Rook. "They kidnapped Aimee."

"If you say so."

"You'll bring her back."

"I don't do rescues." Josiah tilted his head and raised his hands to probe the blood-clotted hair at the back of his skull. The iron bindings clanked and he lowered fists to his lap.

Rook reigned in his temper, scrutinizing him. "Word is you don't take too well to chains, Wyland." The gunfighter stilled, his eyes glacial. "Far as I can see, you don't seem to mind them." Rook saw he finally had the man's undivided attention. "You killed three men yesterday, in my town."

"It was them or me," Josiah said.

"Witnesses say not one got a shot off in return. Folk been calling for your arrest." He might have been threatening a rock for all the reaction the man showed, though Rook thought he saw the blue eyes change hue. "You've got three days. I want her back, and I want the Malloy brothers dead. In four days, I cite you as their accomplice and put out a warrant for murder."

Rook turned to leave, and Josiah rose to his feet. Jerrod Kelly moved his right hand to rest on the forward butt of his left pistol. "Oh, and you'll have some competition." Rook looked over his shoulder. "Silas is already on the hunt."

One of the deputies opened the cell door to let Rook out, then closed and locked it again. Rook told the man with the bruised face, "Give him fifteen to think it over. Then let him go and give him back his guns. Make sure they're empty." Rook, Jerrod, and the other deputy departed. Josiah scowled after them.

When his eyes shifted to the remaining deputy, the man swallowed and said, "I don't reckon you'll be needing them fifteen minutes." Josiah stood silent and still as the man fumbled to unlock the bindings around his boots and wrists. He accepted his gun-belt without a word, fastening it around his hips while the guard stood aside sweating. The battered man's eyes watered as he handed over Josiah's hardware, and he winced a little when the gunfighter inspected each Peacemaker before holstering it. As he watched the gunman step out the door, Dawes considered that working for Rook Kelly might be bad for his health.

The sun was high and hot and blinding. Josiah walked around the side of the building into the shade. He bent over, placed his hands on his knees, and retched. Soon as he'd aired his paunch, he reloaded his guns. His fingers quivered ever so slightly as he drew the first cartridge from its slot on his belt. The tremor vanished by the time he slid the same round into place on the wheel.

***

Aimee sat behind Trace on his horse, her arms around his middle, her hands stacked where his belly widened into a broad chest. She felt his heartbeat drumming steadily against her palm and heard the strong thump-thump where her ear rested against his back. She'd clung tight to him through the first lengths of their journey, as they stole away by the glow of the moon and then pushed for distance and for the hills as dawn breached the horizon and daylight sought them over the flats. Elation gave way to exhaustion over the miles and through the hours, so her body drooped against his. Her mind likewise relaxed, quieted of the anxieties that had dominated her waking thoughts for long months. On matching geldings—colored in patches of brown, black, and white—they meandered through the earthen folds between hills that looked to Aimee all alike. It seemed to her, they could lose themselves in those hills, forever safe from discovery.

The brothers rode side-by-side so long as the terrain allowed, and Aimee listened to them talk, comforted by the cadence of conversation, letting the rumble of words drift about her without attempting to follow their significance. Trace's voice, serious in youth, had deepened into that of a more serious man. Tyler's too had changed but still retained a light-hearted, boyish inflection, like a smile for the ears.

"How's the hand?" Tyler watched Trace make a fist and open it, stretching thick fingers.

"Sore, but worth it. Let me have one of those."

Tyler handed him one of the leftover biscuits he'd stuffed his pockets with while in Rook Kelly's kitchen. "Don't remember the last time we had soft tack. Just like ma used to make too." The brothers' smiles flashed, then wilted.

"Your timing last night couldn't have been better," said Trace.

"I was riding up to the jail, trying to reckon how to go about it when you come strolling out like you was the sheriff. Surprised it wasn't more guarded."

"That's the Kelly ego," said Trace.

"Can't believe he accused us of thieving horses. Think he'll send a posse after us?"

"He'll send his brothers. And Wyland. But Cooper will know what to do."

"Thought you said Cooper retired." Trace told him the old judge would still have influence and connections with the governor who could pardon them of any crimes Rook fabricated. Tyler asked what his thoughts were on Josiah Wyland.

Trace said, "What about him?"

"He saw me in town, but I don't got no bullet holes in me."

"Might be he didn't see you, busy as you said he was with them three bushwhackers."

"He saw me, and I reckon, if he'd mentioned it to Rook, we would have had a harder time back there." Tyler licked his lips and said, "I'm thinking it would be good to have him on our side."

"Wyland don't pick sides," said Trace. "He's a hired gun."

"So, we hire him," said Tyler.

"He's dangerous."

"Exactly!"

"Listen," said Trace. "Wyland was a black-hearted devil when we knew him. His blood runs a lot colder now. We don't want his kind of help."

Aimee dozed, the sun warm on her face. She absently plucked at the bit of cloth around her thumb until it loosened and fell away. Her fingernail grazed the cut, and the nip of pain roused her in time to hear the gunfighter's name. She jolted awake just as Trace's mount swayed. Unbalanced, she began to slide.

"Aimee!" Trace twisted and threw his arm back, snatching a handful of her sleeve and holding her up with it while Tyler jumped from his horse and took her in his arms. She ended up reclined against his chest while Trace dabbed her brow with a dampened handkerchief. They were all three on the ground, flanked by eight painted legs.

"I'm all right," she said, blinking up at the two men. The brothers had identically colored hair—every shade of blond with some browns mixed in. They both had hazel eyes, but up close, Aimee saw that Tyler's were flecked with green and Trace's with gold.

"You gave us a scare," Tyler murmured.

"She got overheated," Trace said. It sounded to Tyler like a reasonable explanation, except Aimee was shivering as suddenly cold.

***

Josiah got his horse and got the hell out of town. He went to the farm, because he needed time and it was as good a place as any—empty but for ghosts and memories that were much the same. He reckoned the Malloy brothers wouldn't be coming home anytime soon. The structures all still stood, like skeletons waiting for life to return. In the fields, the crops were dry at least a year.

Josiah walked along an ancient weathered fence, stooping to pick up old cans and place them as he went. The posts were pocked with misses from another world, before time had molded boys into men. The tin was orange and dented, punctured from prior practice, corroded thin with holes like moths chew in cotton. Josiah pivoted and strode away from the line, not bothering to count paces as they'd once done. He already knew where he'd end up. He turned and faced the fence. When they were boys, there'd been something—and nothing—at stake. The best shooter got bragging rights and whatever bits of junk they designated as prizes. Once a kiss from a girl—someone's cousin or neighbor—had been offered up but vetoed since she wasn't even present. A voice from the past issued the order to fire. Bullets zinged and cans clanked, knocked from their perch to fall to the dirt where they'd rust some more, homes for spiders before crumbling to dust.

Josiah wasn't there to hone his skill. Neither was he there to make his decision so much as to get acquainted with it. He

64

reckoned it was decided the moment gray eyes met blue. He shook out the spent cartridges, loading each cylinder anew, without a thought to the task. Neither did he consider how natural the weapons felt in his hands, how he could aim as easily as pointing his finger, or how taking a life had become as simple as shooting a can. He felt neither pride nor shame at the steadiness of his hands and never reflected upon the acclimation to violence that was necessary to both his livelihood and survival. It was what he did—as much a part of him as those blue eyes. He didn't question whether the skill he wielded had drawn him to do evil or if that taint had always been in his blood. Or whether it mattered either way. He didn't ask if there was any difference between killing one or a hundred, if numbers made him more or less of a killer. He'd never be able to undo that tear.

Josiah Wyland knew what he was. He knew there was nothing of himself he could offer a woman—no kindness, no gentleness, no safe and stable home. All he could do for the wayward wife of Rook Kelly was render a service she already despised him for. Maybe she would despise him a little less if by it, he aided her escape, helping her to find haven with a better man.

Josiah recalled the Malloy homestead as it had been seven years past, with the fields green and chickens clucking about the yard, with linens drying over the porch railing and the scent of supper wafting from open windows. He could picture Aimee there, stepping off the porch, hair blazing golden in the sun, walking toward the corral that now kept his horse. For a moment, Josiah remembered a white horse in its place. Then his mind turned to Trace as a boy.

The eldest Malloy had been the self-appointed leader of the small band of Promise locals that had the Malloy and Kelly brothers at its core with Josiah on the perimeter, included when Silas insisted and excluded when he did not. Young Trace had been serious and strong, mindful of his ma, and protective toward his little brother. He'd been a decent shot and a superior scrapper, authoritative but not a bully. He'd distrusted Josiah intently, never once inviting him inside the Malloy home.

Though he was surprised Trace would set his sights at another man's wife, Josiah reckoned Malloy would do right by any woman, particularly the one he made his own. He didn't much like the idea of her belonging to Trace, but he was convinced Rook cared nothing for his missus—or he wouldn't have sent Silas to collect her.

Josiah recalled Trace had a special respect for Judge Del Cooper. It occurred to him Malloy would turn to his old mentor for aid and advice. Cooper's place was on the other side of what had once been Promise. Josiah had ridden with the Kelly gang long enough to predict that Silas would set up his gang in ambush where the hills opened up into the town. Josiah did some rough figuring of the distance. He gauged where the sun was at in the sky. Then he ran for the corral, swung up into his saddle, and dug in his heels.

7

A coal-black stallion raced across the desert like a demon intent on running down the setting sun, and Josiah Wyland rode him like the devil. They were as two touched by fire—alive only to feel the lick of the flames once more.

Besides his guns, the animal was the only thing upon which Josiah allowed himself to depend. Never ridden before him, it was a horse he couldn't ruin no matter how he pushed it. He'd sought the biggest, orneriest beast he could find, wanting a mount that couldn't be stolen. But sometimes Josiah felt the stallion had chosen him. They were not man and horse so much as brothers. They'd been through blazes together and come out singed but with souls fused in a common struggle.

Josiah kept to the flatlands for speed, following the arcing shadow at the base of the low range. He figured Trace would seek cover within and knew it would slow his party down. Some of the Kelly gang might be prowling those hills, looking to flush the fugitives out, but others would be waiting in ambush at the point their prey was most likely to emerge. That was where Josiah headed.

***

Back on the painted geldings, Aimee and her rescuers snaked through valleys, avoiding the higher, more exposed terrain. The brothers spoke less often, and Aimee feared it was out of consideration for her. The sun slipped slowly from the sky to sit like melting butter on the hilltops.

There was more vegetation in the troughs between peaks—spiny branches plucked at her dress, capturing threads and leaving prickers. Hooves knocked dully against rocks and crunched plants that were dry in the wettest seasons.

They startled up a sparrow. As Aimee watched it flap away, she caught sight of a rider pacing them along the top of an adjacent slope.

"I see him," said Trace. "Keep your chin down, don't let on."

Tyler said, "There's two more on the rise left of us."

"We'll be coming out of the hills soon. They got to make their way down. Be ready to ride hard." Trace reckoned if they could stay ahead of their pursuers, beat them to town, they could take shelter in one of the abandoned buildings and make a stand there. "Aimee, you'll have to hold on tight."

Aimee's heart was already skipping fast. She snuck another glance at the single rider, afraid that his delineation would prove familiar, afraid that Rook had sent Wyland.

The valley floor leveled and opened, Trace and Tyler gave a unified shout, and the two steeds bolted from between the hills. Aimee whipped her head around and saw men on horses barreling down the hillsides. They spread into formation behind the geldings, five riders strung out in a row. Then the men at each end kicked and hollered and swatted their animals' rumps, and the band curved like a net, closing in.

Even with Trace shielding her, the wind tore loose Aimee's braid, making a golden streamer of her hair. Ahead, the horizon was a line of flame. She looked back in time to see a bandit raise an arm over his head and shoot off the pistol in his hand. The others followed suit. Then the first man lowered his arm and aimed his weapon, it seemed to Aimee, right at her. As explosions popped in her ears, she cringed and waited to know what it felt like to die. The man's horse pitched forward, as if it had stumbled. Its front legs bent and its chest angled toward the ground. The animal turned its head and Aimee saw the white of one eye, then its rump and tail and back hooves as it somersaulted. Horse and rider vanished in a spray of dirt.

A mass of brown and white hovered in Aimee's peripheral vision. Tyler's mount had fallen back just behind and to the side of her and Trace. He had twisted in his saddle and his revolver was in his right hand, clutched against his left hip and pointed back at their pursuers. Their eyes met as each turned forward and it surprised Aimee how well she could see the specks of peridot in his.

"They're herding us!" Trace acknowledged Tyler's shout with a glance. He felt Aimee's fingers curl into his chest and hoped she could hang on a little longer. The buildings ahead of them were dark boxes backlit by blinding reds and oranges. As they loomed larger, Trace had an eerie feeling—not that they were empty, but that they might not be.

"When I yell," he said, "break right and make for the inn." Wooden walls deflected back the thunder of galloping hooves. "Now!" Trace jerked the reins and felt Aimee's arms contract about his ribcage as they cut the corner, following Tyler around back of the first building. He didn't have time to spot the man on the rooftop across the street, but when the corner they skirted exploded into kindling, Trace knew he was there. A pair of bandits followed them while the rest charged straight down the main drag of what had once been the brothers' hometown of Promise.

***

When Josiah rounded the last curve of hillside, he saw clouds of dust drifting in the distance, painted rust by a dying sun. He adjusted the reins and the black horse flew like an obsidian arrowhead loosed at the heart of yonder sinking globe.

He found the ghost town alive with eruptions of gunfire, splintering wood, and shattering glass. His horse skidded to a halt in the shadow of the first building. Josiah's palm made two wet smacks as he patted the stallion's neck, once in thanks and once in farewell. He vaulted from the saddle and the horse trotted off victorious in his part.

Josiah added a sixth round to each revolver, listening as he went about it to the staccato beats, the dissonant song of the gunfight composed by Colt, Remington, and Smith & Wesson. He knew by the cadence that he'd need every shot. The Malloy brothers were vastly outnumbered.

***

Veering into the corridor between what had been the inn and a shop, Trace and Tyler brought their mounts to a quick stop. Tyler leapt down and reached for Aimee without needing to be told.

"Ammo." Trace pulled a box out of his saddlebag and tossed it to his brother. Tyler stuffed it in his pocket and took Aimee's hand. His other hand held his gun. They looked up at Trace and he down at them, struck by how much they appeared like children, wide-eyed and trusting him. "Make it count," he said. "Go."

Trace spurred his horse and it darted into the street, across the sights of two riders who shot at him. The gelding took the hits but got him to the other side where he scrambled from the saddle and sprinted toward the nearest door. Bullets broke through a window as he passed it. He spun and returned fire and saw one assailant tip off his horse.

Inside, Trace took a flight of stairs two at a time and found himself in an empty room with a window, its shutters still intact and closed. Through the slats, he saw the remaining riders regrouping in the street. He heard booted feet running to join the action, down the old boardwalk, from the east side of town. From nearby, came four shots in quick succession, the last two so close together they might have been one. The men in the street looked about, and Trace took the opportunity to wing a shot at one. He missed, and their barrels swung in his direction. He dove for the floor and rolled as lead perforated the wall and shutters. Trace took the time sprawled on his belly to reload his revolver. He had only what cartridges were in the loops on his belt—enough to fill his six-gun once more. He heard shouting and shooting outside. He crawled back to the window. Tyler had drawn their aim to the inn's second story. A pair of bandits crowded at the inn's door, ready to rush in once their horsed confederates ceased firing. Trace heard men below him likewise preparing to charge up the stairs.

***

Aimee huddled against Tyler's side as glass rained down upon them. She watched bullet holes appear in the opposite wall. The air grew dense with sawdust and smoke. Coughing, she asked who they were.

"Silas Kelly's boys, I reckon," said Tyler, jamming new cartridges into his gun as fast as he could shake out the spent ones. The casings that accumulated on the floor around him were still hot. When the firing paused, Tyler had a moment to consider how quiet it was when the building wasn't coming apart all around them.

From across the street, he heard Trace yell, "Tyler! They're coming up!"

Tyler jumped to his feet, pulling Aimee to hers and dragging her behind him to the doorway. He eyed the stairwell. In as calm a voice as he could manage, he told her to go further down the hall and hide in one of the other rooms. "Good girl," he said to himself as she scurried to obey, silent as a mouse.

***

One of the horsemen was reloading. The others had pistols raised, ready to fire at whichever of the cowboys showed his mug first. Two men lined up outside the inn, mirrored by two more across the street. The man reloading counted six cartridges into the palm of his hand. By feel, he slid each one into the cylinder, surveying the street and buildings with their shot-up faces. He said, "How many of us did they get?"

"Two," answered another of the horsemen. "Where's the rest of our boys?"

"They're supposed to be rounding up the horses," said a man on foot, holding a shotgun.

"Careful where you aim that pea-shooter," said the horseman now done reloading. "Boss wants the woman alive." More gunfire sounded east of them. The man squinted down the street. "What in tarnation?"

Another man chuckled. "The fight's down here, chaps."

But the man looking down the street wasn't so certain. "Who's that?"

"Looks like Billy."

***

Through the limited scope of the shutter, Trace saw a horse galloping down the main street, its rider waving to get the attention of the others, pointing from whence he came. Regardless of whether they understood him, his pals were inspired to act. Trace heard booted feet below him and watched the men across the way invade the inn. He bellowed a warning to Tyler and stationed himself at the top of the stairs.

***

A breathless Billy panted and pointed as he tried to get his words together. He choked out the news that the others were all dead. "He's coming," he wheezed. Before the rest could make sense of it, a shot rang out and a bullet punched through Billy's skull. The men on horseback all opened fire as a lone gunman dodged back between the buildings.

Josiah whirled out of the line-of-fire as bullets chewed through the edge of the building where he'd been standing. With his back against the wall, he felt the vibrations from each bite. He'd counted seven men—three on horseback and four afoot. The Malloy brothers had obviously separated. He wondered if one of them had Aimee or if they'd dropped her to hide in one of the other structures. With the bandits charging in, Josiah reckoned he'd find out soon enough.

***

As soon as Tyler glimpsed the man coming up the stairs, he loosed his gun, driving him back down. Four shots spent, he reloaded. A shotgun blasted a hole in the floor beside his feet. The man came up the stairs again, followed by a second. This time, the first man didn't retreat quickly enough. His pal didn't wait for him to drop before opening up with the shotgun. The blast hit the first man in the back as Tyler ducked into the room. The next blast came through the wall. The boards took the brunt of the damage, but the force still knocked Tyler off his feet. When he finally managed to breathe, the air felt like daggers in his lungs.

***

Trace heard two sets of steps below him. He waited in the doorway, revolver ready. He let the first man come up the stairs before shooting him dead. He listened for the second, trying to hear over the gunfire down in and across the street. There was a shotgun blast, pistol fire, and then the shotgun sounded again. Trace tried to focus on the fight that was his, to turn his mind from what he couldn't help.

***

Aimee picked the room at the very end of the hall, away from the front of the building, furthest from the shooting. She closed the door and found herself in an empty room with nowhere to hide. A small window let in light from an alley between buildings, so she didn't even have a shadowy corner to conceal her. She crept over the floor, easing her weight from foot to foot. The window panes were still intact. She rubbed grime from the glass with the sleeve of her dress. A man entered the alley below her. He wore a black hat and a dark brown duster. Aimee recognized his lank build and the stiff way he moved. Wyland held a revolver in each hand.

Aimee backed away from the window, no longer cautious with her footing. As the boards creaked, she didn't realize some of the steps didn't belong to her. Kicked inward, the door cracked loose of its hinges.

"Lucky guess." A squat man with a shotgun seized her arm and yanked her out into the hall. He shoved her along in front of him, prodding her with the butt of the gun. As they neared the stairs, Aimee saw a splintered hole in the wall and through it, Tyler's body.

***

The man below Trace was waiting him out. Everywhere, the firing had paused. Trace sidestepped to the shutter, keeping his gun pointed in the direction of the stairs. He noted the dead man still slumped in the saddle and how the other riders searched for movement up and down the street. Trace had just spied a figure in the alley catty-corner to his vantage point when a woman's wail pierced the silence. Trace heard a clatter of boots and saw a man emerge from the level below him to clamber up behind a rider. Aimee tumbled through the door of the inn, driven by the man with the shotgun.

Trace stampeded down the stairs. The man was forcing Aimee up onto a horse. Trace leveled his revolver at him and he raised the shotgun in return, firing before Trace could sight on him. Buckshot disintegrated the doorframe beside him and Trace dropped back inside. The bandits spurred their horses. Trace stepped from the doorway just as Josiah Wyland emerged from the alley across from him. Trace swung his weapon from the men getting away to face Wyland's double irons. He fanned the hammer on his six-shooter, emptying the revolver and driving the gunfighter back into the alley. Then he ran for the inn.

***

Josiah spit curses as he was forced to take cover. He rounded the corner as soon as Trace stopped shooting. He aimed at the escaping gang members, but they were out of handgun range and obscured by dust. He whistled for his horse and stalked into the inn.

At the bottom of the stairs, he paused and called out. "Malloy, I'm coming up," he said. "My guns are shucked." Figuring Trace less inclined to shoot an unarmed man, Josiah suited actions to words and holstered his irons. But he kept an elbow cocked, with fingers tickling one ivory grip, just in case.

At the top of the stairs, Josiah stepped over the bloody mess of a body near cut in half by buckshot at close-range. In the room beyond, Trace knelt beside Tyler. The younger man was in bad shape. Trace hauled him up onto his lap and hugged him. His revolver lay forgotten on the floor. The area was crisscrossed with lines of amber light through holes in the wall. Tyler's eyes rolled away from Trace, toward Josiah. His voice was tight with pain. "They took our sister."

***

Trace Malloy's horse was dead. Josiah lugged his tack into the inn and piled it on the floor, figuring Trace could come back for it. He found Tyler's horse wandering just outside of the abandoned town. He pulled the saddle off it as well.

When the brothers began to argue, with Tyler advocating Josiah's aid and Trace begging him to quit talking and rest, Josiah left to round up their mounts. He hitched his black and Tyler's paint to opposite ends of the post out front. He was rummaging through his bags, dumping the extra canned goods he'd just bought in Prospect, when the cowboys shuffled through the door. Tyler sagged against Trace, one arm across his big brother's shoulders, while Trace supported Tyler with both arms around the younger man's middle. Both men were sweating with the effort, and Trace's sleeve was as red as the front of Tyler's shirt. Trace lowered Tyler to sit against the building and marched up to Josiah.

Blue eyes slanted his way, though the gunfighter continued to adjust his gear.

"Just so we're clear, Wyland, if I was up to my neck in quicksand, I wouldn't call on you to pull me out. But I can't leave my brother."

The taller man nodded once.

Trace said, "This is me asking."

"I'll fetch your sister, Malloy." Josiah began tightening straps by quick, methodical tugs.

"If you cause her any grief or let any harm befall her—"

Josiah interrupted him. "Don't got to tell me what I already know."

It took both of them to get the wounded man up on the horse. Josiah held the reins while Trace climbed up behind his brother. Barely conscious, Tyler slumped back against Trace's chest. Josiah handed up the reins.

"We'll be at Cooper's," said Trace.

Josiah shook his head. "I can't go there," he said. "There's a place in Tucson called The Wishing Well."

"I know it," said Trace.

"I can get her there, and the owner will hide her until you follow."

"Aimee," said Tyler, though Josiah didn't realize he was speaking to him until the younger Malloy brother opened his eyes and looked down. "Her name is Aimee."

"Aimee," Josiah repeated. He felt the name resonate in his chest.

8

Aimee hurt all over. She'd been driven from the inn, prodded in the back with the butt of the shotgun and sent sprawling by forceful shoves. She'd stumbled off the sidewalk onto her hands and knees in the street, only to be plucked from the dirt by bulky arms about her torso. All she could do was wiggle and scream and watch Trace scramble for cover as gunfire tore through wooden walls like they were paper. She hardly noticed the bite of a rope being tied around her wrists, but when it was tossed over a saddle and given a yank, she felt fire clear to her armpits. A boost from behind had her slung over the saddle on her belly. Her captors routed the rope under the horse and across Aimee's back before winding and knotting it at the horn. She lifted her head, saw Trace emerge from the splintered doorway, saw Josiah Wyland step from the alley across from him. Guns were raised and pointed. Aimee heard shots and a crack in her neck as the horse surged forward. After that, all she heard was the hammering of hooves.

She struggled to draw breath as each bounce was a blow to her stomach, pushing the air back up and out of her lungs. All she could see was the dizzying blur of desert passing beneath her. By the time they cut her down, her arms were numb, her ribs bruised, and she'd bitten her tongue. She slid from the saddle and lay gulping on the ground. A couple of riders swapped positions and Aimee was made to sit up behind the man who'd shot Tyler, her arms on either side of his trunk, her wrists bound in front of him.

It was nightfall. Somewhere in the darkness, coyotes yipped and mewled. Ahead, mountains rose to block the starry sky. The open range narrowed into a valley between sheer rock walls that became taller and closer, until they were forced to ride single file through an artery-like crevasse leading into the mountain's heart.

They came to a clearing where a campfire projected a flickering light that made shadows dance upon the rock. Aimee was cut loose from the stocky man only to be bound hand and foot. She was left to lie within the ring of light while the men saw to their horses and joined others around the fire.

Whenever Aimee closed her eyes, she saw one or the other of her brothers—either Tyler covered in blood or Trace diving from bullets. So, she rolled her back to the fire and the men huddled round it and stared into the shadows. She felt that they stared back.

***

From a spot along the canyon wall, crouched down where neither moonlight nor the glow of the flames could reach him, Josiah studied Aimee. He was familiar with the rocky refuge from his days riding with the Kelly gang. He knew every route in and out. He'd made it to the hideout ahead of the group and had been in place to observe their arrival.

She wasn't hurt. Weary and sore, he reckoned, but uninjured. She'd been able to stand. Josiah determined she'd be able to walk

80

the distance, through another crevasse too narrow for mounts, to his horse. He thought to approach her once the bandits had settled down to sleep. He'd steal her away at gunpoint if she couldn't otherwise be convinced to accompany him. Until then, he was oddly content to watch the firelight glint off her hair.

She lay quietly but didn't sleep. Josiah could tell by the way she'd startle then go still again that her mind wouldn't let her rest. Her face was in shadow, but he could picture her gray eyes.

Josiah had known her brothers when they were boys, had even been to the Malloy farm a time or two, along with Silas, Rook, and Jerrod Kelly. But he couldn't remember any mention of their having a sister. She would have been no more than ten. Josiah scoured his memory for a forgotten glimpse of her and out of it came the vision of a small girl reaching up to touch a white horse. She was a blithe little angel in an ivory smock, with a halo of corn-silk hair, balanced on her tiptoes in the dust.

Josiah sat back against the rock wall. The horse had been his—too old for work, too big for speed, but in the memory unfolding in his mind, he watched it gentle as a lamb under her touch. He remembered never being so pleased that something was his. He'd been bold enough to approach her, though he half-expected, as he closed the distance between them, that she would shimmer and fade like a mirage. He couldn't recall what he'd said, but she turned and looked up at him with curious, downy-gray eyes.

How old had he been, fifteen? Old enough to have already grown accustomed to seeing suspicion and distaste in people's expressions when they looked at him. But she'd let him stand beside her, let him place his hand over hers on the animal's neck.

Aimee Malloy. He never saw her again, not until Mrs. Rook Kelly opened the door and looked up at him with those very same eyes.

They rode the white horse, Josiah remembered. He laced his fingers together, she put her foot in his hands, and he boosted her up onto its back. She held out her arms and leaned back against his chest, with eyes closed and face tilted toward the sun. Josiah reckoned Trace Malloy would have beaten him bloody if he found out, then he remembered having received such a pounding around that time. Trace hadn't cited a reason and Josiah hadn't made the connection. Soon after that day, his life had altered—substantially and irrevocably—and he'd forgotten both the ride and the beating.

***

The barking of dogs echoed through every canyon crag. Aimee picked up her head and looked around. Josiah muttered a curse and touched fingertips to pistol grips.

Silas Kelly entered the clearing from yet another footpath, holding a ham hock over his head as three hounds bounded around him. He chucked the bone and the dogs chased it, snarling at one another.

One of the bandits rose to meet him. "We got her." He pointed to where Aimee pretended to sleep. "We got her for you, and the Malloy boys are dead."

"Rook will be pleased," Silas said to himself as he studied the small form, very still, at the edge of the light. He scanned the seven faces looking at him from around the campfire. He frowned. "How many did we lose?"

"Two of us stayed to guard the camp," said one man.

"We lost twelve," said the man standing. "But they had help."

"A real gunman, not just a cowboy," said another.

"I don't suppose you shot this real gunman," said Silas.

"We hardly saw him, Sir." The man blanched when emerald eyes narrowed. "Sorry, Boss," he corrected.

Silas unbuckled and coiled his cartridge belt. He left it with his gun and his hat on a rock and walked over to squat beside Aimee. Her eyes were closed, but she shuddered when he placed a hand on her shoulder. "My condolences," he said and guided her to sit up.

"It was your men that killed them," she said.

"That doesn't keep me from sympathizing," he answered. "I have brothers too." Silas drew a long, thin knife from a sheath in his boot. He moved to Aimee's feet and sawed through the ropes binding her ankles.

"What would you do if a man had them killed?" Her voice was as stiff as her body.

Silas freed her wrists next. "I'd disembowel the wretch," he said. Then his voice softened. "But gently. He'd live for when the crows started picking." As he eyed her, the corners of his mouth curled. He said, "I don't think you have it in you."

Silas set the dirk aside and took one of Aimee's hands in his. A shiver vibrated through her as he massaged one wrist then the other. When he released her, Aimee turned her back to him. And jolted when his fingers delved into her hair. He combed out the tangles and began to braid. "Do you know who he was, the man your brothers had helping them?"

Aimee couldn't stop her body or voice from shaking. "There was no one helping us," she said. She felt his fist at the back of her neck, grasping the braid at its thickest point. He used the grip to direct her forward onto her hands and knees. He leaned over her, planting his free hand in the dirt next to hers. Aimee could feel the line of his body, barely touching. She glanced at the blade, firelight winking off it. Silas lowered his cheek beside hers. He too looked at the knife, then at her.

"Your husband doesn't want you marked," he said. "But I'm certain you can still show me a good time." He let go of her hair and smoothed the braid down her back, hand gliding between their bodies. At her waist, he rotated his wrist and skimmed his palm over the curve of her backside. Aimee grabbed for the knife. Silas was quicker. He reared up, moving his hand from the dirt to her cheek and slamming her head down upon the hard ground. Aimee moaned. He continued to hold her there like an eagle might pin a rodent in its talons.

Josiah rose up off the balls of his feet. He eased a Colt from its holster.

Aimee stared into the darkness, still feeling that someone stared back. Her head ached, squashed beneath Silas's hand. She whimpered to feel his pelvis against her backside, his other hand groping to raise her skirt. He didn't notice the shadow that detached itself from the rocks and stalked towards them.

Before Wyland's shape materialized out of the night, Aimee saw the raised revolver. She stopped squirming and froze. For a moment, hard blue eyes met hers, then he fired. The explosion rolled like thunder around the clearing.

Josiah shifted his aim to the outlaws coming off their bedrolls and scrambling for their weapons. Aimee snatched up Silas's blade as she stumbled to her feet. She dashed for the shadows. Josiah shot a bandit who was leveling a shotgun at him, then followed.

Gunshots chased them. Aimee collided with a rock wall, turned and hurried along it, blindly searching for a way out. She was caught by strong fingers that dug into her shoulder and spun her around. She lunged with the knife, and it lodged in something solid, tearing the handle from her grasp. A harsh whisper said, "This way." She fled in the direction he pushed her and would have missed the gap in the rocks, but his arm came around her, yanking her back against him before shoving her into the crag. Behind them, gun powder flashed and the dogs barked.

Silas roared, "Blood for blood, Wyland!"

When Aimee glimpsed moonlight, she rushed for it, breaking into a night that seemed bright by comparison. Behind her, the gunslinger let out a sharp whistle. There was an answering whinny and a conglomerate of shadows trotted toward them. Aimee gaped as Josiah drew the dirk out of his thigh. He flung it to the ground and swung up into the saddle. He held out a hand to her.

She could hear the shouts of pursuit somewhere in the rock tunnel. Louder came the braying of hounds. The stallion danced with excitement, wanting to run. Josiah kept a tight hold on the reins with one hand. The other he still held out to her. Aimee took it and he pulled her up behind him. The mutts broke from the mountain and charged them. Josiah snatched a gun from his hip, popped off three shots, and gave the horse its head.

They flew across the desert by the light of the moon, hooves and heartbeats racing, each caught up in the wild rhythm, neither daring to conject how the ride would end. Though she'd taken his hand, it was not trust that kept Aimee clinging to his wiry body with all her might, not a sense of safety that his strength evoked in her, that made her unwilling to loosen her hold. What she felt was more akin to fear.

A gunfighter knew the excitement of predator stalking prey, of riding fast, of staking his life on his skill with a gun. None of those things were new to Josiah. And he'd known when he held his hand out to her, that if she took it, it would be because he was the lesser evil and at that moment, she feared something more than him. But knowing couldn't spoil the triumph of her reaching out and placing her hand in his. As they raced away, it was not the threat of pursuit or the exertion of riding hard that had his heart beating wildly, but the thrill of Aimee's arms tight around him, her small hands splayed over his chest, her soft body pressed tightly against his back.

***

"I've lived too long." Beth Cooper glanced at the aged man, saw that he wasn't really speaking to her—he seldom did. His lamentations were directed to the embers in the hearth or to the picture on the mantle in front of him.

"Eat your supper, Pa," she said and turned her attention back to the books she was dusting. Volumes of law and ideology penned by Jefferson, Paine, Franklin, and others—they hadn't been touched in three years, except for cleaning. She replaced the last one on the shelf, sliding it flush with the others. The candle at her father's elbow sputtered, drowning in its own wax. Beth took it up and carefully crossed the one-room cabin, pulling back the curtain separating her bed from the rest of the room. There was another candle on the stand beside the wash basin. She lit it before blowing out the dying flame and brought it to him.

A newspaper on his lap was opened to the shooting in Prospect. The headline read, "Three Lives Snuffed Out." It took only a glance for Beth to locate the name Josiah Wyland in black type. She didn't care to know any more, so she adjusted the blanket over her father's legs and went back to her dusting.

"The world's in a bad way, son," the man said with a sigh, gazing up at the boy's portrait framed in tin. "I won't be sorry to leave it."

Beth fetched a cup and poured brandy from the bottle kept on the table beside her father's bed. She took one swallow for herself then set the cup beside the candle. Because he was easily chilled in his later years, she knelt and added another log to the fire. She picked up the plate on which his supper had gone cold, took her shawl, and stepped outside.

She scraped the plate into the hogs' trough before sitting on the front porch swing. The moon was a full silver-blue orb. She gazed at it until the dark and light spots blurred, then she wiped her cheeks. Her father wouldn't ask her to explain her tears, but she still preferred he not see them.

Beth sat surrounded by quiet night, the snoring and snorting of pigs the only sound. She grew less warm. As she adjusted her shawl, she heard a clip-clop, slow and heavy in the dark. For a long while, she stared at nothing. Finally, the shadows took on shape. "Pa." She jumped to her feet. "Pa." She fled inside.

***

Trace kept one hand on the reins and one hand bracing his brother's head, stroking his hair when he moaned and checking his pulse when he was silent. The horse would only move so fast, burdened with the weight of two men. Trace would have gotten down and prodded the animal along if he'd thought Tyler could stay upright by himself.

Trace feared they'd find the house abandoned, that the lawman had settled elsewhere after his retirement. But he saw the flicker of light within, and Del Cooper himself waited on the front porch, rifle raised. Trace slowly spread his arms wide. "State your name and your business." The voice was hoarse with age but still commanding.

"It's Trace Malloy." He kept his hands up as the bent figure approached. "Sir, my brother's been shot." The old man's hair and mustache had gone gray, the face lined, but the eyes were the same.

Del squinted up at Trace and Tyler, then turned back toward the house and hollered for Beth to come take the rifle.

*****

Josiah coaxed the stallion down from a gallop to a trot, to an eventual halt. Moonlight frosted the desert for miles around them. The animal's breathing was the only sound. Aimee's arms remained tight around his ribs. He could feel her face pressed between his shoulder blades. He tried to turn his head, but she was hunkered down out of view. His touch slid down her forearm, over her hand. He gave it a squeeze, then a small shake. But her grip didn't loosen.

"Hey." He cleared his throat. "I need you to get down so I can get down."

Aimee felt the pounding of his heart as though it were housed in her own breast. But the low, raspy voice sounded strangely far away—it didn't rumble as Trace's had. "We can't stop for long," he said. Josiah moved his head and hair brushed across her forehead, tickling the bridge of her nose. His coat had a strange smell, and it was wet. The front of her dress too was moist. Strong, slender fingers pried at hers. Then he pinched the thin skin on the back of her hand.

She gasped and pulled away and might have fallen to the ground had he not caught her arm and eased her decent. Once she was down, Josiah dropped heavily from the saddle. He moved a slight distance away, scanning for movement. They had a decent head start. He got down on his knees and put his ear to the dirt. It would take some time for the bandits to navigate their mounts back out of the canyon.

Aimee stayed by the horse, hugging herself, watching him. She shivered as the air cooled the damp patch on her dress. She looked down and noticed a dark stain. She touched it, and her hand came away covered in blood.

"It's mine," he said. She watched him peel off his jacket. There were dark splotches on his shirt. He pulled it over his head, tore it to pieces, and tied one strip around his thigh. He held the remains out to her, telling her to tie a section around his arm. She took the cloth and inched closer. He turned his elbow out from his side so she could bind the bloody scrape where a bullet had grazed his bicep. Small, timid fingers felt like butterflies brushing his skin. "Tighter."

His voice was quiet, but Aimee quailed at the emotionless tone. She wondered how many wounds he'd sustained to make him indifferent to the pain. When she'd bandaged his arm, he pivoted on the balls of his feet so that she faced his back. There was a dark hole oozing a dark stream that ran from his shoulder down to his waist, where it soaked into the seat of his trousers. He waited as she stared. "There's still a bullet in there," she said.

He angled his head. She knew he looked at her, but she couldn't see his face beneath his hat. "It'll keep," he said. Aimee held a swatch of shirt to the wound with the palm of her hand, winding the rest over his shoulder and under his arm. She trembled to feel his blood, warm between her fingers, and his skin, hot beneath her hand.

Josiah closed his eyes and inhaled deeply. In the middle of the desert, leaning over him like that, her scent flooded his senses. She finished and he stood, unsure if it was her or loss of blood that made him woozy. There were bruises—or maybe only shadows— on her face. He reached up to tilt her chin, to get a better look. She shrank away and he dropped his hand.

Josiah eased back into his coat, climbed back atop the stallion, and helped Aimee up behind him. He noticed she hesitated to take his hand and only gripped the sides of his jacket, careful not to touch him anymore than was necessary to stay secure on the mount. Again, Josiah remembered when the horse had been white instead of black. There was no doubt in his mind Aimee was the girl from his memory. He wanted to ask her if she remembered that bright day, but he knew she would never be able to recognize him as that boy.

9

Since he settled in Arizona Territory, Del Cooper had lived in the same small cabin. He built it for him and his wife when Promise was a fledging little hope of a town. He always planned to build larger, when it was more than just the two of them. But when Beth was five, his first wife succumbed to dysentery, and it was eight years before he remarried. She was a widow whose grown daughter had left her alone. Again, he'd thought to add on to the home, but reckoned Beth herself would marry soon. After two years and twice as many miscarriages, his second wife died bringing Cooper's son into the world. Before a fine house was more than a thought, the boy too was taken from him. By that time, Promise was no more, and it was clear to Del that he would die in the same one room.

The cabin was more crowded than it had ever been. Trace Malloy sat in a chair pushed away from the table, his elbows on his knees and his hands fisted in his hair. They'd put his brother on Del's bed. Beth sat on a stool by Tyler's side, meticulously digging fragments of shot, shards of wood, and bits of cloth out of the wounded man's bloodied chest. She worked stoically at the task, depositing the debris in a bowl set on the mattress near his hip.

Del sat opposite Trace, sipping a cup of coffee and contemplating the younger man. Now and then, he'd ask a question to distract him, though Trace still flinched each time Tyler moaned. Malloy explained they'd been herding cattle in Texas when Aimee's letter found them, bringing months-old news of their parents' violent deaths and their sister's unexpected marriage.

"The worst of it is she'd been writing all that time, pleading for us to return for the funeral, begging for advice on how to answer Rook Kelly's proposal." Trace shook his head. "How abandoned she must have felt." And how scared, when months later she went to clean out the stove and discovered scraps of parchment with her handwriting among the ashes. That's when she'd begun to write and send her letters in secret.

"It's not your fault," said Del.

"We shouldn't have stayed away so long," said Trace. He'd taken it for granted that at home Aimee would always be safe, that nothing would change there. "I always thought Tyler was the one I needed to look out for, keep out of trouble." He glanced over at the bed. "Protect."

Tyler's eyes were rimmed in red, his lips rimmed in white. He inhaled with sharp gasps and exhaled in huffs, while the woman picked at him like a bird pecking seed from suet. "Stop," he said. "Give me a minute, before I disgrace myself." The invasive fingers fell away.

Beth placed the dull utensils across the rim of the bowl and dropped both her hands and her gaze to her lap. Tyler blinked several times then looked at her out of the corner of his eye. She'd tended to his injuries, tirelessly, for more than an hour. Throughout the torturous process, he stole countless glances at her, if only to have something to concentrate on other than the pain. But he hadn't a moment, uninterrupted, to assess the details.

She was tall for a woman, emphasized by her straight posture. She seemed to Tyler as contained as her hair in its bun — dark hair, like her father's had been. Tyler might have decided she was a stern, unaffected creature, if it weren't for her eyes. They never rested, but flitted about, evading capture. Her sure hands had been moving over him since he lay on the bed, but she hadn't truly looked at him in all that time. He didn't think it was the blood or torn flesh, but maybe rather that he was flesh and blood.

Tyler swallowed and hoped his voice didn't croak. "You're very capable, Beth Cooper," he said. He watched her carefully, ready when surprised eyes finally made contact with his. They were brown eyes but warm, and far gentler than he expected. He tried valiantly to smile at her but could only manage to make the corner of his mouth twitch. He was rewarded nonetheless, with a blush — visible even in low light — that brought a rosy hue to her cheeks and neck, and warmth to his blood. She averted her gaze the next moment, and he was free to stare and appreciate the sight.

The reprieve was short-lived. A snippet of conversation, something that Tyler failed to catch, stole the color back out of her complexion. Her shield of composure slid back into place, and she picked up the tools, asking with a glance. Tyler gave a slight nod and took a deep breath.

Del said, "It wasn't Apaches that killed your ma and pa. These parts haven't seen a raid in years. I reckon it was highwaymen with no other quarry."

Trace said, "You mean like Silas Kelly and his gang?"

Del mulled it over. "They usually operate in the surrounding counties, out of Rook's jurisdiction. But they hole up and hide their loot in the nearby mountains, until they can journey back to Canyon Diablo."

"So, Silas has a sanctuary in central Arizona, while Rook gets credit for keeping his element out of Prospect," said Trace, thinking peace had become a charade and the law a ruse.

As if reading his mind, Del said, "The side of justice was brought low the day Rook Kelly pinned on that star. Folk will have no choice but to let him keep it, unless someone steps up to challenge him and Silas both. Folk been waiting a long time for you to come home, Trace."

Trace swallowed. "I know you're retired," he said. "But how could you let it happen?"

The old man raised his eyes to a frame on the mantle. "My threat to the likes of Kelly was neutralized before Rook ever sought the office," he said. "But I'll go with you to see the governor."

"I've got to get to Tucson." Trace told him how Wyland had agreed to help, how his sister's best and only hope was the cold-blooded killer.

Del stroked his mustache and listened. "We'll go to Tucson first, then Prescott."

When Beth had done all she could for Tyler, the brothers were able to rest. Tyler slept where he lay in the bigger bed, and

Trace was persuaded to accept Beth's. Del resumed his position by the fire, but he did not take up his study of the embers or cocoon himself in blankets and sorrows. Instead, he plotted.

The return of the brothers Malloy awakened a dormant purpose in the old lawman. He'd dedicated his career—first roaming the mesquite brush as a Ranger, then passing down judgement from the bench—to persecuting the scourge of society. With one pursuit, his fate had become entwined with that of his prey, never to be extricated.

Two men. One name. Wyland. Del had seen the sire strangled only for his spawn to replace him. Arrest and incarceration had put Josiah out of Del's reach, then Rook Kelly's appointment provided him a rock to hide under. No longer, thought Del Cooper.

Her father didn't appear to notice when Beth donned her shawl and went out to tend to the brothers' horse. Neither did he seem to note her return. She washed her hands and face, scrubbing them with plain soap and rinsing with water from the basin beside her bed. She brushed out her hair, slipped off her shoes, and because there was no other place, she eased down atop the quilt beside Tyler Malloy.

Tyler awoke at dawn and made the mistake of scratching a spot high on his belly. When the itch turned to fire, he swore. And swallowed the curse when he noticed the woman asleep beside him. She lay on her side with her back to him, wearing the same cotton dress, with wool stockings on her feet. The rays through the window turned Beth Cooper's dark hair to shades of warm chocolate and vibrant nutmeg. Still propped up with pillows, he looked down at the side of her face. In sleep, she was finally unguarded, even vulnerable. He watched her and did not hear his brother roll out of the smaller bed.

"Do you need anything?" Trace stopped midstride when Tyler whipped his head around and scowled at him, index finger pressed to his lips. Tyler pointed at a blanket folded over the back of a chair and Trace fetched it, then stood and watched his little brother endeavor to spread it over Del's daughter without waking her. "Give you a hand?"

"Got it."

"You sure?" Trace grinned when Tyler glared at him.

"Go put your trousers on, will you?" Long underwear fit Trace's muscular form like a shrunken sock. He ruffled his brother's hair before strolling back across the room.

***

During the night, Aimee had been too desperate to care who delivered her from danger, too terrified to consider whether she traded one threat for another. All she'd wanted was distance. But come dawn, they were riding into the breaking sun, and she was forced to remember whose company she kept and for whom he worked.

Josiah felt her tense and scanned the horizon. It was empty, so he reckoned she'd just concluded her closest danger was now him. He thought if they could both ignore it for a time, if she could bear his presence a little longer, they could get to where they were going.

He knew news of his betrayal would already be on its way to Rook, that he'd lost the four-day window before every bounty hunter in the West would be after him for reward and reputation. He knew Silas would be out for blood with an army of cutthroats behind him. And he knew there would be one other, one who'd undoubtedly been waiting for Josiah to stray across the line of the law and wouldn't rest until justice was done, the one man who didn't fear the name Wyland.

"Don't," he said. But she slid down from the saddle. He pulled on the reins so the horse was nearly stopped when her toes touched the ground. She backed away, looking up at him. There was courage in those big gray eyes again. Josiah realized he admired it. But he didn't have time for it. "Don't do this." He held out a hand to her, but she shook her head.

"I'll go no further with you," Aimee said. He looked around as if to ask what choice she had, where else she would go. Aimee looked too. There was a greenish-yellow haze, the color of an old bruise, where cloudless sky met shapeless desert. Man, woman, and horse were the only beings for miles.

Aimee thought it strange her heart could be as barren as the landscape yet feel so heavy. She'd heard her kidnappers confirm that her brothers were dead. She was certain Wyland had killed Trace and if she went with him, he would return her to her husband, a man who'd proved he cared nothing for her.

The bounty hunter continued to hold out his hand. Aimee looked up into sapphire eyes, cold in the shade of his hat. She decided it would be a waste of breath to try to appeal to a man like Josiah Wyland. She turned and started back the way they'd come. She heard him sigh and drop his hand. But he didn't ride off and leave her. He didn't dismount. He didn't even turn the horse around. Instead, he coaxed the animal backwards, keeping pace with her as if to emphasize the futility of her situation and taunt her with it. She reckoned he was waiting for her to come to her senses, to concede defeat. Though uncertainty hounded her every step, Aimee continued to walk.

She glanced sidelong at him. His left hand hung at his side. The reins were loose in his right. He leaned slightly in the saddle, toward her. What she did next, he could never have anticipated. It surprised even her.

The seeping wound in his thigh was too obvious a target for Aimee to have to think about—she whirled and drove her elbow into it, exerting all her strength and fear. When he doubled over, she grabbed ahold of his jacket and pulled with her full weight. It was enough to unseat him.

Before what she had done caught up with him, Josiah fell head-first off his own horse. He came down on his injured shoulder at the stallion's hooves, and pain shot through his arm like a lightning bolt, leaving the limb numb. He felt Aimee stumble over his legs and looked around in time to see her scramble up to take his place in the saddle.

The horse was dancing about, and Aimee was struggling to catch the fallen reins when the gunfighter staggered to his feet. Pain, rage, or a combination thereof twisted wolfish features into a snarl. His eyes were icy slits. One arm hung limp, but a pistol appeared in his other hand. Clutching the stallion's mane in one small fist, Aimee leaned forward, almost lying along its neck. She stretched the fingers of her free hand to reach the reins fluttering like ribbons in the wind. The horse tossed its head and the saddle horn smacked her in the chest. The animal was churning up a storm of dust, turning in circles so that Aimee caught periodic glimpses of Wyland gauging her struggle, tensed like a predator about to pounce. She didn't know if he would shoot or grab for the reins himself. A leather strap brushed her fingers and she grasped for it madly, finally catching hold.

Aimee brought the horse around. She gave a breathless, inarticulate shout and kicked at its flanks. The stallion's front hooves came off the ground, then it lunged forward.

Josiah straightened up and watched them go, woman and horse fighting each other as they zig-zagged in an erratic westward direction. He tapped the barrel of the Colt against his leg. Except for the black horse shrinking in the distance, there was nothing to see in any direction. He holstered the gun since he wasn't going to use it. His shoulder throbbed and his arm tingled as feeling returned. The leg supporting much of his weight trembled just standing. Josiah propped his hands on his hips and shook his head. He was stunned but had a strange compulsion to laugh out loud. Maybe it was another symptom of blood loss. Maybe it was her.

The ground was still cool. He lowered himself to the dirt and stretched out on his back, tucking his good arm behind his head and dropping his hat over his eyes.

***

Aimee felt as if she'd been struggling with the spirited horse for hours. The animal wanted its head, and she had to fight to control the mammoth creature. The stallion would take off at a pace that nearly swept her off its back, then when she pulled on the reins, it would shake its head and hop in protest, almost bouncing her off. She had no idea how many miles they'd covered or where their confused course had taken them. The animal seemed inexhaustible, while Aimee was beyond tired. Her hands were raw, her arms burning, and sweat stung her eyes. Her thighs were cramped, and it felt like her throat had been swabbed with a feather. She needed to rest and get her bearings, but the horse ignored her plea of *whoa*.

She hauled back on the reins to stop, and the horse reared up. Aimee felt herself begin to slide. She clutched at the mane, grabbed for the saddle horn, but she was falling. She landed hard on her bottom. The animal bolted.

Aimee sat on the hot dirt, not quite believing what she'd done or where it had gotten her. The desert was as empty where she'd ended up as where she'd left Wyland. She remembered him pulling the revolver and decided if he tracked her down, it would be to shoot her for the trouble she'd caused him. She imagined him furious and justified in his fury. It occurred to Aimee that she didn't fear his wrath as much as Rook's calm. Alone in no man's land, Aimee wobbled to her feet and began walking once again.

***

The thud of hooves resonated through the hard-packed soil, rousing Josiah. He raised his hat and squinted at the approaching horse. Big and black, it was his, and it was without rider. He labored to his feet with a groan and waited for the mount to come to him.

"I hope you enjoyed your gallivanting," he scolded. The stallion proved difficult for even its owner to handle on occasion, so Josiah wasn't surprised it had lost little Aimee Malloy. Aimee Kelly, he reminded himself. After cinching the saddle, he hauled himself up. "Show me where you let her off," he said.

By the time he picked out small footprints at the end of the meandering horse tracks, Josiah could see the figure in the distance. Though she must have heard him approach, she didn't look around or stop walking.

Josiah dismounted a short distance behind her—he wasn't giving her the chance to commandeer his horse again. He removed his gun-belt and looped it over the saddle horn in case it occurred to her to steal one of his six-shooters next. He called for her to hold up, not really expecting she would, then started after her. He gained on her, despite his bad leg. Her pace was little more than a shuffle. When he'd about reached her, she tried to run, stumbling only a couple steps before he caught her. "I said stop."

His arms came around either side of her, pinning hers at her sides, and drawing her back against his front. Aimee allowed herself to be captured only a moment before going feral in his hold, kicking and screeching. Josiah hugged her to his chest and dropped to his knees, dragging her down with him. He leaned his full weight against her back, trapping her between him and the ground. Still she squirmed, all the while screaming that she wouldn't go back, that she wouldn't let him take her. She said that he'd have to kill her too.

His hand clamped over her mouth, slipped when she jerked, and she bit him. His other hand fisted in her hair and yanked her head back. Aimee felt his facial hair, wiry against her jaw, and his breath puffing against her neck. A low voice competed with her high-pitched panic, telling her he wasn't going to hurt her, that he wasn't taking her back.

"You are," she said, her voice reduced to a squeak. "I'm not," he insisted, out of breath.

He told her he was taking her to Tucson, to her brothers. She cried that her brothers were dead, that she'd seen Tyler not moving, that she'd seen him shoot at Trace. He told her he hadn't shot Trace, that they were both alive when he'd left them.

"You're lying," she cried. He said, "I'm not."

She said, "You work for Rook." He hissed, "I'll kill Rook."

Beneath him, Aimee went silent and still, and Josiah knew he'd once again said the wrong thing. He released her and fell back upon the sunbaked ground.

Aimee stayed on her hands and knees, blinking as his words sunk in. She believed him, perhaps only because she needed to. All thoughts of running deserted her, replaced with a queer, quiet relief. Tasting a metallic bitterness, she wiped blood from her lips. She sat back on her heels and peered at him over her shoulder. Josiah lay with his eyes closed, his chest heaving, and his arms flung wide. There was fresh blood soaking through his jacket and bandages. The meat of his right hand showed angry red marks left by her teeth. Again, she wiped a sleeve over her mouth.

The duster gaped open, leaving his torso bared from the band of his trousers to the bandana about his neck. Aimee's focus shifted from new wounds to old. A white slash spanned his tanned belly from left ribs to right hip. The rash of scars that pocked the side of his face and neck reached further down, over his upper chest to the nipple. Other spots looked like flat white marbles—one between a pair of ribs, another above his collarbone, and two to the left of his sternum where someone had aimed for his heart.

It occurred to Aimee that Josiah Wyland had bled for her and killed for her. He'd risked his life for hers and vowed to kill for her again. She had no idea why—nothing about him allowed her to anticipate it. He was a complete stranger to her.

The sun through Josiah's eyelids made a fiery collage of reds and oranges. The heat of the earth sucked the energy right out of him and with it, the anger. It was an emotion he'd felt acutely in his youth but learned early to keep stifled, a dangerous emotion for any man and particularly for a gunfighter. Josiah never declared his intention to kill and never expressed regret or boasted of it after. Out of anger, he wanted to murder Rook Kelly. In that anger, he'd gone and told Aimee as much. He reckoned she'd never trust him now. It occurred to him it wouldn't matter either way if he continued to lie there. So, he rolled and pushed to his feet.

Aimee watched him pick his hat up out of the dirt. The horse had stuck around. A low whistle summoned it to Josiah's side. He unhooked a canteen and took a long swallow. Aimee climbed to her feet and approached, hopefully. She still tasted blood. When he handed her the container, she drank greedily and gratefully. He unhooked another and emptied it into his hat for the horse.

After horse and humans had their fill, Josiah secured the canteens. He tried to decide what would be the right thing to say—easiest for him to speak and Aimee to hear—to get her to come with him. He didn't think either of them had the strength for any more fuss. Before he said anything, she touched his arm. Small fingers curled around his wrist. He relinquished his hand to the gentle pressure and watched her take a handkerchief from a pocket in her dress, wrapping it around the torn and swollen flesh. The bandage wasn't very tight, but he didn't correct her.

When she was done, Aimee let go of his hand and peeked up at him. As his eyes roamed her face, she wondered what she ought to say. Sorry and thanks both seemed like too much and not enough. She was a little afraid he might leave her there if she didn't say something. She was about to speak when he reached up and removed his hat. He lowered it onto the top of her head and she forgot what she'd intended to say.

He moved aside and gestured her toward the horse. Aimee took a small step forward and reached out to touch the stallion's neck, hesitating when the animal shifted. Josiah placed his hand over hers, pressing her palm to the hot horseflesh. "It's not his intention to frighten you," he said. "He only wants you to be certain." His long fingers and wide palm dwarfing hers seemed very familiar to Aimee. He withdrew before she could make sense of the brief sensation.

She raised her foot to the stirrup and stretched for the saddle horn, arms trembling with fatigue. She hopped up off the ground, lost momentum, and came back down. She tried again, without success. Josiah moved alongside the stallion's shoulder. He linked his fingers together to make a cradle of his hands. Aimee felt another jolt of familiarity. She carefully put her foot in his hands and he lifted her up. He handed her the reins, took ahold of the front and back of the saddle, and heaved himself up. It took two attempts before he was positioned behind her. They were both slim enough to fit together in the seat, sandwiched between the pommel and cantle. He turned the horse in the right direction with his heel against its side. "Keep east until dusk," he said to her. He clucked to the horse and they were underway.

10

Silas Kelly rode into Prospect, down the center of Main Street, tall in the saddle of a palomino with members of his gang fanned out in his wake like the tail of the peacock. Townspeople stopped what they were doing, stood and watched with that peculiar reverence folk have for the things they both fear and admire yet do not understand. From the shade of the porch out front of the jailhouse, the younger Kelly brothers watched as well—one with bemused pride, the other with covert envy.

Silas wore black boots, vest, trousers, and hat, and a white shirt. All were remarkably clean, as if the dust didn't settle on him the way it did everybody else. His clothing was accented by shining spurs, polished pistol, and a band of silver scallops around the crown of his hat. The palomino was outfitted with silver-studded black saddle and bridle. As their older brother rode up to the jailhouse steps, Jerrod met him with a wide grin and Rook with a scowl.

"Nice day for a parade," said Jerrod.

Silas waved his hand and his entourage dispersed, drifting in the direction of the saloons and brothels. He slipped from the saddle and landed lightly like a cat. "Maybe if I weren't a dozen men short," he said.

Without a word, Rook turned on his heel and stalked into the building. Silas swaggered after him. Jerrod followed.

"Get out," the sheriff growled at two nervous deputies who skittered like roaches out the door. "Two cowboys killed twelve armed men?"

"Not by themselves," said Silas.

The Kelly three faced one another, forming a circle on the jail's floor. Silas posed with chin held high, one hand behind his back and the other slid into his vest pocket. Rook crossed his arms over his chest and lowered his chin. Jerrod stood with boots planted shoulder-length apart. He tucked one thumb into his gun-belt and nibbled the other cuticle.

"After a running shootout and some hide-and-seek in old Promise, my boys left Trace and Tyler for dead," said Silas.

Rook said, "Then where's Aimee?"

"The plow-chasers had some help." Silas unbuttoned his vest and drew back the black fabric to reveal a red stain where blood leaked through a bandage beneath his shirt. "He stole her out from under me. I told you that was one stray you couldn't tame."

"Wyland." Rook's eyes flashed and his nostrils flared. Silas only smiled. Rook told Jerrod to go saddle up. "You ride as soon as I write the warrant."

"Where am I going?"

Rook looked to Silas who said, "Wyland turns up, he isn't found. But if he needs patched up, he'll go to Tucson."

When their younger brother had left, Rook turned to Silas. "I'll send a deputy to confirm the Malloy brothers' deaths. How long will it take you to recruit more men?"

"For you or for me?"

"If Trace Malloy survived, if he ousts me," said Rook, "the next time you promenade through this town will be on your way to the noose."

***

It took four and one-half strides for Trace Malloy to cross the floor of Cooper's cabin. His brother counted from his seat on the edge of the bed. Trace turned and Tyler counted again. It gave him something to concentrate on besides the impending prick and subsequent burn that came as Beth Cooper slowly peeled away his soiled bandages. Her gentle touch and the fact that she was positioned between his knees made the process a special kind of torture.

"I won't die if you go to Tucson," he said to Trace. "Not with this one fussing."

"We can stall another day." Outside, Tyler's horse was saddled and waiting for Trace. A mare as gray and bent as the old man was prepared for Del Cooper.

"I don't reckon I could stand another day of your worrying," said Tyler.

"Kelly men might find you here," said Trace.

"They'll be looking for Wyland, not us." Tyler winced when Beth inadvertently tore open a scab. "Blazes woman, I ain't a chicken you're plucking." When she stilled, he had a moment to regret his language and tone. Then in one movement, she straightened and ripped off the last of the dressing. In four paces, she marched out the door. "Please," said Tyler. "Go to Tucson. Bring home Aimee."

Trace said, "I can't believe we sent him after her, a man like that."

"Can't think of anyone better qualified, can you?"

Trace looked at his brother's chest and grimaced. He glanced toward the door to confirm Cooper's daughter was out of earshot. He said, "That woman might kill you, but I don't think she'll let you die."

"Speaking of women," said Tyler. "Say hello to Holly for me."

Tyler watched from the doorway as the horses trotted toward the southern horizon. Beth watched them too, standing at the porch railing, her back to him. When he stepped out, she said, "You ought to be in bed."

He said, "I need to use the privy."

"Let me replace the bandages first." He followed her back inside and sat on the edge of the bed again, leaning back on his hands to give her better access.

Beth had misplaced the net she used to secure her bun. Loose hair kept slipping forward over her shoulder, and she kept tossing it back, away from Tyler's wounds and out of her way. When both her hands were engaged in her task, he gathered up the wayward locks and held them at the nape of her neck. His hand was still in place, and the gooseflesh on her arms had not yet dissipated by the time she finished.

Tyler waited for her to peek up at him, to meet his eyes for the first time since he'd snapped at her. "I like it down," he said. "And I rather like your fussing over me." He leaned forward and reached out his other hand to cup her jaw. He only wanted to prolong the connection. It surprised him to see real fear in her eyes a moment before she pulled away. And it surprised him how quickly she fled, snatching up her daddy's rifle on her way out the door. She left strands of hair tangled around his fingers.

When Tyler stepped outside, Beth was nowhere to be seen. He used the outhouse then returned to the cabin. He waited. She couldn't have gone far. He paced the cramped cabin and limited length of porch until he was trembling from exertion. Dizzy, he lay on the bed, sweating and worrying. It was dusk when she returned.

Beth trudged back into the house with a rabbit ready for the spit. She leaned the rifle against the wall and went straight to the fireplace. Tyler got up and moved to stand behind her. She didn't acknowledge him but went about starting a fire over which to cook their supper.

He said, "I'm not going to touch you again, if you don't want."

"Yes, I would prefer that," she said. "Thank you."

She knelt and sat back on her heels, waiting for the flame to take. He continued to hover over her. She could practically feel his gaze. She set her lips in a firm line and turned her face upward. Her mouth fell open at the sight of him. "Sit down," she cried and shot to her feet.

Tyler's hair was wet with perspiration, the bandages soaked with blood and sweat. His face was chalky and his eyes too bright. He looked as bad as when she'd first seen him. He blinked at her and backed away until his calves bumped the mattress and he plopped down. Beth leaned on the bed beside him, discovering the linens on that side were drenched. She felt his face, finding his forehead clammy and his cheeks warm. Clumsily, he followed her urging until he was situated on the other side of the bed.

Beth rushed across the cabin and pawed through a small cabinet, looking for medicine. She cursed the time it took to dissolve in a cup of water. When she returned to Tyler, his eyes were closed. She had to wedge herself behind him to get him to sit up. Her hand shook as she held the cup to his mouth. But when he parted his lips, it was to apologize. He murmured that he was sorry if he'd said or done something—she pleaded with him to stop speaking and drink. She spilled half the mixture when he turned his head. Beth flattened her hand against his cheek and tried to turn it back, but he resisted.

"It wasn't you," she said, whispering against the back of his ear. He relaxed enough to let her turn his head. Hazel-green eyes fixed on hers from inches away. "It wasn't you." Her thumb stroked his cheek. When he lowered his eyelids, Beth noticed the lashes were golden. He drank from the cup. She rewarded him with a tiny kiss to the brow that she doubted he even felt. He was asleep when she scooted out from behind him. She lit a candle and went about collecting new bandages, a wash cloth and basin full of water. She climbed back onto the bed beside Tyler, prepared for a long night.

11

Aimee lost all conception of distance and time as they plodded over parched terrain. It seemed a feat of folly and faith that folk would come to this land and attempt to reap life from the cracked soil. The stallion seemed to know the way and she was glad of it.

The saddle shifted in synch with the horse's gait, causing its riders to sway slightly in their seat. When she looked over her shoulder, Aimee saw Wyland's chin had dropped to his chest. Dark, stringy hair hung in front of his face and through the soiled curtain, she saw his eyes were closed. His arms hung at his sides, hands bumping against the leather skirt of the saddle. It took Aimee much consideration and a long while garnering her courage before she reached down and closed her fingers about his wrist. She lifted his hand, draping his arm around her hip and settling his injured hand in her lap. She gazed down at long, boney fingers and pondered the growing sense of familiarity.

Josiah drifted in and out before wakefulness won out over sleep. He was instantly aware of two things. First, he needed to piss. Second, his hand had somehow ended up in Aimee's lap. He ignored the discomfort of the former in favor of prolonging the latter. Not only had she not flung his hand away, but hers was softly curled around it.

The hand in her lap twitched. The index finger straightened, sliding beneath her sleeve to caress bare skin. "Mr. Wyland?" Aimee swallowed. "Mr. Wyland, I need to use the privy." In answer, his hand lifted, fumbled for the reins, and brought them to a halt. He leaned forward to swing his leg over the horse's rump, chest brushing her back in the process, and dropped to the ground, going all the way down to one knee. He rose stiffly and guided her descent, hands open on her hips until Aimee's toes reached the ground. It was then she noticed there wasn't a shrub in sight.

"You stay on this side of the horse," he said. "I'll go around to the other."

He moved opposite her and stood facing away. Aimee could see his head and shoulders over the animal and his legs below. After a few moments, she heard his stream where it splattered the dirt. She crouched down and adjusted her skirts, peeking nervously at his boots pointed away from her.

While he waited for her to finish, Josiah stared into the distance. He noted a faint haze, different than the waves of heat rising from the earth, and recognized where they were.

Aimee announced that she was finished, and he came back around. She was able to pull herself back up into the saddle, though his hands hovered ready to render aid. He climbed up behind her and pointed to a spot yonder that she couldn't make out. He said, "We'll make camp there."

By the time they reached the site, the sun was at their backs, the sky shifting from blue to mauve. Steam rose from a rocky chasm where an underground river bubbled through the surface to form a string of gurgling pools that grew wider and deeper as they ventured into the fissure. The canyon opened as if they'd entered a cave with no ceiling. Moss blanketed flat stretches of stone and brush grew against jagged walls.

They dismounted and Aimee stood aside, unsure what she could do to help, as Josiah unburdened the horse, grouping saddle and bags against a boulder. He refilled the canteens and snapped off pieces of brush for a fire, moving purposefully despite his injuries. He spilled grain over a flat stone for the horse.

The water made the air humid, and Aimee grew drowsy as she watched him. He peeled away his jacket. The scraps of shirt were stained a dark reddish brown and his torso was crusty with splotches of dried blood. He rummaged through a bag, mumbling something about flint and beans. "Eat. Get some sleep," he said. "I'll be back."

She blinked at the half-full bottle of whiskey in his hand. "Where are you going?"

"Round to one of the deeper pools." He indicated the general direction. "Got to clean these wounds out some." She just sort of stared at him. Josiah scratched the back of his neck. He walked over to her, picked his hat off her head and placed it on his own, nudging the brim up with his knuckle. "Do you know how to shoot?"

Aimee shook her head. Her brothers learned growing up, but at that age, she had been frequently ill. Those lessons were only one of the things she'd missed. He slid one of the Colts from its holster and showed it to her. "This here's an equalizer," he said. "You got to pull the hammer back each time before you fire." He tapped the lever with his thumb, mimicked the motion of drawing it back. He tilted the revolver sideways. "To shoot, pull the trigger." He curled his index finger to demonstrate. "Five cartridges, five shots." He grasped the gun around the barrel, holding it pointed at the ground. Aimee reached for the ivory handle. "Don't shoot me, okay?" His lips twitched in what might have been a smile. Hers curved in response. He frowned.

She said, "What is it?"

"You smiled," he said.

"Yes?"

"At me." Josiah watched her smile falter and was sorry he'd ruined it.

Aimee looked down at the weapon in her hands, studied its shape and scroll-engraving, felt its weight and the coolness of the metal. She imagined it must seem to him as familiar as it was foreign to her. It was only a tool—one wielded by almost every man in the West. As she watched him limp away, she wondered how it had come to define him. It was as much a part of his identity as his name, yet she was beginning to sense there was more to him than his profession or his reputation.

She set down the gun to untie the bedroll from behind the saddle and spread it over the smooth but hard stone. It smelled of the smoke of previous campfires. In a bag, she found boxes of ammo and cans of beans. Digging deeper, she discovered a tin of peaches and a wadded-up shirt. When she shook it out, something hard landed at her feet. Almost giddy with delight, she snatched up a small chunk of soap.

Aimee clambered from small pool to small pool until she found one deeper than a puddle. She hesitated, glancing all around. Then she pulled off her shoes and stripped out of the dress that was stiff with Josiah's blood. It had soaked through to the light shift she wore underneath. The bodice was ruined, but the skirt was still clean. She tugged the garment over her head and her skin pimpled with gooseflesh. The water was warm. She knelt on the moss at the pool's edge and washed her hands, arms, and face. She dunked and scrubbed her dress then used the wet cloth to sponge her neck, chest, and stomach. Droplets rained down upon her thighs and streamed into the seam between, making her shiver. She wished to rinse her hair but didn't think the pool deep enough to submerge her head, so she combed it with her fingers and braided it anew. She dipped, soaped, and dipped her feet, and splashed her legs. She dressed in the wrinkled shirt which was just long enough to cover her knees. She had to roll the sleeves several times to shorten their length to her elbows. She found a knife to cut her underskirt into strips, knowing Josiah would need new bandages. She went back to the pool to scrub his coat with the last of the soap. She wrung the garments until her forearms ached then draped them over the bushes to dry. She was just finishing when she heard a sound that caused fear to seize her heart. She didn't have to look to know the gun was out of reach.

***

Josiah found a warm spring deep enough and not too hot to sit in. He tugged off and dropped his boots to thud on the rock surrounding the pool. He set his gun-belt within reach but far enough to not get wet. Last, he kicked out of his trousers. When he lowered himself into the water, the heat nearly made him faint. He peeled off the soggy dressings and let the swirling water cleanse his wounds. He took a long pull from the whiskey bottle

115

and propped it against a rock. He put both hands on his thigh and squeezed the gashed flesh, gritting his teeth against the pain, until the blood ran free of infection. After another gulp, he raised his knee and shifted to his other hip, bringing the wound above the surface. He doused it with whiskey. The arm supporting his weight gave way and he splashed down, almost losing the bottle to the bubbling depths.

He drifted in the heat as color slowly faded from the darkening sky. Before he could fall asleep and drown, Josiah crawled out of the pool. His legs were wobbly as a newborn foal, so he stretched out on the warm rocks that were gritty with minerals.

***

For once it was a gunshot that awakened him, not merely a hollow click. An actual gunshot, not dreamed. He heard its echo as he came alert. He'd dozed off on his back on the flat rock beside the pool. His hand found one of his revolvers and he was rolling off his spine when a second shot rang through the chasm. His senses were searching, his mind scrambling for recollection. He remembered he'd left Aimee armed with one of the Colts. Its twin in hand, he rushed to reach her.

He discovered her standing, facing the spiny bushes. He knew by the natural sounds of the place, by instinct, and by the annoyed demeanor of his horse, that hunters hadn't tracked them or happened upon them, that they weren't being stalked by hungry predators, solo or in pack. There was no danger, but she was scared.

He approached her, coming up to her side, slowly to avoid spooking her. She had both hands around the pistol grip, wide eyes fixated and barrel trained at ground level. It wasn't until he stood adjacent, a few feet to her side, that he saw the rattler.

She'd blown the serpent's head clean off. The body lay coiled beside it. A splash of snake's blood darkened the stone. He scratched his chin as he took in the sight.

"Decent shot," he commented.

Startled gray eyes turned toward him. She whipped her head back to face forward. She wore a man's shirt she must have found in the saddlebag. Her dress was stretched out over the brush by the snake's remains. The shirt left her calves, ankles, and feet exposed. He realized she must have bathed beside the shallow pools. He also realized it was more likely his state of undress rather than her own that unsettled her. He'd rushed from the rocks as naked as he'd left the water. She swallowed nervously as he stepped closer and pried the weapon out of tight, small hands. He stepped away again.

"I left some things." He gestured back toward the deeper pools, though she kept her eyes straight ahead. He mumbled that he'd be right back. He moved, feeling aches and pangs forgotten in his hurry.

"Mr. Wyland?" He half-turned and looked at her over his shoulder. She licked her lips and swallowed, careful to keep her face forward. He kept silent and awaited whatever she had to say, likewise careful to keep his gaze above her shoulders. When she looked downward, he reckoned she had changed her mind and he should go. But she turned her head, eyes traveling the ground between her feet and his.

Josiah kept still as her gaze climbed his rangy form, scaling long limbs, moving up. His height and frame emphasized his slimness, the muscle not bulky enough to conceal jutting bone. Gray eyes reached his face, flitting over it too quickly to be caught by his blue. Her gaze drifted back down his body, stalling in the vicinity of his hips.

Josiah glanced down his front. He was semi-erect, cock arching up from a bramble of dark hair. He looked back at Aimee and blinked to find her waiting. He sucked in a breath and held it, shuffling his feet just enough to face her.

For one long moment, she stared at him. Josiah reckoned it was time enough for her to form an opinion, though she gave no indication as to what it might be. Without a word, she faced away from him again. Josiah resumed breathing. His eyes wandered to the hem of the shirt and down limbs more lovely than the painting at The Old Mare.

"Mr. Wyland." Her voice jerked his attention up from her ankles. She was still facing away from him. "I made new bandages," Aimee said. Her mouth felt as dry as when she'd been wandering the desert afoot. When she considered he might expect her to apply them, she felt her whole body go hot and cold at once.

Strips of white were draped over the saddle. "I'll take them and leave the gun." Her consideration felt odder to Josiah than standing bared to those gray eyes.

***

When he came back, Josiah was clad in clean bandages and stained trousers. He carried his hat and boots. Aimee sat, swathed in a blanket, feeding twigs to a small fire. Smoke drifted up to make the constellations dance. The climate in their camp consisted of warm eddies of rising steam competing with a draft of fresh night air through the chasm. She wasn't cold so much as self-conscious, having had time to reconsider her attire and behavior in the aftermath of her encounter with the rattlesnake and Josiah's sudden and shocking appearance. As if sensing or sharing her discomfort, he gave her a wide berth. He replaced the gun he'd left opposite its double and looped the belt over the saddle horn. He took up the knife she'd used to cut bandages and went to inspect the snake. When he brought the beheaded reptile back to the fire impaled on the blade, she asked if he meant to cook it.

"Better than beans," he said. Soon she was absorbed in watching the process and stopped clutching the blanket so tightly, letting it slip off her shoulders when she grew warm. She was hungry enough to try more than a few bites of snake meat. She even sipped some whiskey to wash it down when he offered her the bottle.

They ate and drank in silence and when the meal was gone, the silence stretched. Josiah nodded at the bedroll she'd spread out and suggested she get some sleep. "If we ride all day tomorrow, we can make Tucson by nightfall." When she asked where he would sleep, he indicated the flat stone. "I've slept on worse ground," he said.

She asked if there were more snakes. He said that they liked the rocks and she'd be safe in the open area by the fire. She lay down and he started to do the same. "You're rather close to the rocks," she said. He glanced at her, at the space between them. "You can move closer." He shifted, cutting the distance in half. He watched her eye the remaining gap. "A little closer," she whispered. He moved again.

They were near enough that neither would have to fully extend his or her arm to touch the other. "That's close enough," she said. He stretched out, resting his ear on his arm. She curled beneath the blanket. Somewhere in the black, the horse swished its tail. They didn't speak but stared at one another as the firelight dwindled, until each was only an outline against the clouds of steam. Then they slept.

***

In her dream, Aimee was a child again. It was a summer evening and her mother had allowed her outside before supper to see that the chickens were all in their coop for the night. All afternoon, she'd listened to the pop and zing of gunfire as her brothers and their friends practiced shooting. She'd begged to watch and been denied.

Heading back to the house by way of the corral, she noticed the big white horse. She ducked under the fence and hopped over clumps of manure to reach it. The animal lowered its head and allowed her to run her hand down its face. *What's your name?* The answer came from behind her. *He don't got one.* She looked over her shoulder at a boy she'd never seen before and wouldn't see again. He was as tall as her father and had very blue eyes. He walked toward her. Up close, she had to tip her head back to see his face. There were pink lines on his skin she knew were scars. He reached up and put his hand over hers on the horse's neck. His touch was light, his fingers long and slender. *Why don't you name him?* He shrugged boney shoulders. *What would you call him?* She answered almost immediately. *Belvidere.* His lips curved, the smile wistful. It turned self-deprecating when she asked him his name. *Nothing so fine as that.* The dream ended with her looking up into the sapphire eyes of a boy grown.

"Josiah?" His name was on her lips when she woke. The only answer was the garbling of water against rock. She reached out and her hand met warm skin, his heartbeat behind it. The hair on his chest was as sparse and patchy as that on his face. Long fingers touched hers, skimmed up her arm to her shoulder and around to splay over her back. His arm settled around her and Aimee felt herself drawn toward him, sliding over the bedroll, out from under the blanket. His breath stirred her hair. His heart thudded against her palm. His cock grew against her belly. Then he jerked as if shot.

***

It was a different dream that awakened Josiah. He came out of the nightmare with a start and found Aimee in his arms, the heels of her hands against his bare chest, her breath puffing against his skin. Her shape conformed to his, her body warm through the single layer of shirt. He felt his cock throb, restricted by his trousers. She trembled and he realized she too was awake.

His skin smelled of sulfur from the hot spring and Aimee had the wild thought that if she stuck out her tongue, she would be able to taste the salt on his skin. His erection, solid against her softness was a revelation. For the first time, she thought of him as a man foremost and a gunfighter second, dangerous in a different way.

They both lay silent and still. It was pitch-black, the bubbling spring still the only sound. Josiah moved first. He inched his hips back. The pressure of his hand and fingers eased and the weight of his arm lifted. Night air stabbed into the broadening gap between them, frigid after their shared heat. Rough words drowned out the water's melody. "Go back to sleep," he said.

She made a small sound of protest, no louder than a sigh. At the same time, her fingers convulsed, nails just grazing his chest. She didn't know why he'd reached for her, or why having done so, he'd withdrawn. She understood her own reaction even less—inexplicable dread at his pulling away and relief, equally inexplicable, when he paused. She sensed a tension within him, felt an answering desperation within herself. When her fingers curled, his breath caught—and held as the tentative touch trailed down his sternum, over his quivering belly, to sift through the hair below his navel.

Aimee explored him by touch, in terror and awe of what she found, in terror and awe of her own boldness. The moment her wandering fingers encountered the coarse cloth of his trousers, his hand captured hers in a squeezing grip. She gasped.

The rough palm of his hand covered the back of hers, intertwining fingers rotated, and he moved her palm down slowly over the front of him, forcing her to take measure of his girth. A repressed groan rumbled in his throat as he pulsed beneath her hand. He released her, tossing her hand away.

Josiah waited for her to shrink away, to heed his warning. Instead, she surprised them both by tilting her head back and touching her lips, then her tongue, to his throat. Her fingers returned to gently, curiously squeeze him. His groan was almost a growl, and Aimee thrilled to feel the vibration against her lips. Her grip tightened a fraction.

He rolled toward her, over her, momentarily catching her hand between their bodies. Then he shifted his weight, wedging his hips between her thighs. His hand skimmed down her side, over her hip, finding the hem of the shirt. Long fingers clawed at the cotton, drawing it into his fist and bunching the shirt above her waist. He worked his hand between them, fumbling to open his trousers, and Aimee felt his knuckles brush skin that had never been exposed to a man's touch. A prick of fright moved through her as she realized she'd started something she couldn't stop. His fist moved between her thighs, guiding his cock. She felt its tip, smooth and hot and solid.

Josiah leaned onto one elbow, his other arm snaking under the arch of her back, pulling her up against him even as his hips pushed. He thrust into her in one swift movement punctuated by their mutual cries of surprise—hers at the overwhelming sensation of being suddenly and completely filled by him, and his at the dizzying intensity of being enveloped in her moist, tight heat. Aimee slid her arms under his, around his sides to his back, clinging. His arm around her waist tightened, hugging her closer. They were anchored to each other, the connection simplified by darkness, reduced to undeniable need. He rocked his hips to delve into her and her pelvis tilted to accept him, harder and faster until the force was bruising and the speed breathless. They each gave and took all, desperately and greedily. Aimee couldn't differentiate between pain and pleasure and so accepted both. Josiah was torn between a craving for release and a desire to ride that edge forever.

He reared up, planted his hands on the ground, arched his back, and gave himself over to the violence of climax. A mix of rage and ecstasy washed over and through him. Aimee felt suspended in air like she'd been thrown, then the fall came unexpected and glorious. Josiah felt her body quiver beneath him, around him, echoing his release and glazing every sensation with renewed feeling. Josiah Wyland was suddenly grateful for every wretched second of his life which had brought him to that moment in the dark, with her.

Aimee felt her body grow heavy. Her arms slipped from around Josiah and plopped to the ground. His gave out and he sank to his elbows, cushioned by her body. The only response she could manage was a sigh. Before he could settle too heavily upon her, he rolled off in one last feat of strength.

***

Josiah awoke when day was only a suggestion, the stars above him lost in the gray of impending dawn. The air lay cool on his exposed skin, but there was a line of warmth from his hip to his knee. He lifted his head and could just make out the figure beside him. Aimee had drawn her knees up to her chest. It was her naked shins and the tops of her bare feet that Josiah felt along his thigh.

He reached a hand down the front of his body, dread cramping his belly even before he discovered the evidence of his crime still sticky on his skin. Recollection came like the recoil from a Big Fifty. With a groan, Josiah rolled away from the woman he'd ravished and climbed stiffly to his feet. Sore muscles attested to certain violence. He made it to the bushes before he retched, on his hands and knees, body shaking.

In the cold morning light, he was able to assimilate what hours before he could only absorb. The awareness had been there, that she was too small, delicate. He knew the sound of pain, should have recognized it in her cries. But he'd been too caught up in sensation to comprehend the obvious. In the night's blindness, he hadn't questioned her mouth open on his throat, teeth grazing his skin, or her hands clutching his shoulders, nails scratching. Maybe if he'd been able to see her face he'd have realized he was bound to hurt her.

As he knelt at a pool, washing away the tackiness with trembling fingers, he was very much afraid nothing would have stopped him. He'd never been so lost in a woman before. And now it was done. A whore he could compensate with money, but she was no whore. Josiah learned long ago—at fifteen years old—the only woman allowed him was the sort a man paid for, that touch came at a price. But he'd taken Aimee anyway, ruining her and condemning himself. He picked up the blanket, spread it over the ball she curled into, and waited for her to wake.

When Aimee peeked out from under the blanket, the sun was up and so was Josiah. He was packing up their camp, strapping bags to his horse. He'd put on jacket, boots, hat, and guns. His pants, she remembered, he hadn't taken off. His back was to her. She glanced at the brush where her dress was still spread.

She abandoned the blanket and flitted to the bushes, forgetting the danger of snakes. She shed the borrowed shirt and scrambled to step into her dress. Tiny apricot buttons kept slipping out of frantic fingers. But a quick glance over her shoulder showed Josiah shaking out the blanket and bedroll, paying no attention to her.

He'd heard her move. He bent to inspect the horse's hooves next, covertly watching Aimee walk back, smoothing her stiff dress, tucking a strand of hair behind her ear. He expected some show of feeling, testament to her violation. Instead, she was silent. Her composure unnerved him—he'd rather she spat at him, beat her fists against him, threw stones, bit, kicked, hissed.

Aimee sat on a rock and put on her shoes. She was relieved to be dressed again before he spoke to her or looked at her, except he hardly glanced in her direction and said not a word. Her sore thighs and the sharp ache between them were the only confirmation anything had happened between her and Josiah. With a confused heart, she approached him.

She brought him the shirt she'd worn. She held it out and he snatched it from her and jammed it into a bag. He swung up into the saddle with a fraction of the previous day's difficulty. When he held out a hand to help her up, Aimee noticed he wore gloves. She cringed at the leather barrier. As they left the spring and emerged from the crack in the desert monotony, Aimee sensed they were also leaving behind whatever connection they'd found in the night.

The sun glared down at them from a cloudless sky. The distance traveled seemed to stretch out between them. Only once did Aimee attempt to peer around Josiah's shoulder to see his face—his eyes stared straight ahead at the horizon. After that, she watched the shadow that rode beside them, first lagging behind, then marching ahead, changing shape as the day waned.

Past midday, a wind picked up and a current of red silt swirled about them, turning the sun a chalky orange. Dust caked on sweat-dampened clothing and settled gritty on exposed skin. It made Aimee's eyes itch and muddied the shine of the horse's black coat.

Josiah pulled the brim of his hat lower and worked the bandana up over his mouth and nose. For hours, he kept his body too rigid to doze, rarely shifting to relieve restlessness or cramped muscles. He was aware of Aimee behind him, her arms crossed.

He wished she would wrap them around him, rest her cheek against his back. But she only touched him by accident. He felt her wind-loosed hair play along his neck and tangle in his jacket's collar.

Whole bushes bounced across the empty land, coming from miles away, destined to travel miles more. The desert began to slope into low hills dotted with sage and treed with cactus. Then appeared the meandering line of greenish-brown foliage that marked the Santa Cruz. They turned south, following the gallery forest toward Tucson.

12

Worse to Tyler than being an invalid confined to the cabin was realizing he'd been absorbed into Beth Cooper's routine. First thing, she stepped into an old pair of her papa's boots and went out to feed the animals, milk the cow in the barn, and let the chickens out of their coop. She returned, started breakfast cooking, and saw to his bandages. She dished up and served his meal, barely eating anything herself. While she waited for him to finish, she cleaned the one-room hovel of whatever dust had sifted in through the door, window, and cracks in the walls. Tyler found he could not entice her into conversation, though he invited talk with many an inane comment or observation. Beth washed the dishes and bundled up the linens from each bed to haul out and air on the line, declining his offers to help.

"How come you ain't married?" Tyler finally asked the question that had been tickling his noggin since the first morning he awoke with her beside him. Nearby Prospect, like most startup towns, had an abundance of men and comparatively few womenfolk. A man in want of a wife couldn't afford to be choosey or wishy-washy when courting might begin before a girl had outgrown her dolls and resume the month after a widow buried her husband. Beth Cooper was still of child-bearing age, in good health, and the daughter of a respected man. Tyler reckoned her status must be in deference to her father's health or opinion—unless she was holding out for some particular fellow, a possibility that soured Tyler's humor. She didn't pause or look at him but had her answer ready. "That's none of your concern," she said and went outside.

For hours throughout the day, she left him alone. On his trips to and from the outhouse, he'd spy her weeding or watering the small garden beside the cabin or patching a line of fence. She carried her father's rifle wherever she went and though she kept her distance, Tyler was aware of her discreetly watching him. He didn't know if her vigilance was solely that of nurse toward patient or if she harbored a more personal concern for him. Though she'd offered him use of the judge's library, Tyler passed a lot of time simply thinking, wondering if Beth Cooper had any interest in him as a man.

At midday, she made them a snack of bread and cheese. He told her about his sister being often ill as a child and said that until now, he'd never considered the extent of the boredom she must have endured cooped up indoors. Beth told him he ought to rest until his wounds had scabbed over and the risk of infection had passed.

"I could rest just as well sitting out on the porch and make myself useful as a lookout."

Beth shook her head. "You really ought to sleep." She put a kettle on the stove then went out to fetch the linens. By the time she tidied the beds, the water was boiling. She filled a tin cup before emptying the rest into a wash basin.

Tyler knew the drill. She would use the heat to soften and remove the old dressings then apply fresh ones. He reclined against the pillows, closed his eyes, and decided he would go stir-crazy by the time Trace returned. He heard Beth pull up a chair to his side and felt her fingers pick at the buttons of his shirt. He wanted her to linger over him, wished to see her blush at the task, but when he opened his eyes, her expression was apathetic. She spread open his shirt and he flinched as her fingertips brushed his skin.

"Does it hurt?"

"It tickles." Tyler slid his hands over hers. "What if I want you to be my concern?"

She didn't raise her eyes to him right away. When she did, they were steady. And her voice didn't falter when she said, "You don't."

Tyler pushed her hands away. "Leave the bandages," he said. "I can manage myself."

His rebuff stung more than Beth expected but no more than she supposed she deserved. Her avoidance was an insult to his friendliness, her honesty an affront to his pride. She stood and put some space between them before he could insist again. He was by nature good-humored, likeable, and non-threatening. She wanted to respond to him, but it was those very qualities that made him a danger to her. He might make her fall in love with him before he realized he didn't want her after all. She moved to start supper, but he said, "If you want to sit down at the table and share a meal with me, I'll eat. If not, don't bother fixing anything."

Tyler studied her back, awaiting her decision. She picked up the cup, stirred something into it, and brought it to him. "Drink this, at least," she said, her eyes asking. She left him staring into it, his stomach grumbling in admonishment.

The cabin in which Beth had lived all her life with her father proved too small for her, Tyler, and the tension between them. Beth fled, seeking distance. She was halfway to the barn when she realized she hadn't taken the rifle, but she wasn't ready to face Tyler so soon. She was afraid he would ask her secrets and that she would tell them. He would not look at her the same way once he knew.

Beth tried to ignore the uneasy sensation that came of being unprotected. But each step further from the cabin felt wrong. She told herself she would round up the chickens and then head back. Even the animals seemed restless. She heard the hollow moo of the cow inside the barn. She found the chickens all huddled in the back of their pen. She closed and latched the door. And froze at the sound of a revolver being cocked.

A shadow joined hers on the dirt floor beyond the wire mesh. It advanced until the man was close behind her, towering over her. "Where's daddy left you and gone off to this time?"

Beth's eyes filled at the sound of Silas Kelly's voice. "Prescott, to see the governor," she answered, her own voice weak.

"Who all's inside?"

"No one."

Silas tilted his head to scrutinize the side of her face. He said, "I've been watching Tyler Malloy walk in and out all day."

Tears spilled down Beth's cheeks. "He's hurt. He's no threat to you," she said. "I put a sedative in his tea. He'll be asleep by now."

"Is that right? So, if you scream, he won't come running out to rescue you?" Silas placed one hand on her shoulder and rested the wrist of his gun hand on the other. He directed her and together they walked toward the cabin.

Out of the corner of her eye, Beth spied Kelly men concealed in the shadows of outbuildings. At Silas's nod, they directed their attention and the barrels of their guns toward the front of the cabin. Silas guided Beth to halt a few paces from the bottom porch step. He planted his feet wide and moved his empty hand from her shoulder to her front, holding her in place with his palm over her belly.

"Give a holler," said Silas. "Let's see if he's asleep."

Beth shook her head. She could see Tyler rushing out to save her, right into the gang's line-of-fire, gunned down at her feet, before her eyes.

"You need some help finding your voice," Silas said. He straightened his arm, leveling his revolver at the wall of the cabin. He fired two shots into the wood.

"No!" Beth cried out. Silas waved the smoking six-shooter in front of her, bringing the barrel close to her cheek so that she shied from the heat of it. "Please." Fear choked her, making the plea strangled. He aimed again at the building, staggering his shots. Beth counted.

Five shots spent, she wrested free and darted for the cabin, Silas on her heels. She hoped to make it inside, to get her hands on the rifle. But he tackled her on the steps. The impact scraped her chin and elbows. Strong fingers seized her shoulder and turned her over. Silas straddled her. His empty hand closed around her throat. When he raised the pistol, Beth realized he meant to hit her with it. She threw her hands up and jerked when her pa's rifle exploded over her and her assailant's head. Tyler stood above them, holding the barrel inches from Silas Kelly's face.

Silas rolled his eyes upward and met Tyler's furious glare. He smiled at the conviction in hazel-green eyes. He kept his gun hand in the air, loosened his hold on Beth Cooper's throat, and slowly raised his other hand. He rolled back onto his heels and stood. Beth scrambled up the steps on her hands and knees.

"Keep your hands high and your eyes off her," said Tyler.

Silas cocked his head. "Staking a claim, Malloy?" He looked the younger man over. His shirt was open and past wounds were seeping blood, but there were no new bullet holes. Tyler was in a fair bit of pain, but Silas reckoned he still had the wherewithal to pull the trigger if he—or any of his men—made a move. At that range, Malloy was unlikely to miss. Silas would come away even uglier than Wyland, if he survived at all. The bandit leader smiled and called out to the others. "Head back to town, boys. What we're after ain't here."

While his men dispersed, Silas stood with his hands up. Tyler held the rifle steady, his finger ready on the trigger. Still looking at him, Silas said, "He's sweet on you, Miss Cooper. Might not matter to him how many men you've sheathed." He watched Tyler's brow furrow and his nostrils flare. Silas backed away smiling. He turned and began walking, twirling the empty gun around his trigger finger. He called back over his shoulder, "Fuck her in the dark, Malloy, my advice to you."

Tyler kept the rifle raised and aimed until Silas Kelly was out of range. By the time he lowered it, his muscles were cramped. He leaned the rifle against the wall of cabin. He reached the mattress before he dropped. He closed his eyes and concentrated on breathing. Hearing Beth approach, he said, "Don't touch me right now." She'd raised her hands to do just that. At his growled words, she lowered them again. He opened his eyes and squinted up at her, taking in her mussed hair and the scrape on her chin. When she spoke, he noticed she'd tamed the waver Silas Kelly had put into her voice. She told him she wanted to change his bandages. "Not now," Tyler said, unwilling to let her escape into her routine.

"I told you—"

Tyler snatched the tin cup off the bedside table and chucked it. It ricocheted off wall and floor. "Nothing," he said. "You told me nothing."

Beth stood her ground. Still striving for order, she said, "I knew what you'd think—" She stopped when he turned his head. His sigh seemed to deflate him, making his shoulders sag and his chin droop.

"You ought to get to know me better if you aim to tell me what I'm thinking." He'd been mad, but as the anger faded from his voice, Beth saw he was also hurting and not just physically.

She realized he'd taken her silence as a lack of trust, that under his jovial demeanor, he had the same deep-rooted sense of honor as his older brother. She'd cut him deep enough to find it. She sat down on the bed beside him.

"A few years ago, Pa went to Prescott to oversee the murder trial of two Kelly men," she began. "While he was away, Silas showed up here." When she paused, Tyler looked at her. The sympathy and patience in his eyes was all the encouragement she needed. "When Pa came home, his son was dead." Beth nodded to the picture on the mantle.

Sic'em. Silas had loosed his hounds on the boy — a bit of sport for his band of degenerates — but it was a bullet that killed him. Beth had heard the command, the barking, and the shot.

"And his daughter?" Tyler breached the quietude gingerly. "Does he know what was done to you?"

Del hadn't asked and Beth hadn't told, but she reckoned her father knew. "I didn't fight him." Her confession was a whisper. "He said it would be worse for me if I disobeyed. I was eighteen and afraid of pain." She told Tyler that when Silas had finished, he'd marked her, and when he was done with her, he'd given her to his men.

No man would be able to take her to bed without knowing Silas had been there before him, had branded the proof on her body. The thought filled Tyler with warm rage. But the idea of rejecting her, of her being rejected by any good man, made him cold. He realized they'd have to contend with her past. She'd have to face the damage done to her and he'd have to face it with her. He might only ever have a fraction of her trust — what they could piece together from that which a pack of scoundrels had shattered. He'd never have her innocence — Silas Kelly had stolen that. Tyler once thought of love as a limitless well of possibility. Now he knew purity could be poisoned. Whatever he might have with Beth Cooper could only be bittersweet at best. She thought he wouldn't want to concern himself, once he knew. But he was concerned, whether he wanted to be or not. He lay his hand palm up between them and waited for her to place hers in his.

13

Aimee's first impression of the A. and H. Pueblo was that it looked like a massive patchwork quilt unfurled over acres of desert. The streets were wider than the river and for all she could see, just as long. Tucson was no shantytown, but a maze of blocky buildings ten times the size of Prospect. She heard a shrill train whistle but nowhere did she see the tracks. In the midst of the storm, the streets were sparsely populated as blowing dust drove folk indoors and kept shutters closed.

Josiah directed the stallion to a small stable reserved for guests of The Wishing Well Inn. It was musty within and eerily quiet with the wind howling outside. Aimee dismounted with the aid of Josiah's gloved hand. She was stiff from long hours on horseback after sleeping on rock and felt dried out and worn down by exposure to the elements. Worse was the sick feeling in her heart, the loss of something barely found. She stood by, aching, as he tended to their mount.

Josiah kept moving, methodically and mechanically, fueled by anger that sparked each time she shied away from him and by self-disgust that grew whenever he caught his thoughts turning toward the creamy sweetness of her body.

Aimee wanted to offer help but sensed his rage and didn't dare. Besides, it was all she could do to stay standing, to not collapse from exhaustion and dejection. She jumped when he shoved his duster and hat at her, ordering her to put them on. While she struggled to navigate too-long sleeves, Josiah rooted in his bag for the spare shirt. He couldn't resist holding it to his face for a moment, inhaling the scent of smoke and of her. He pulled it on and stalked out, leading the way from the stable.

The wind caught the long coat and nearly jerked Aimee off her feet. She held the hat on her head with both hands. She followed Josiah into a narrow alley where buildings blocked the gusts. There, he halted so suddenly Aimee nearly collided with the back of him. She wobbled on her heels, weariness putting her off balance. When he spun around and whipped the hat from her head, she was too stunned to flinch. She could only gape as he set to adjusting her disguise with a scowl, hat held by its brim between his teeth.

Josiah stood up the coat's collar with a simultaneous tug to each lapel. He tucked the rat's nest remains of her braid within, and nimble fingers fastened every single button from her chin to her knees in quick, unerring succession. He was intent on the task, and Aimee was free to watch the dance of agile fingers no longer gloved. She noticed a perpetual tension in his features. She wanted to touch him, to see if the tight brow would loosen, if the clenched jaw would ease, if those frozen blue eyes would thaw. When the last button was done, he pushed up from the ground. Aimee noted the effort and imagined the pain and fatigue he didn't let show. She wanted to reach for him, wanted him to draw her close again.

He brushed hands over her hair, taming the unruly strands with swipe after swipe. His touch gentled when he raked fingertips back from her temples, through tangled tendrils. She searched his face, hoping for a hint of tenderness, but he screwed the hat on her head, blocking her view. Like her first glimpse of him, all she could see was the wall of his chest. It seemed ages had passed since he was a nameless, faceless threat on her doorstep. She wasn't sure how she'd gotten from fear to reliance, from dread to longing.

Josiah indulged for a few seconds more in what might be their last moment alone, before he returned her to the bosom of society where she belonged, where even a little battered, even tainted, she would be welcomed. Then he turned and led the way into the saloon after which the inn was named. He was two long steps away from her before Aimee remembered to follow.

Josiah didn't pause to observe the layout of the room but made for the dim corner where bar met wall, aware of Aimee trailing like a stilted shadow behind him. He took her elbow long enough to direct her into the corner then put himself between her and the rest of the room, turning to challenge any pair of eyes that might have followed their entrance. He touched fingers to one Peacemaker, a habitual precaution, unnecessary since no man was watching to note the warning, all absorbed in their cups or preoccupied with the women.

Aimee leaned to peer around him. His hat low on her head blocked much of her vision, and his tall form backed up next to her blocked more. Even in church, she had never seen so many people crowded together in one place. And church this definitely was not. Men congregated in rowdy groups, sitting or standing around tables. Some smoked, some played at cards, nearly all had a glass either in their hand or at their elbow. But she'd seen all manner of men on the streets of Prospect. What arrested Aimee's attention was the women—serving girls, dancing girls, and whores—attired to capture notice, either by what they wore or what they did not. Some sashayed through the throng. Others perched on men's laps or hung like living shawls over masculine shoulders.

Wide gray eyes absorbed visions of impropriety—groping hands, sloppy kisses, the suggestive bumping of bodies. The sights triggered memories of intimacy with the man standing right beside her, close enough to touch, yet too far to reach. She realized this would be the sort of place he would come to when he had the itch, that these would be the type of women to scratch it for him.

Somewhere a woman was singing, occasional notes soaring up out of the drone of conversation, drifting back into obscurity. Aimee felt she too was dissolving, dwarfed by the coat and hat, overrun by the noise and an onslaught of feeling. She felt herself sinking, weighted by a leaden heart. Then she was being lifted, by a pair of hands under her arms. Her bottom was set onto a stool. Josiah ducked to peer under the hat's brim. She saw his lips form her name and realized she'd never heard him speak it. She wanted to. She opened her mouth to speak his. Someone else spoke it first.

"Josiah Wyland." The smoky voice sounded from the other side of the bar. Aimee found herself the focus of rich chocolate eyes. They belonged to a woman with dark red hair threaded with hints of silver. She wore burgundy velvet and gold jewelry and held herself like a queen. "Figured the next time I saw you would be in hell."

"I'll get there eventually," Josiah said as he straightened and turned toward her.

The woman glanced over him, but her bold gaze returned to Aimee. "Sooner rather than later, by the looks of it." She produced two glasses from under the counter and splashed amber liquid into each. Josiah tossed back the contents of one and slid the other in front of Aimee. She took a swallow and coughed as it burned her throat, bringing tears to her eyes. Through them, she saw the woman smirk.

Josiah said, "We need a hot meal, clothes, and beds for the night."

"Separate rooms?" she asked. Aimee flushed, but Josiah ignored the question.

He said, "I've got lead in my shoulder and a cut that needs stitching."

The woman nodded. Aimee thought she didn't look at all surprised. Neither did she seem uneasy conversing with the gunslinger. Aimee felt a twinge of envy, realizing the woman knew him well. The feeling subsided when the woman's smirk softened into a sympathetic smile.

She said, "The inn offers baths now."

"Oh, yes." Aimee blurted it out. Checking her enthusiasm, she said, "Please, ma'am." Her voice softer yet, she added, "We would each like one."

The woman laughed, and her eyes danced merrily between Aimee and Josiah. When Aimee peeked up at him, she found Josiah staring down at her, blue eyes speculative. He glanced down at his front, skin and trousers the same red-brown as the Arizona soil. He'd already sweated through the shirt. Aimee couldn't suppress a shy smile as the redhead laughed. The woman held a hand out over the bar.

"Name's Louanne Fitzgerald, owner of The Wishing Well. Call me Lou," she said.

"Aimee." She tentatively held out her hand for Lou to shake.

"Just Aimee?" She hesitated, and Josiah answered for her.

"Malloy," he said, his tone brusque.

Aimee took back her hand, clasping it with the other in her lap.

Josiah glared at Lou, as irritated at the madam for her assertiveness as he was glad she'd made Aimee smile. He took out his money and handed it to Lou without counting, and she put it away likewise without counting. He glanced sidelong at Aimee. "Anything else you need?" He tried to soften the edge in his voice, lest she think his anger was for her. He hated that he'd gone and ruined the smile. He'd pay Lou double to bring it back. Aimee shook her head.

"What about you?" Lou's eyebrow arched. "You want a girl?"

Josiah didn't notice the gray eyes snap to him, but Lou did. Aimee held her breath, awaiting his answer. When he gave it, she dropped her gaze, quick enough that no one saw her anguish.

Lou gave directions to their rooms and handed over the keys. She said, "I'll send Holly to fetch you when the water's ready."

***

Aimee followed Josiah out of the saloon, not really noticing where he led. They exited through a side door, back into and across the

141

narrow alley. One of the keys let them into the inn's lobby. It was a small space that served no purpose other than to give and restrict access to an indoor staircase that led to the rooms above. The rest of the inn's lower level was kitchen and bathrooms.

Josiah trudged upstairs and Aimee trailed after him, down a hall to the last room. He opened the door and she followed him inside. Josiah crossed to a window that looked down on the stable. The storm was dying, but the streets remained empty.

The room was of good size with a vanity and four-post bed, not extravagant but comfortable. Aimee kept her head down and only saw the floor.

"If you think of anything you need, ask Holly," Josiah said. "I'll settle it with Lou." Her only answer was a sniffle. When he turned from the window, he watched her quiver in quiet contention. She didn't look up when he crossed back to stand before her or when he tipped the hat backward off her head, not even when his thumbs brushed her cheeks. New tears spilt to replace the ones he'd swept away. He swallowed and said, "I didn't intend for what happened."

Aimee lifted both hands, placing one over the other, over her mouth. Josiah turned his head and glimpsed himself in the mirror atop the vanity. "People say I got my daddy's eyes," he said, looking at them looking back at him. "They say we're the same, me and him." He saw Aimee lower her hands and tilt her face up toward him. He turned back to her. "But I never had a woman I didn't pay for," he said.

Until her, Aimee realized. She finally understood his anger. "You didn't hurt me, Josiah."

"There was blood," he said.

Her eyes widened and her mouth dropped open. "Oh," she said. "Well, Mrs. Finch told me there might be." Her gaze dropped to her clasped hands. "The doctor's wife, when I was married, she said that the first time…" Aimee stopped fidgeting and faced him. "It's because no man had ever taken me to bed," she said.

Until him. Josiah realized it made her his, more than she'd ever been Rook's.

When he didn't respond, Aimee lifted her chin. "And you can tell Lou you have a woman of your own now," she said. A glance at the mirror reminded her she wore his jacket and a filthy dress beneath it, that at her best, she still lacked the pronounced bust and wider hips most men preferred, that she hadn't any experience pleasing a man. "That is, if you want me," she said.

His hands returned to her face. "From first I saw you," he said.

Aimee licked her lips, and his eyes followed the retreat of her tongue. Slowly, he lowered his face to hers. When Josiah's mouth grazed hers, Aimee's lips parted on a sigh. Their noses touched. His breath mingled with hers.

There came a knock on the door—Aimee jolted but Josiah didn't move. He waited for her attention to come back to him, for gray eyes to meet blue. Then he kissed her. He expected a tiny taste would suffice, but the curious little craving exploded into hunger.

The knock sounded again.

***

Holly Watson had been dancing when she caught the name Malloy out of a snippet of conversation near the bar. She wished

143

to seek out the speaker at once and learn the context in which he'd mentioned it, but she had three more paid partners awaiting their turn to spin her around the floor. She exhausted them all then made her way to the bar, followed by a young corporal with a polite offer to buy her refreshment and an earnest request for her hand.

Lou had been waiting, with a knowing smile for Holly and a consolatory beer for the besotted soldier. The madam explained to the young man that Holly's heart was reserved for another, but he could take her to bed later if he could afford her price. To Holly, she said, "We have a guest I'd like you to attend to."

Holly knocked and was standing outside the door, eager to make the acquaintance of Aimee Malloy. Lou had told her the young woman was running from trouble further north, that she'd come into Tucson in the company of Josiah Wyland and would be staying until her brothers came for her. Holly had readied a bath and rushed upstairs. "She will like you," Holly assured herself. "Tyler likes you. Trace does." She squared her shoulders, shook back honey-brown curls, and knocked again.

When the door swung open, she recoiled at the sight of Josiah Wyland, though Lou had warned her. It wasn't that Holly had a personal reason to fear the gunfighter—his dealings with Lou had acquainted them years ago, and Wyland had always respected Lou's regard for Holly—but an encounter was never pleasant. He gave a nod toward the interior of the room and stepped aside, giving her space to enter.

Holly leaned forward to peer inside. There stood a bedraggled woman looking much like a child, with gray eyes wide and small form lost in a man's coat. Recent tears left smudges where they'd been wiped away and tracks where they had not. Her cheeks were pink and the bridge of her nose was blistered with sunburn. With that first glimpse of Aimee Malloy, Holly forgot Wyland. She started toward the poor creature but halted halfway, belatedly aware she had intruded upon some exchange of intimacy.

Aimee's attention was directed over and above Holly's shoulder. Wyland was still there—his gaze devoured the small woman with predacious, male intensity. Holly planted her hands on her hips and cleared her throat. Blue eyes glanced over her, wary and annoyed.

"Lou is waiting for you downstairs." Holly glowered at him and he shuffled out. When she turned back to Aimee, her expression was all compassion. "You poor dear," she said.

The pretty brunette with cornflower blue eyes must be the Holly that Lou had mentioned. She surprised Aimee by coming toe-to-toe with and then embracing her. The woman was only an inch taller but had becoming curves emphasized by a corset and scooped neckline. She smelled like gardenias. Holly took Aimee's arm and guided her downstairs.

Aimee was led to a small room with a private tub. A tall window let in sunlight and vented steam. Holly deposited her in a chair. "I'm so glad to meet you," she said. She tested the temperature of the water and turned to a small table with a tray of perfumes. "What scent do you prefer?"

"I'm pleased to meet you too," said Aimee, unsure whether it was true. She was dazed by the heat and humidity, by the other woman's openness and jubilance, and by the lingering effects of Josiah's kiss. The press of lips and sweep of tongue had intensified from the moment he touched her to the moment he tore himself away, becoming torrid, possessive.

"Something understated." Holly chose the oil for her and added a few drops to the bath. "You must be a great deal younger than your brothers," she said. "Here, let me help you with that." She glanced up from undoing the jacket's buttons and watched flaxen lashes flutter in bewilderment.

"Do you know my brothers?"

Holly had got to babbling and it had just come out. She ought to have considered the Malloy brothers would have no cause to mention a saloon girl to their sister. "Trace and Tyler, of course," said Holly. She smiled and reached for the tiny buttons at the collar of Aimee's dress, but small hands flattened over them.

"How do you know them?"

Holly had been giddy to meet Aimee, predisposed to like her on account of her brothers, and anxious to make a good impression. She realized the other woman was unlikely to share her enthusiasm. Proper women weren't as accepting toward prostitutes as were their men. Holly stood and gave Aimee some space, reining in her natural exuberance. But she wouldn't lie.

"I know them the same way I know many men."

Holly wasn't sure those gray eyes could get any larger, until they did. Aimee's mouth fell open and her cheeks flushed a deeper pink.

"Your bath will be cold." Holly gestured toward the still-steaming tub but didn't attempt to resume helping her undress. Aimee gulped the humid air.

"Did you… do you… know Josiah… in that way?"

"Wyland?" Holly blinked and for once had no words. She slowly shook her head and kept shaking it as she saw gray eyes flood with relief and mortification.

When Aimee finally reached to unbutton her dress, her hands shook. She set them in her lap and looked up at Holly. "Would you help me, please?"

14

I don't know how a woman could stand being within three feet of you without a brisk wind," said Lou as she poured one last pot of heated water into a tub. "Getting wet ain't washing, you know."

Josiah unbuckled his belt and the familiar weight fell away from his hips, making him feel already naked. He worked the thick leather into a loose coil and handed his guns to Lou. She set them aside with his hat. His boots went next to them. The rest of his clothing and bandages she burned as fast as he stripped out of them. He tried suggesting the shirt could be spared, but she tossed it with the rest into the stove used to heat water for the line of tubs.

"What happened to your hand?"

"A misunderstanding." Josiah stepped over the rim of the tub into the near-scalding bath.

"And your leg? How'd he get that close?"

"It was dark. I don't think she knew it was me." He gripped the sides and used his arms to lower himself to sit on the zinc bottom. The water level came to the middle of his chest.

"Wasn't her that shot you, was it?"

He glared, but she only chucked a bar of soap at him. While Josiah scrubbed, Lou gathered new bandages and the utensils she'd need to remove the bullet and sew up his wounds. She was no doctor, but many of his injuries had been patched by her over the years. He always paid her for it, for the use of the whores she employed, and for whatever supplies he needed that she got for him. It had been that way between them for seven years.

Lou grimaced when he dunked his head between his knees. She reckoned there was dirt from three counties in her tub. Watching him grind the hunk of soap into his hair, she knew she'd have to cut out the knots.

When the water in the first tub was the color of rust, muddy with silt, and topped with a film of bloody suds, she made him move to another. He hissed when she walked over and upended a bottle of booze over the hole in his shoulder. But when she pulled up a stool and got to work extracting the bullet, all Lou heard was the sloshing of water and the grinding of his teeth. She'd never tried to dissuade him from the life he led and had only advised him on one matter long ago, never expecting it would come up again.

"She don't belong to you," Lou said, once the task was done and Josiah was getting dressed. He pulled up new trousers and shoved his arms into a clean shirt. "Even if she weren't Rook Kelly's wife." Though his eyes blazed in warning, she continued. "She comes from people, Josiah. You come from nothing."

He focused on buttoning the shirt. It was blue and appeared already faded compared to his eyes. "I know that," he said. "Her brothers asked for my help." He didn't need to tell her they'd had no other option. He tucked the shirt and fastened the trousers.

Lou crossed her arms and watched him put on his boots. "You best be leaving in the morning," she said. "Her husband will send *his* brothers."

"My horse could use a few days' rest." He reached for his belt. "As could I," he said. They both knew it was a luxury he didn't have. He secured his weapons back at his hips.

"Leave tomorrow," said Lou. "Or you'll be resting on Boot Hill." Blue eyes looked at her. In them, she recognized the shade of a fifteen-year-old boy who had stood in front of her declaring he'd met the girl he wanted to marry. It had been impossible then. It was impossible now.

"Lou," he said. "I don't want any other."

***

While Aimee soaked in a bath of milk and rosewater, Holly brushed out her hair, gently undoing every tangle. She talked as she worked, so Aimee soon knew her better than anyone else outside the Malloy family.

Holly Watson came from Chicago. She was the second of eight children and the only girl. Her father and older brother worked in a factory, but it was a struggle to feed and clothe the younger siblings, so Holly had been sent west. It was arranged for her to marry a cousin, but he was killed over a gambling dispute before Holly arrived in Tucson. She hadn't enough money to buy a train ticket home—that's when she met Lou, three years ago.

"She offered me a means to make my own way," said Holly. "I started out as a waitress and dancing girl, but that didn't provide me much to send home. A lot of men thought I was pretty and kept asking for more." Holly saw curiosity and uncertainty clash in gray eyes. "I'm not ashamed," she said.

"Do you like it?"

"What men pay me for isn't the only reason they come to me," said Holly. Aimee nodded, more in encouragement than understanding. "Some are just lonely, far from home and missing their wives and sweethearts," Holly continued. "For others, it's a chance to be themselves apart from the expectations of their women, of each other, and even of themselves."

"What do you mean?" Aimee remembered her brothers were among those men of whom Holly spoke.

"They can be vulnerable without it costing more than they can afford, without having to show their weakness to anyone who would judge them. Sometimes men need talk as much as the other, and sometimes they just want to be held like they were boys again. I do like being able to give them that."

The water went still while Aimee listened. The dirt sank below the milky surface and the bubbles dissolved. Aimee drew her knees up to her chest. But for the bruises and sunburn, her skin was as white as the bath.

"What about love?" said Aimee. "Don't you wish to be held in return?"

"The man I love isn't ready to settle down yet. When he is, I hope he'll remember me."

What if he didn't? How long would she wait? Holly saw all her heart's questions reflected in Aimee's eyes. They were full of innocence the world had not yet challenged. Holly reckoned this recent adventure had been the woman's first. And an ordeal it had been, evident in the marks on her body—chaffed wrists, sun and wind burn, bruises large and small. Holly knew there were bound to be other marks, invisible ones inside. And she feared the worst had yet to be inflicted.

"Love is a respite, in our struggle to make peace with ourselves," said Holly. "Sometimes that respite is a permanent place in the heart of another, and sometimes it is only an hour between the sheets. I believe our ability to give and accept love has more to do with how we feel about ourselves than each other." Holly debated whether she ought to comment on the scene she'd walked into upstairs. She said, "I don't think Wyland's ever felt that peace."

Aimee said, "I'm getting cold now."

Holly poured a bucket of clean water over Aimee's head to rinse her hair. When she was out of the bath, they scented and moisturized her skin, and Holly insisted she choose a dress from her own wardrobe. It was a dark plum color with lace at the neck and wrists, much finer than any Aimee owned and only a little too big. They left her hair loose to dry.

Holly stayed behind to clean out the tub, and Aimee went back to her room. She found Lou and a hot meal waiting for her. "Feeling civilized again?" Lou gestured for Aimee to sit in the other chair she'd placed at the vanity table.

"Thanks to Holly."

"She's a sweet girl." Aimee detected a mother's pride in the older woman's voice.

"You're close to her," said Aimee. Lou nodded. "You've known Josiah a long time too."

Lou smiled. "Long enough to tell you that whatever you're looking for, you won't find it in Josiah Wyland."

"But you don't know me," Aimee said.

"I know your husband wants you back, Mrs. Kelly. Perhaps you're hoping Josiah will make you a widow." Before Aimee could say anything, Lou continued. "I know you're not cut out for the life of a long rider. You value your roots. You'd want a home, a family, a man who'd not just pass through from time to time."

Aimee couldn't refute it, as much as she wanted to.

Lou said, "Why do you think he's survived as long as he has, when there isn't a gunfighter alive who wouldn't like to boast he'd been the man to kill Josiah Wyland?"

"He's better than them," said Aimee.

"I just pulled a bullet out of him," Lou said. "It only takes one. Granted, this wasn't his first, but there'd be more if he was compelled to come back to someplace in particular."

"Or someone?"

When Holly went up to check on her, she found Aimee curled on the bed, her supper cold on the vanity table. "Weren't you hungry?"

Tears leaked from the corners of her eyes. "I'm no good for him."

Holly sat on the edge of the bed. "Lou once told me a story about Wyland, about where he came from." A light flickered in fog-gray eyes. Holly lay down, facing Aimee.

She told her of a soldier for the South who did such terrible things during the fighting that his superiors surrendered him to be tried by the North. Only he escaped out west and continued his violent ways, drifting from town to town, creating havoc.

"He was chased by this ranger, all the way to Arizona. Before the lawman could catch him, the scoundrel stole a girl from a county fair and had his way with her. Lou said that the vigilantes lynched him before his pecker could wilt. The girl ended up in an asylum back east, but before she left, a baby boy was born."

"Josiah."

Holly nodded. "The young mother took one look at those blue eyes and would have nothing to do with him. It was a whore with a babe of her own that nursed him."

"Lou," said Aimee. "She was like a mother to him."

"Not quite." Holly's voice lowered to a whisper. "Her baby, a girl, died. The doctor said there wasn't enough milk for both of them."

More tears flooded Aimee's eyes. "Did she blame him?" She wondered if he blamed himself, if that was the child he'd killed.

Holly shrugged. "The ranger did. He settled in the town and made sure everyone knew the orphan's name and origins." She took and squeezed Aimee's hand. "You may be the only good Josiah Wyland will ever know."

***

Aimee and Holly were still sequestered in one of the private bathrooms when Josiah left Lou. He ate a plate of chili and cornbread standing at the kitchen door then went out to the stable. He chased a curry comb with a brush over his horse's coat while one thought chased another through his head. The stallion shone black again before Josiah had decided his course. He reckoned the mount was rested and ready to depart, and he ought to make ready himself.

***

When the gunslinger stepped into Murphy's Mercantile, the storekeeper sidestepped over to the bulletin and discreetly removed Josiah Wyland's poster from the wall. He knew some men got a kick out of seeing their picture with a price affixed, but others didn't care to be reminded of their notoriety. Either way, Murphy preferred not to risk exciting a wanted man. He waited by the cash register for Wyland to approach.

Josiah selected his usual ammo and air-tights and counted out his payment while the clerk wrapped it all in paper and tied the bundle with twine. "How much does it say I'm worth?"

"Two-thousand," said Murphy after swallowing the bile in his throat.

"Dead or alive?"

"Doesn't say."

It would have been a waste of ink if it had—anyone coming after him should know that Josiah Wyland wouldn't be taken alive, and Josiah knew there'd be no glory in letting him live.

***

Originally strictly a saloon, The Wishing Well expanded to include a parlor house when a whore-turned-businesswoman from old Promise moved to Tucson and bought the establishment. The inn was Lou's most recent venture. In addition to their wooden architecture, the three businesses shared signage and street frontage, with the saloon in the middle acting as a buffer between hotel and brothel. Neither of the adjacent buildings was accessible from the main street, the saloon being the common point of entry. A staircase inside the saloon led directly to the girls' rooms on the second floor of the parlor house which was built to share a dividing wall. Lou lived on the first floor. The small corridor between saloon and inn was designed to separate noise from quiet and to give guests access to the stables. Holly was waiting when Wyland entered through the door from the alley.

Whether he came from the saloon or elsewhere, she had no means to determine. He stopped when he saw her in the lobby, though his gaze continued up the stairs in the direction of the rented rooms.

Holly said, "If you're going to keep a lady waiting, you should bring her a token."

Disconcerting blue eyes turned on her. "A token?"

"Flowers. A bauble." Holly doubted she would have dared to address the gunfighter had she not been speaking for Aimee's benefit. Devotion to her new friend made her bold. She asked Wyland where he'd been, was encouraged that it wasn't at the brothel and surprised that he seemed just as uncomfortable talking to her as she was talking to him.

He glanced up the stairs then back at Holly before taking something from his pocket and holding it out to her. Holly took the small tin, opened it, and smiled. Inside were two combs, delicate metal inlaid with silver butterflies. She closed the tin with a nod of approval.

Before she handed it back to him, before she could lose her nerve, Holly said, "Do you know how to make love to a woman, Josiah? Do you know the difference between being with a sweetheart and being with a whore?"

He blinked at her, started to glance at the stairs but redirected his gaze to the floor. He scratched the back of his neck then focused on her, giving the slightest shake of his head.

Holly said, "You still touch her where you want, but you touch everyplace else first." She watched his throat move as he swallowed. "And you make it last until it hurts."

She held the tin back out to him. He didn't take it. His attention was directed out the front window of the inn. A trio of riders passed by in the street beyond, slowing to stop at the saloon. Holly recognized Jerrod Kelly among them. Wyland's hands moved to his guns.

"Wait," said Holly, stepping toward him. "They haven't seen you. We can keep Aimee hidden, but you need to leave now, before they discover your horse."

When he slid one revolver from its holster, Holly reached out and put a hand on his forearm. Josiah looked down at it, small like Aimee's. She said, "Please don't make her watch you kill or be killed."

He said, "What does a man say to a woman when he leaves her?"

"He promises to return, no matter what it takes. He says her memory will sustain him, wherever he goes. He assures her their hearts are tethered, no matter the distance."

"Seems it ought to be more honest than all that," said Josiah. He nodded toward the tin still in Holly's hand. "Give her that. Tell her, if she'd come to the window, I'd like to see her once more." Holly nodded. Josiah made sure the way was clear and slipped out into the alley. Holly rushed up the stairs.

Josiah crossed the street to the stable. He slung his saddle over the stallion's back and secured it. His senses were on alert, his instincts ready. Practiced motions left reluctance to lag behind like an afterthought. In a matter of minutes, he was set to leave. He swung up onto his horse. Outside, in the street, he waited where anyone might see, watching the window for her to appear.

The inn's door opened and Holly emerged. She held out the tin for him to take. "She said to tell you she meant what she said."

Josiah tucked the metal box into his shirt pocket and turned his eyes back to the window where Aimee had appeared. She seemed to him like an angel on high, framed in light. He longed to worship her as Holly had described.

For a long moment, they looked at each other. She blew him a kiss. In reply, he touched long fingers to his hat.

Wyland rode off into the shadows and the light went out in the window above. Holly walked back through the alley. By the time she reached the door to the saloon, unshed tears were in her eyes. The door opened before she touched it. Holly found herself face-to-face with Jerrod Kelly.

15

Jerrod glanced beyond Holly at the closed door leading into the inn, then up and down the empty alley. But his focus was pulled back to her like the needle of a compass toward north. Tear-darkened lashes lined her eyes, emphasizing irises the color of a violet sky. As a gunfighter, Jerrod knew how to quell his fear, harness his anger, put aside his pride, but seeing tears in Holly Watson's eyes almost severed the reins.

He took her arm and led her out of the doorway, to the bar. When he asked her what was wrong, she denied that anything was the matter. She turned her face from him, gaze wandering down the bar to where Lou poured drinks. Part of him wanted to nuzzle her neck, inhaling the scent of gardenias. Part of him wanted to close his hand around her throat, securing her undivided attention. He fought to keep his grip gentle on her arm.

"Is your family all well?" A small smile touched her lips and her eyes returned to him.

"Yes, thank you, Jerrod," she said.

"When's the last time you saw Malloy?" He couldn't keep himself from asking. Fresh tears welled up before she averted her face again with a sniff. Jerrod sighed and pulled a square of paper

159

from his pocket, unfolding it and smoothing it flat upon the counter. "What about him?"

Holly studied Josiah Wyland's likeness, rough and formidable in black ink but lacking the intensity blue brought to his eyes. She told Jerrod that it had been months. He withdrew another, smaller picture and placed it over that of Wyland. It was a portrait of Aimee. She looked exceedingly pale in black-and-white, gray eyes haunted.

Two men approached, both with deputy-sheriff badges pinned to their shirts. Jerrod instructed Lucas to go check the stable and Dawes to inquire at the general store. When they were gone, Holly slanted her gaze toward him and said, "She's pretty, Jerrod."

"My sister." He was quick to clarify. "By marriage to my brother Rook."

"Oh." There was a trace of disappointment in her tone. "She looks sad."

"Her health is poor," he said. "It's made her life rather dull."

"That's tragic." The bandana about Jerrod's neck was skewed. Holly adjusted it, noting the flare of desire in his moss-green eyes. She said, "What's life without a little fun?" His hand covered hers, the tension in his fingers a warning. He asked if she would be available later.

"For you, Jerrod." She gave a sugary smile he knew was fake. "In fact, I'd better go take off my armor." She indicated the apron she wore while doing chores around the inn. "And put on my war-paint."

She started to go, to step around him, but he stopped her with an arm across her middle. He moved to the back of her, his arm curving around her waist, and stepped close. He swept her curls aside and touched his lips to the nape of her neck.

"It's good to see you, Holly," he said. "I'll keep coming back, you know." She hummed in answer, but he heard more incredulity than pleasure in it. He said, "If only to see whether you've stopped pining for him." She went rigid in his embrace. It was rotten retaliation, he knew, but he hated her treating him like just another patron. He'd had her too many times to be dismissed as one of her typical admirers.

"The inn offers baths now." Polite words were delivered in a frosty tone. "If you've had a long ride." She pushed his hand down and away. As he watched her climb the stairs and go into the parlor house, admiration eased his irritation. He collected the pictures off the bar, refolding the poster, putting both back into his pocket. Lou also claimed that Wyland hadn't been in the saloon for months. Brotherly duties done, Jerrod decided a bath sounded swell.

***

Unlike the other girls that Lou employed, Holly lived at the parlor house. Since she'd come to Tucson, The Wishing Well had been her home and Lou her family. Still, her room was far less cluttered than most. Her armoire held a comparatively modest number of dresses—a couple for dancing and entertaining in the saloon, one plainer for working in the inn, one finer for going out that she hadn't occasion to wear in a long while. She had a dresser for smaller articles and accessories. She kept the top clear as a table for visitors to set their effects. There was a coat rack for patrons to hang their hats, that Holly used to hang-dry her laundry. She kept a hairbrush and selection of perfumes and toiletries atop the vanity. Her only jewelry was what she'd brought from home or been gifted by admirers, and most of the latter she gave to the other girls. It wasn't a lavish existence Holly envisioned for herself—the life she wanted was simple.

She washed using the basin in the corner opposite the door and dressed in garments she wore only for a select number of men and never outside her boudoir. The ruffled tulle petticoat was the same light blue as her eyes. The floral-embroidered corset was ivory silk. She pinned up her curls, leaving her neck, shoulders, and cleavage bare. She dabbed on her scent and a little rouge. She slipped ivory stocking up her legs and tied blue garters above each knee.

Holly sat at the vanity, scrutinizing her reflection in the mirror, adjusting her expression in search of the perfect mix of flirtatious and demure. It was harder for her to affect the right attitude with Jerrod—he had come to want more than she was willing to give. His knock came at the door. Holly bit her lips, gently to encourage a little color. She called for him to enter and turned to welcome him with a smile. It dissolved as Trace Malloy filled her doorway.

She could only stare as he closed the door behind him and locked the knob. He stood with his hat in his hands, his hair mussed and longer than she'd last seen it, his eyes bright but his face drawn. From opposite sides of the room, they took in the sight of one another, each suffering feelings long repressed. Then he crossed the space in long strides that shortened her breath.

Trace sank to his knees before her, letting his hat lay on the floor so he could take Holly in both arms, use both hands to slide her to the edge of the chair. Her arms encircled his head and fingers delved into sand-blond hair as he pressed his ear to her breasts and his strong arms banded her body.

"Tyler was shot, Aimee taken by bandits," he said. "Our parents are dead."

Holly pressed kisses into his hair and wept to hear the brokenness in his voice. She kissed his brow and cheeks. Their lips met and clung.

Trace lifted her from the chair and lowered her to his lap, her stocking feet sliding across the floor until she straddled his hips. His hands roved up her back then held her head clamped between wide, rough palms. His kissed her, filling her mouth with his tongue. Then they rested with their foreheads together, catching their breath. His eyes were sun, hers were sky.

"I need you now," he told her. His fingers skimmed along the top of her garters and she moaned his name. He hoisted her back up to her seat but stayed between her thighs. She tugged to untuck his shirt and he hurried to unbuckle his belt. The holstered gun clunked against wood as he shoved it aside. His hands tore at the strings of her corset. Hers plunged into his trousers. He stood and pulled her up with him, walking her backward toward the bed. She was down to stockings and garters before they reached it. She fell back upon the mattress. He yanked off his boots and shucked his pants. Holly opened for him—arms, legs, and heart. Trace fell over her, into her.

An hour later, they were still in each other's arms, in her bed. She still had on stockings and garters. The rest of their clothing was strewn across the floor.

"I was afraid you weren't coming back," she said.

He said, "I couldn't stay away."

"Did you try?"

He hesitated and she hoped he'd lie. But he said, "Yes."

Holly asked about Tyler. Trace told her he was on the mend. She asked if he'd seen Aimee. He said that Lou had told him she was asleep. He was ashamed to admit he'd been glad to see Holly first.

Holly said, "She's in love with Wyland, you know."

"She couldn't be," said Trace.

"It only takes a moment," she said, willing him to remember.

"I'm going to challenge Rook Kelly for sheriff," he said in a rush.

"I can wait." She watched him sit up, reach for his clothes, and begin to dress. "Until after you're elected?" She sat in the tangle of sheets, growing cold.

Only when he was done did he turn to her. "I can't marry you, Holly." She saw regret in his eyes, but conviction was stronger. She continued to watch, stricken as he withdrew a roll of bills from his pocket and set it on her dresser. "I'm not coming back." Like that, he left her.

***

From his seat alone at a table, Jerrod Kelly watched Trace Malloy descend the stairs into the near-empty saloon. The storm had dissipated and the crowd with it. A few blurry-eyed gamblers still squinted at cards, trying to summon their wits for one last hand, betting whatever they had left. A couple men sat in queue at the bar for their turn with a favorite lady. Jerrod reckoned that by then, the prostitutes would be too worn out to be worth the wait and the men too drunk to notice. He reckoned he was no less

164

foolish, waiting the better part of an hour for Holly, nursing a warm beer and his resentment for golden boy Malloy.

The cowboy had just reached the bottom of the stairs when Holly stormed through the door at the top in a show of temper made ever more magnificent by the fact that she was clad only in stockings and a crown of brunette curls. "Take your money, Trace," she said. She flung out her hand and greenbacks rained down. "I only wanted you." She spun—a whirlwind of pink flesh and brown hair—and doors slammed in her wake.

Trace made his way to the bar and Lou poured him a drink. Jerrod collected the scattered money then joined him. Trace seemed to contemplate the whiskey, not looking up when the other man moved onto the seat beside him.

"Howdy, Malloy." Jerrod received no reply. "What brings you to town?" Trace picked up his drink and tipped back the glass. Jerrod turned to Lou and said, "Is Holly ready for me yet, do you reckon?"

Lou knew it wasn't the liquor that made Trace snarl. Furious gold-flecked eyes forbid her to answer. She refilled his glass. Her steady brown eyes met his and watched the sun-fire go dim when she said, "Go on up, Jerrod."

Outside her room, Jerrod paused and tried to find a less risky state of mind. Having no luck, he knocked and entered without awaiting an answer.

Holly sat on the chair with elbows atop closed knees, her head in her hands, and one foot curled over the other. She was crying. Jerrod locked the door. "Are you all right?" he said, placing Trace's money atop the dresser.

She glanced at him, managed a bleak smile, and shook her head.

"Will you let me spend the night with you?"

"No, Jerrod," she said.

He took out his pocketbook, counted out her rate, and added the amount to the pile on the dresser. "Then I'll take what I can get," he said, "same as you."

He crossed to the bed and pulled off the used sheets, dumping them on the floor. He hung his shirt and hat on the coat rack, placed his gun-belt on the dresser and his boots at its base. He took Holly's arm, pulled her up and walked her to the bare mattress. She whimpered as she lay back on it, closing her eyes. They remained closed while he finished undressing, even when he gripped her ankles, spread her legs, and knelt between her thighs. Jerrod untied each garter and peeled the stockings down her legs, one at a time, letting them flutter to the floor. He ran his hands up her calves to the backs of her knees, pushed the tops of her thighs toward her chest, and opened her with his thumbs. He rested the tip of his cock between the folds of flesh and bent his head to release a stream of saliva onto the juncture.

His initial plunge was sudden and deep and had Holly's eyes flying wide open. He told her to say his name. A little confused, a little unsure, she stuttered it. He withdrew all but the head of his cock. "Say it again," he said. He sank into her slowly and his name soughed from her lips. "Keep saying it."

Jerrod had bedded many women, but Holly he'd taken the time to know. He watched her face and listened to her breathing as he touched her, inside and out, until need shone through the haze of uncertainty in cornflower blue eyes, until his name became a chant. Each time she said it, he rewarded her, delving swift and deep, pushing them both toward that purifying brink.

Holly's thoughts shredded and swirled away in a rising storm of sensation. She anchored herself to Jerrod lest she too drift away, hands clutching his shoulders, thighs squeezing his hips. She fixed her stare on the vision of him above her, black hair curling the more he sweat, green eyes bold when everything else blurred.

Finally, his name was a fractured scream Jerrod hoped would ring in Trace Malloy's ears. For a moment, Holly was liberated. Too soon, he watched the confusion eke back into her eyes, and regret with it. She turned her head, though her body hadn't fully relinquished him. Jerrod brushed his lips over her cheek. Her cringe was enough to have him pulling out before he was done. He snatched a spittoon off the floor and relieved himself in two hard, angry tugs.

Before he was dressed, she began to weep again. There was nothing he could do—her tears were for another man. He left her no better off than Malloy had.

Downstairs, Trace was gone. Another man had taken his seat at the bar.

***

Lou reckoned Trace Malloy had a lump in his throat too big to swallow, because he left the second glass of liquor untouched. She felt a grudging respect for his resolution and a twinge of pity for what it cost him, but her allegiance was to Holly. She left him to brood alone and went about wiping down the otherwise empty bar, thinking it must be a quirk of the universe that the old be made to watch the young repeat their mistakes.

When a familiar figure pushed his way through the saloon doors, Lou mistook him for a figment of fancy prompted by that very thought. But he came closer, and time moved backward with each step, until Lou recalled herself as a girl younger than Holly, just as hopelessly in love.

Del put his hand on Trace's shoulder and gave it a squeeze. "Why don't you check on your sister and get some sleep? We ride out with the morning stage." Trace nodded and Del took his place at the bar. He stole a sip of the abandoned whiskey and said, "Hello, Louanne."

The years had weathered him, and the wiser woman Lou had become could recognize the flaws. But she knew he had an infallible core she would find unaltered. She looked into dark brown eyes and saw the compassion that had always been there for her still shone.

He said, "You probably thought me dead."

She shook her head. "I would have known."

"I was dead enough."

She said, "I heard about your son."

"Then you know why I'm here." His tone warned that she couldn't dissuade him.

"He's gone, Del," said Lou. She wasn't referring to his son. Her eyes pleaded with him to leave it at that, once and for all, for all their sakes. Del had never seen more persuasive eyes.

"It's different this time," he said.

"It is. He's in love." She thought she'd squelched it years ago, when she'd introduced a fifteen-year-old boy to his first whore. "He'd never admit it." She hesitated to add, "No more than he'd admit to mercy."

"Shooting my boy was murder."

"Josiah was no older when that wild pack got ahold of him." The mauling had left him with the first of his scars.

"If he'd shot Silas Kelly's dogs instead, I'd still think you give him too much credit."

"I give it where it's due. I trusted your guidance over my own heart and helped you make him what he is—you made sure he got his daddy's name and I refused to love him. But Josiah Wyland survived in spite of us. And what he's done is on us too."

"You blame me for my son's death?"

"No more than you blame me for that of my daughter." Lou sighed. "The world isn't just, Del," she said. "But you made me believe it could be. I remember the day you rode into Promise, larger than life, too good to be tempted by a fourteen-year-old whore."

"I remember that girl," said Del. "Town tried to bury her in disgrace, but she rose out of it like a phoenix with an elegance all her own. She tempted me sorely."

"I never knew that." And she didn't believe it, he saw.

"You could now. Let me take you to bed." He reached across the bar, his hands warm on her face. Her eyes closed as he leaned over the counter. She felt his mustache tickle her lips. His mouth was as firm as she always imagined it would be.

"You used to ride a high horse, Del Cooper," she said, pulling away. She knew she'd be the easiest vice to start his downfall, because he genuinely cared for her, because it would feel like loving. Though her eyes filled with tears, she smiled at him. "Even if I'm the only one, I'll hold you to your principles."

16

The shrill chirp of a locomotive awoke Aimee just past dawn. She lay listening to the rattle of horse-and-cart traffic and other noises of civilization, missing the bubbling spring and the sound of quiet. She'd slept with the combs between her palms, and the metallic butterflies left winged indentations in her skin.

Trace dozed in a chair beside the bed, long legs stretched out in front of him and crossed at the ankles, arms folded over his chest. With hazel eyes closed, he seemed oddly unfamiliar to her, as if it had again been years since she'd seen him instead of days. Aimee rose and crept past him to the window. She'd fallen asleep atop the linens, still wearing the dress Holly had given her. A borrowed nightgown remained folded upon the vanity.

She gazed out at Tucson, its pueblo buildings tinted pale pink, and thought of Josiah. Over those few days in the desert, he'd become close to her while everyone and everything she knew before him had grown distant. Now that he'd gone, she felt a yawning emptiness inside and wondered what had been there before him. She wondered too if that glimpse of one another through the window would be their last.

In that final look, she had seen him apart from his profession, his reputation, and his daddy's blue eyes. And she felt he'd seen her as no one else could. She'd wanted to look well for him. She'd hoped the connection forged blindly in the dark of the canyon would be reaffirmed in the light, within that very room.

When Holly brought her his gift, Aimee feared he'd already gone. She would have flown down the stairs after him had Holly not stood in her way, pleading sense and assuring her that he had reason to return. But Aimee's doubts rose with the sun, with the realization that they were now separated by the same perils that had brought them together.

When she happened to glance back at Trace, his eyes were open, studying her. He was frowning. Aimee wondered if she looked as altered as she felt.

For Aimee's comfort and added protection, Del Cooper secured a seat for her on a mud wagon headed north out of Tucson. He and Trace would accompany it on horseback.

Holly bid them farewell out back of the inn. The women hugged like girlhood friends instead of recent acquaintances. Trace thanked Holly for her kindness toward his sister but said nothing more. Neither did he glance back at her—Holly had been watching and from the stable's doorway, so had Jerrod Kelly.

He crossed the street to where she stood, took a handkerchief from his pocket and offered it to her. She only eyed it—and him— distrustfully. "Why aren't you rushing back to report to your brothers?" she said.

He scowled down the street. "No rush," he said. "I wired Rook last night and sent his deputies back earlier this morning."

Holly slapped him. He took it without a word, but the look he gave her warned he'd only allow it once. "I don't ever want to see you again, Jerrod Kelly," she said.

He watched her stomp away. He continued to stand in the glare of the rising sun, cursing her, himself, and Trace Malloy.

In the saloon, Holly leaned back against the shut door and began to sob. Lou came out from behind the bar and embraced her.

"The frontier breeds a species of man hard to hold," she said. "Some women depend upon that hardness, some break upon it, and others develop a hardness of their own."

Holly continued to cry. "I don't want to be like you, Lou," she said.

***

For the pastor of Prospect's one church, it stole some fire from his brimstone to have one of the sinners he'd been preaching against wander into Sunday service, a serpentine smile on his lips and devilish gleam in his eyes. When the sermon stalled, Rook and the rest of the congregation glanced about for the cause.

Silas met many an indignant glare as he strolled down the aisle between pews, his spurs singing and his frock coat drawn aside to show shining six-gun. He winked at Mr. Brown's twin daughters then took an end seat in the row behind his brother. In his peripheral vision, Rook saw him bend one long leg and prop his boot on the seatback in front of him. He only shrugged when Rook shook his head.

The remainder of the pastor's speech was broken by distracted pauses and blighted with misspoken, repeated, or forgotten clauses as Silas smirked, yawned, and polished his pistol, rolling the cylinder down his arm when he was through. As soon as the service concluded, the shepherd's flock scattered.

The outlaw's presence didn't deter Mrs. Finch from stopping to inquire into Mrs. Kelly's absence. Rook told her that Aimee had stayed home with a headache and declined the biddy's offer to send the doctor on a house call.

"Your wife is missed," Silas said. "By all but her husband, I reckon."

The pastor descended from the pulpit and approached them. Silas met the man's sour look with one of disinterest. The pastor said, "Your father was a God-fearing man."

Rook waited to see which way his brother's mood would turn. If the preacher thought Lord or lawman could spare him from Silas Kelly, he had too much faith in both.

Silas answered with a wolfish smile. "Sir feared many things which I do not." The pastor split a stern look between the brothers and left the church, blessedly oblivious to the myriad ways his death was being contemplated behind green eyes.

Seeking to distract him and avoid a career-ending catastrophe, Rook asked Silas where he'd been. He answered the other side of Promise, meaning Cooper's cabin.

"Has the old man had any visitors?"

"Tyler Malloy."

"You said he was as good as dead."

"He has a newfound reason for living—Cooper's daughter."

"What about Trace?"

"Gone to Prescott with the judge," said Silas. "Reckon he's still after your star."

Rook cursed and started to pace.

"Why do you want that piece of tin?" Silas spread his arms wide to encompass the church, the town. "Is it even any fun, being sheriff?"

"I suppose your plan is to retire a highwayman." Rook scoffed. "The Wild West is being tamed, Silas. The outlaw is a dying breed. I've got longevity on my side."

"I've outlived plenty of lawmen." Silas shrugged. "I reckon I'll outlive a few more."

And when they were all dust, the names of Silas Kelly and Josiah Wyland would live on, thought Rook. Even Jerrod would be remembered. Rook was reminded of the telegram he'd received that morning. He told Silas there'd been no sign of Aimee and Wyland in Tucson.

"Little brother missed something," said Silas. "It's the only place he could take her."

Rook said, "How far did you get with my wife?"

Silas cocked his head. "Still as pure as on her wedding night. Unless she and Wyland have made a cuckold out of you."

"Go to Tucson," said Rook. "Send Jerrod back. You can have Aimee, provided you can find her. No restrictions."

"I was kidding about her and Josiah," said Silas.

"I know," said Rook.

He remained in the empty church for a long time after Silas left, contemplating the blood and secrets he and his brother shared.

***

As the Southern Pacific stage started north, directly up Main Street out of Tucson, a few seasoned travelers were able to appreciate the spare inches afforded by the slightness of the

174

female passenger huddled into the corner behind the driver. They knew not whether the small blessing was owed to girl or woman as her face was angled outside the compartment and obscured by a new bonnet.

Six mules made up the team that hauled the mud wagon crammed with nine passengers including Aimee and laden with their luggage and the mail. They broke from town at a bruising pace that churned up dust like another sandstorm, made Aimee's teeth chatter, and continually knocked travelers' knees together. Through the stage's open side, Aimee could see Trace and Del Cooper pacing them on horseback, the dizzying whirl of one spoked wheel, and the red dash of desert soil beneath the carriage. Mostly, she watched the adobe blocks of Tucson shrinking in their wake, blurred by dust and tears.

Aimee found the ride no less taxing than horseback, the sway of the wagon unpredictably jostling, the same route along the Santa Cruz both faster and longer. When there was only open range in all directions, it occurred to her that a man like Josiah Wyland could lose himself in that vastness, vanishing forever if he so chose. She felt the accumulation of each mile traveled as an increasing congestion about her heart, a physical testament that she and Josiah were moving further from one another. Aimee wondered if he too could feel the pull, if he would be compelled to follow it back to her.

***

Ever further to the south, Josiah Wyland rode, paced by the shadow that had stalked him all his life. Sometimes to his right, sometimes to his left, leading or trailing behind, it was a solitary figure without a face, sometimes hunched, sometimes stretched

175

tall and thin. Like him, the phantom rode a black horse. It dismounted when he did, met him when he turned to face it.

Josiah studied the form cast against the trunk of a towering saguaro. Without the smaller figure that had accompanied it for the past few days, near enough at times to be melded together, the shadow was just another reflection to be despised—if it had eyes, they'd be blue. Josiah knew it was the one man he could never outdraw. But that didn't stop him from giving in to his frustration. Just then, he didn't give a damn about preserving ammo or the futility of fighting a shadow.

Josiah pulled his right revolver and mimicking his motions, the phantom pulled its left. The instant he went for his left gun, the shadow went for its right. They couldn't even kill one another. The shadow shot blanks. Josiah's bullets tore bites out of the cactus beyond, and when the Colts were empty, the phantom still stood. The gunfighter and his shadow reloaded, holstered their irons, and remounted.

Before he continued south, Josiah looked back the way he'd come. The desert appeared no less desolate than in any other direction, yet something beyond his sight tugged at him with an insistence that made his heart ache. He was homesick for Tucson, for the desert camp beside the springs, even for the small kitchen in Prospect and the corral at the Malloy farm. For Aimee. Trace would take her home, where Josiah had never been welcomed. She belonged there, he reckoned. He belonged nowhere.

17

Forty miles northwest of Tucson, the stage finally halted to swap its exhausted mules for a fresh team before continuing north toward Prospect. Passengers disembarked, eager to stretch their legs after the eight-hour first-half of the journey. The driver took Aimee's hand to help her down, passing her off to Trace who led her to the shade of a lone adobe building. Del took their horses to water at the trough next to a rickety mesquite corral.

The station served as a juncture for both the stage line and railroad. Aimee overheard that a train from the East was due within the hour. Some of its travelers would join the party going north, while the rest would ride further, to Tucson. It occurred to Aimee that Holly Watson might have come west by that very route. She wondered if her brothers knew the sad story that had brought Holly to The Wishing Well. She might have asked Trace had he not looked as weary as Aimee felt.

Even standing on solid ground, she seemed to feel the vibration, up through the soles of her feet, of wagon wheels turning in sun-hardened tracks and the sway of the chassis churning in her stomach. The creak and rumble of the coach and the clamor of so many hooves echoed dully in her ears—until a piercing whistle heralded the approaching train.

The locomotive glided to a halt with a harsh sigh, spewing soot and steam, wafting heat and the pungent scent of hot iron. It didn't stop so much as pause, hissing and chattering its readiness to set off again. Trace had gone into the building. Aimee drifted toward the great iron beast that breathed like a man-made dragon. Through the windows in the passenger cars, she could see folk from the East—women and children traveling to join their husbands and fathers, or whole families migrating together—coming to settle the territories or continuing on to California, driven by faith, drawn by hope.

Aimee's gaze came to fixate on the steps that led aboard. Her heart thudded with the realization that the train could bring her closer to Josiah. She longed to do something to close the distance between them. She glanced around. Trace was still inside. Aimee felt a pang in her chest at the additional grief she might cause him. But her focus returned to the steps, her thoughts to Josiah. She wanted to believe he would turn back and that they could meet again in Tucson. Though it seemed a great weight anchored her, Aimee took a step forward then another. Legs shaking, she climbed aboard the train, falling into the first available seat. She clasped trembling hands together and stared at them in her lap, afraid that if she glimpsed Trace out the window, she would abandon her chance. Tears rained down upon her fingers as the bell atop the train began to ring.

"Ma'am." A voice spoke down at her, and a worn hand moved into her line-of-vision. Aimee peeked up at the aged lawman, felt her face flush with shame, her heart rent by despair and gratitude. Del Cooper waited patiently for Aimee to put her hand in his then led her off the train. Moments later, the locomotive gave a hoarse hoot and surged into motion.

Aimee walked numbly, her arm linked with that of the old judge. Ahead of them, Trace was looking about, bewildered. When he spotted them, Aimee's eyes filled at the relief that broke over his face. She turned her head as if to watch the train depart, its rhythmic huffing increasing in tempo as it gained speed leaving the station.

To Aimee's surprise, Del told her brother they'd taken a turn around the other side of the locomotive. "She wanted to see the running gear," he said. Trace told them the stage was almost ready to depart. Once he'd gone to get the horses, Del patted Aimee's arm and said, "I reckon you've worried him enough, don't you?" Aimee blinked at him.

"You're the ranger from Holly's story," she said. "He's not his father."

"I believe deeds make a man," he said. "Josiah Wyland was fifteen when he shot his first victim. Would you care to know how many he's killed since?"

Aimee recalled standing in her kitchen, awaiting that very answer from the gunslinger himself. She lifted her chin as she had then.

The look Del gave her was pitying and patronizing. "The life of an outlaw is uncertain. Full of hardship, short on comfort," he said. "I've hunted plenty of bad men and can tell you, they all turn desperate when the noose tightens. Believe me, his leaving you in Tucson was the best possible outcome."

The mud wagon left the stage stop with four additional passengers seated atop amongst the mail and baggage, like rats in a flood might cling to a scrap of bark. Nearly another forty miles and more than eight hours later, it stopped within sight of Prospect to let off its lady passenger.

***

It was twilight when Tyler spotted the trio, their shapes merged with those of the two horses, darker against the grainy horizon. He'd kept vigil since dawn, sitting on the front porch, the rifle across his lap. In the later afternoon, Beth had joined him and they'd watched in silence as the sun set.

Tyler found her proximity both gratifying and agonizing. Her willingness to sit near him, he took as progress. But things unresolved yawned between them and he couldn't figure how to bridge the gap. He sensed winning Beth would be a marathon of hobbled steps and hoped he had the patience and fortitude to stay the course.

Tyler was happy to see Aimee safe again and glad to have the other men back in case Silas and his bandits returned, but most of his relief was for his brother's advice.

Though their journey was at an end, Tyler noticed a collective glumness about the party. Del seemed distracted, Trace was surly, and Aimee appeared down-trodden. Del dismounted and passed his reins to Beth. He drifted toward the fire-lit cabin, hardly acknowledging her kiss on his cheek. Tyler helped Aimee down from behind Trace. She gave him a weak smile and a brief hug, careful to not press against his chest. Without a word, Trace turned the gelding toward the shack that was the Coopers' barn.

Tyler asked Beth to help Aimee inside, took the lantern from her, and followed him with the mare.

Trace said, "Any trouble?"

"Some," answered Tyler. "What happened to you?"

"Nothing." Trace loosened the saddle cinch and tugged strap through buckle.

"Like hell," said Tyler. "Easy with my horse." He relieved the paint of its bit and slipped head-collar over drooping ears. "You see Holly? She disremember you?"

Trace shot him a dangerous look. He dragged the saddle off the gelding's back and lugged it over to a stand fashioned out of an old barrel. Tyler hung the bridle on a nail that had worked its way out of the warped wall. Together they moved to unburden the mare.

"Why don't you make an honest woman of her, now that we'll be settling back home?"

"I aim to be sheriff," said Trace. "It wouldn't suit the folk in town, to have their lawman marry a soiled dove." Trace stowed the other saddle. Tyler hung the rest of the tack.

"Nobody in these parts needs to know what she done in Tucson."

"I'd know," said Trace.

Out of deference to his brother, Tyler had never been with Holly. He always believed anonymity had spared Trace being bothered by the others.

They went to get water for the horses. Since Tyler's wounds were still healing, he carried the lantern and left hauling the buckets to Trace.

Back inside the barn, Tyler asked, "What's the matter with Aimee?"

"Fancies herself in love with the bastard," said Trace.

"Might be she is," said Tyler. "Did something happen between them?"

"He knows I'd kill him," said Trace. Though an adequate deterrent for the average man, Tyler doubted Trace's threat would have the desired effect on Wyland. But he left the thought unsaid.

"Silas Kelly was here." Tyler saw concern replace the frustration in Trace's eyes. He told him the gang had come looking for Aimee and Wyland. "Beth told them you'd gone to Prescott."

"We go tomorrow," said Trace. "You all should come with us."

Tyler asked if he thought Aimee was up to it. Trace shook his head. "I'd like to take her home," said Tyler. "Beth could come too, as a companion for her."

Trace said that the farm wouldn't be any safer than the cabin. But he understood his brother wanting to be home and reckoned it would be good for their sister as well. "Let's head in," he said. "Was there something else?"

Tyler hesitated, wondering if it was Trace that needed his advice for once. "She's still a good, kind-hearted woman," he said. Trace didn't answer. Neither did he wait. By the time Tyler reentered the cabin, Trace and Del were already planning, Aimee had gone to sleep in the bed behind the curtain, and Beth was dishing up a late supper. Tyler paused in the doorway and watched her. He realized that besides going home at long last, he wanted to have Beth on his territory, away from the cabin and its reminders of pain and loss. He wanted to heal her wounds as she had his, wanted to keep her safe and make her happy. When she glanced up at him and smiled, he thought it might all be possible.

In Beth Cooper's bed, Aimee lie awake. Her body hummed with the vibrations of the stage she'd ridden all day. She was too exhausted to follow the conversation beyond the blanket-wall. Instead, her mind dwelled on the comments Del made after he escorted her off the train. Aimee wondered if Josiah leaving her in Tucson was indeed the end for them, if the kiss from afar and the reminder she had Holly pass along would be enough to bring him back to her, if the tipping of his hat had been farewell, forever. Before she went to sleep, Aimee plucked the butterfly combs from her hair, enclosing them between the palms of her hands as she had the previous night. She closed her eyes… and reached up to touch a white horse.

18

Early afternoon was quiet at The Wishing Well. The inn's guests had checked out, their rooms readied for the next. Most of the men who filled the saloon come evening were returned to their livings for as long as there was light to labor by. Those who remained were professional gamblers or freelancers who worked when their money ran out. Between the bar and tables and the parlor house rooms, there were only a half-dozen customers in the establishment. With hours left to don their frilly costumes and rouge, a group of Lou's ladies passed the time with cards and gossip around one of the tables.

Lou took stock of the liquor, entered tallies in a large ledger laid out upon the bar, and contemplated the pretty young woman sitting opposite her, folding napkins for the inn. Lou had always anticipated losing Holly to an adoring patron, had come to hope it for her dearest girl. But the darling had fallen for the one man who would not concede to honor her love. For two years, Lou had watched Holly remain loyal to her heart though Trace Malloy returned less and less often to Tucson.

"You ought to go back to Chicago," said Lou. Cornflower blues lifted and Lou could all but see Holly's thoughts wander back from afar.

"I could never forget him," she said.

Lou shook her head. "You don't have to forget. You just have to move on."

"Who would help you with the inn?"

When Lou looked beyond her right shoulder, Holly knew it was at the other women, any of whom she could hire to take over Holly's tasks. When Lou's gaze moved over her left shoulder, Holly knew it was toward the entrance. She turned to see what drew the older woman's attention.

A man parted the swinging doors and stood with his hands resting over each, ambient light flooding in around his slender form. He looked lazily about the room before stepping inside and releasing the doors to flap back and forth.

"Silas Kelly," said Lou. Holly had heard the name, often in conjunction with that of Josiah Wyland. She realized the two men had more than their association in common—they shared a likeness. And yet, somehow their similarities were also their differences. Silas was tall and lean, though not to the extremes of Wyland. His hair was long and dark, but also straight and shiny. And when he came closer, Holly saw his eyes were as bright and deep a green as Wyland's were blue.

He moved across the floor with a casual grace that made her think of a predator stalking prey. And his presence made ripples—men put down their cards and cups, eased from their chairs, and inched toward the exits. Sensing danger, some of the women moved to escape as well but were blocked as members of the Kelly gang filed in. Two men flanked the saloon's entrance, two jaunted up the stairs, and two went out the side door into the inn. Their leader sauntered straight up to the bar.

As Silas Kelly's twinkling eyes roved over her, it occurred to Holly that this was one of Jerrod's brothers. Oddly enough, they seemed different species—one warm-blooded and one cold. Holly turned back to Lou and tried to ignore the outlaw, though he came to stand so close beside her that his coat brushed her skirt and his voice seemed to slither over her when he spoke.

"I'll start with tequila," he told Lou. "Leave the bottle."

The outlaws who'd gone out the side door returned, reporting the inn empty. From the parlor house rooms, a pair of prostitutes and the disheveled men rousted from their beds were herded downstairs, their clothing bundled in their arms.

"The Wishing Well is closed to the public for the time being," announced Silas as its patrons—clothed and not—were prodded out the doors. "My men require refreshment and entertainment," he said, turning to Lou. "I trust you will accommodate us."

Bandits trespassed behind the bar, handing bottles across it to their confederates. They ogled and declared their pick of the women who crowded confusedly together, outnumbered by the rugged bunch.

Silas finished his first drink in one prolonged sip. He said, "My brother has lost his wife. I have reason to believe she was recently your guest."

"I don't discuss my guests with ruffians," said Lou. "And I expect you to pay for that liquor." Silas ignored her resolute words.

He shifted to face Holly, resting his forearm along the counter's edge. "She's a timorous little confection, not unlike this one here." Holly's mouth had gone dry, and she shivered with nerves made worse by the way the man studied her, like a cat might watch a cornered mouse, with his head tilted and amusement tugging at his lips.

Not able to bear the suspense, Holly told him Jerrod had already inquired after Mr. Wyland and Mrs. Kelly, that there was nothing else to divulge. Like the cat that got the cream, Silas smiled.

"Did he have those legs wrapped around him at the time? No doubt he believed every word. But I'm not so easily convinced." He gestured toward her skirt. "Show me what my little brother found so diverting."

Before Holly could react, before she could register movement behind the counter, Silas pulled, cocked, and pointed his revolver at Lou. "Put it on the bar," he said. Lou raised the sawed-off shotgun she kept below and placed it with the ledger. Silas eased the hammer forward and returned six-gun to holster. His eyes hadn't left Holly. "Go on," he said. She gathered her skirts in stiff fingers and drew the cloth up her legs. He plucked the bottle off the bar, but rather than raise it to his lips, he lowered it. Holly gasped to feel the cool glass touch her inner thigh.

"Silas!" Jerrod Kelly plowed through the saloon doors. He'd been swilling firewater at one of Lou's competitors when patrons chased out of The Wishing Well arrived with news of the gang's occupation. Jerrod took in the scene as he strode toward his brother. A gaggle of whores huddled in the back of the room. Armed men—some he knew and a few new faces—all ready to draw on him at their boss's command, were dispersed throughout. Lou stood behind the bar and Silas in front of it. As his brother turned to greet him, Jerrod caught sight of Holly sliding off a stool, her dress falling to cover her legs. Their eyes met before she turned away and Jerrod's stride faltered. He'd never seen her spooked.

"Glad you could join us," said Silas. He offered the bottle of tequila.

Jerrod declined with a shake of his head. Lou moved from behind the bar, guiding Holly to an empty table and sitting with her. Outlaws resumed their drinking, dropping into chairs or leaning against the bar. Some headed for the stairs, resigned whores in tow.

"What are you doing here?" Jerrod struggled to keep from looking at Holly.

"Rook sent me for the answers you didn't get," said Silas.

"I got answers," said Jerrod.

"A woman will tell you what you want to hear, not what you want to know."

Jerrod couldn't help it—his gaze slid toward Holly.

"Rook needs your guns in Prospect," said Silas. "I'm to send you back."

"I'll go if you come with me."

"The boys and I just arrived," said Silas. "Rest and a little revelry are good for morale."

Jerrod watched Lou mouth Holly's name. "Let me take her with me."

"Rather unbrotherly of you," said Silas, "not wanting to share."

"You don't share women well," said Jerrod.

"Fair enough," said Silas. "Let's settle it with a contest." He motioned to Lou. "Five shots of tequila each, for my brother and me. Line them out on the bar." She got up to pour the drinks. To Jerrod, he said, "Remember the rules?"

Part drinking game, part target practice, Five Shots was a favorite pastime within the gang. "I'm not going to play," said Jerrod.

Silas walked over to Holly, took her elbow, and pulled her to her feet. He led her to the wall between inn and saloon and positioned her back to the wood. He picked two drinks off the bar and crossed over to Jerrod.

"It won't be a challenge if I have to get Wall-eyed Willie to play instead." Silas grinned. "The man can't hold his liquor."

"If I win," said Jerrod. "She leaves here with me."

"Deal." Silas placed one of the glasses in Jerrod's hand, clinked its rim with his own, and threw back his shot. He strode over to Holly, grasped her jaw between his fingers and thumb, and balanced the empty container on the crown of her head. "Ten paces," he said and counted them off, making his way back to Jerrod. Holly's eyes jumped between the brothers and Lou. Silas pivoted, drew his revolver, and fired. The glass exploded above Holly's head. She shrieked.

Jerrod downed his shot and marched toward her. He took ahold of her quaking shoulders and put his lips to her ear. He told her to just keep steady and it would be over in a matter of minutes. When she shook her head, he moved his hands to her cheeks. "Look at me." Her eyes were wide and wet. "Do. Not. Move." He placed the glass atop her head and backed away, not breaking eye contact even when he drew his gun, only when he fired. Another bullet punctured the wood, and more shards rained down about Holly's feet.

"Stop this," said Lou, coming out from behind the bar in front of Holly, prompting boos from the men following the game. Silas downed his second tequila and tossed her the glass. She caught it and glared at him. "You're wasting your time here," she said. "Wyland's moved on." She flung out her arm to point, and with Silas's shot, the glass in her hand shattered. The bandits cheered.

Jerrod guided Lou back behind the bar. The bullet had clipped her finger. He whipped a napkin from the stack and helped wind it around her bleeding hand. She could smell the tequila on his breath but also whiskey. She said, "How drunk are you?"

"Worse off the longer this draws out," he said.

Though his eyes watered when he swallowed more of the tequila, they remained steady on hers. And his whispered words were clear when he swore he wouldn't hurt Holly. Lou said, "Get her away from here." He nodded.

Jerrod moved to where Holly was rooted rigid and pale, with sawdust powdering her hair and bits of glass glittering on her dress. "I'll take you wherever you want to go," he said and settled the empty glass among her curls. "Close your eyes," he urged. "Think of Trace." Jerrod tried not to. As he walked back, he tried not to think about the six shots of tequila left on the bar or the four cartridges still in his revolver, of Holly bleeding out or running into Malloy's arms. At ten paces, he turned, leveled his arm, sighted his target, and fired.

Silas took his turn. Then Jerrod. When it was Silas's turn again, he approached Holly and said, "So, they *were* here." She watched him smile at her confusion. "Mr. Wyland and Mrs. Kelly," he reminded her. "Did they leave together?" Slowly, Holly shook her head. "Did her brother come for her?" She nodded. She was still puzzling over his questions as Silas took his shot.

With two cartridges left in his gun, Jerrod lifted his arm to position his fourth target. He lowered it again when Holly said, "You lied." Her eyes searched his. "In the telegram you sent to your brothers, you lied."

Vivid in sky blue was the question she wouldn't ask. "For the same reason you lied to me," said Jerrod. He placed the glass atop its perch and went back to stand beside Silas. He dried his palm on his trousers, hefted his gun, and scored his fourth point.

It wasn't something Holly wanted to hear. Jerrod preferred her, she knew. Once or twice, he'd made talk about keeping her. She'd never considered he might truly love her.

"He's a crack-shot, my brother," said Silas, after he picked his last drink off the bar and walked over to Holly. "But he has to win this contest to walk out of here with you. I could lose and he might win, or I could lose and he might also lose." Beyond him, Holly could see Jerrod, his final tequila shot in his hand. She trusted he had the skill and tenacity to see the game through. But Silas's turn came first.

"What happens if you both win?"

"According to Hoyle, in the case of a tie, we load another round and step out into the street." Silas emptied his glass and placed it in her hand. "I won't let it come to that."

Holly studied the unbroken container. She recalled that Jerrod had lied to her too—to distract her, she reckoned. When she wouldn't be comforted, he provoked her and allowed her to hate him, or took her to bed and made her forget. If it bothered him to see her tears, what would it do to him to see her bleed?

"Holly?" Jerrod started toward her the moment she stepped away from the wall. She set the glass back on the bar. He touched her sleeve and she turned to face him.

She said, "You needn't have come back. I told you not to."

Jerrod dropped his hand. "You don't know what you're doing," he told her.

"She made her choice," said Silas, though his gang grumbled in disappointment.

Jerrod searched her face, saw her determination and realized his brother was right. "So long, Holly," he grumbled.

Silas saw him to the saloon doors, where two bandits loitered, looking out for trouble. "You might send a telegram on your way out of town," said Silas. "Tell Rook his wife might be closer to home than he thinks."

Jerrod said, "Don't you reckon she's made her choice too?"

Silas shrugged. "Her brother thinks he'll make a better sheriff than our brother."

"That's Rook's business," said Jerrod.

"It's Kelly business," said Silas. He studied his youngest brother for a moment. "How's about you send that telegram, get some sleep, and we'll ride back together come morning?"

***

Holly was able to maintain her composure until Jerrod left. After that, she could do nothing to dam up a river of tears. She covered

192

her eyes with both hands and pressed until it hurt. The seemingly endless flow confounded her—she didn't want to weep over Jerrod Kelly.

Lou asked Silas to let her take Holly next door. "She isn't accustomed to being shot at."

"Willie will help her locate an empty room." Silas signaled to one of his subordinates, an ox of a man who seemed made to follow orders and excelled at guarding prisoners. "You can tell me about my pal Wyland." Silas gave the man Lou's sawed-off shotgun and instructions that Holly wasn't to be disturbed.

When Holly and her squire went into the inn, Lou reached for the shot of tequila Jerrod had left on the bar. Silas refilled his own glass. Lou said, "What do you want to know?"

Despite the distracting revelry of his increasingly drunken confederates, Silas remained attentive, studying her as she answered each question. He seemed to digest each piece of information, perhaps checking it against his recollection of his former associate. Lou kept her replies simple, neither hiding nor embellishing the facts. She wanted to keep Silas engrossed, until he was too drunk to remember Holly, until the marshal in Tucson could get together a posse and come liberate Lou and her girls. She would sell out Wyland to save her own.

Silas said, "Wyland takes Aimee from me, but rather than return her to Prospect for easy reward, he troubles himself to bring her here. He crosses Rook, essentially biting the hand that feeds him, to curry favor with Trace Malloy, a foe. Did he buy a whore?"

"I asked if he wanted a girl," said Lou. It wasn't the question she expected his incredulity to lead up to. "He decided against it," she said.

"He had time for a bath but declined a fuck?"

"Might be he had more pressing matters on his mind," said Lou. "Or he was too tired."

Silas smirked. "A man is never too tired to toss up a skirt." He reckoned the madam of a parlor house ought to know, since her business depended upon it. "It'd be the first thing on his mind, traveling with a woman." Silas lifted his drink but seemed to forget it halfway to his lips. The smirk faded. His eyes swung toward Lou and he cocked his head. "Well, well, well," he said. "I wouldn't have thought him susceptible to *that* particular malady."

Silas set down his drink and reached for the bottle instead, dragging it off the edge of the bar as he rose from his seat. Tequila sloshed when his arm dropped to his side. He mumbled something about a disposition that sonnets would never soften and blood hellfire couldn't warm. He weaved toward the side door, graceful even when drunk.

***

Holly ended up in the room Aimee had stayed in. She lit a candle and sat at the vanity, inclined her head and shook glass from her curls. Shards bounced across the wooden surface like crystallized teardrops. She picked them up, one by one, and collected them on the rim of the candleholder. "He loves you," she told her reflection in the mirror. "But he isn't coming back." She didn't know which man she meant, couldn't think of one without seeing the other.

194

As the flame grew brighter, the shadows huddled closer and Holly realized dusk had fallen. She blew out the candle. The dark surrounded but would not protect. Eventually, Silas would come for her. Before long, she heard booted steps moving down the hall and doors being opened and closed, one at a time. She slid from her seat and slunk across the floor on all fours to the other side of the bed. There, she lowered her chest to her knees, leaning on her elbows and hands on the hard wood.

The door opened and light from the hall projected a man's silhouette against the wall. Holly tried not to breathe. When her jaw quivered, she clamped hands over her mouth to prevent her teeth from chattering. A hushed voice spoke her name. She saw his head turn, scouring the darkness. He called to her again, in a whisper earnest and familiar. Holly lowered her hands. The door closed, leaving the room black.

"Trace?" Her voice didn't seem to work. Her throat wouldn't let the air out of her lungs. Her lips and tongue wouldn't form the sounds. "Trace!"

Holly scrambled over the bed on her hands and knees. The mattress sucked her in, the linens tangled around her. The door opened again, just as she tumbled off the edge. Hands caught her, arms came around her. She was flipped onto her back with a man's weight pressing her into the mattress.

"Shh." His lips touched hers and warm breath, potent with liquor, gushed against her face. His nose dug into her cheek. "Shh," he said, and Holly realized her voice was working after all. She also realized it wasn't Trace.

"Jer-rod?" A ragged breath hacked his name in two.

"That's the one," he said. He eased off of her. "Come on."

She huddled close behind him as he poked his head out into the hall and listened. He closed the door and said, "We'll have to go out the window."

Holly turned and shuffled through the dark, Jerrod's hands on her hips urging her to hurry. There were steps coming down the hall again. Jerrod went out first then helped her over the sill. The roof slanted toward the ground. Jerrod crawled across it on fingertips and the toes of his boots. Holly clambered after him, dress snagging on rough wood, splinters spearing the meat of her hands. Reaching the corner, Jerrod swung over the edge and dropped to the ground. He gestured for Holly to do the same. She clutched the ledge and let her body slip over, lost her grip and fell. Jerrod half-caught her, and they landed in a dusty heap. Inside, a door slammed.

Jerrod set Holly on her feet and took her hand tightly in his. They ran, keeping close to the buildings until they rounded the corner where Jerrod had left his horse. He pulled Holly up to sit sideways across his lap. She turned into him, tilting her hip away from the rigid saddle horn, slipping her shoulder into his armpit, and tucking her head beneath his chin.

Jerrod had gone back to The Wishing Well resolved to take Holly out of danger. Anticipating her refusal, he'd been prepared to drag her out of Tucson. He hadn't expected to leave with her face burrowed into his chest. Her reaction unsettled him. He could cope while resistance fatigued and fear faded. But he hadn't counted on and didn't know how to handle this outright panic and terrible need. They weaved their way out of Tucson, a long ride ahead of them.

19

Seems smaller," said Tyler.

"It's the same as it ever was," answered Trace.

The brothers gazed upon their home, from whence they'd been four years gone. They came half a day ahead of Aimee and the Coopers, circling around to the north to survey the homestead from higher ground.

The house and barn had been built by their grandfather with the second story and two more outbuildings constructed by the time their parents wed. The corral was added when Trace and Tyler still wore short pants. Beyond the house lay the fields on the north bank of the Gila River. They'd worked that land with their father, had seen one season's efforts washed away by the flood that claimed much of Promise across the river and to the west. Back-breaking days and sleepless nights bagging sand and shoveling mud had saved the Malloy home. Aged by desert wind and sun, it endured—a picture of their youth.

"There's no one left to greet us," said Tyler.

Trace glanced at him and saw Tyler's eyes were misty. He realized that in his reluctance to come back too soon, he'd kept his brother away too long. Easy-going Tyler had been content, even cheerful, in many of the places they'd gone. But here his brother was happy, here he belonged. Trace envied him the simplicity of it but knew it wasn't for him. Though they'd talked of returning, of improving and expanding, Trace had come to understand he could never be satisfied back where he'd begun.

There was no one to welcome their return, but at least there was no one to contest it. Trace reckoned any men Rook might have stationed there had been summoned back to Prospect. He reached over and put a hand on his brother's shoulder.

"Welcome home, Tyler."

Tyler grinned. "Race you."

To the barn to do their chores, down to the river to cool off, to the table for supper, the brothers had always competed to see who could get there first. So, they raced their horses down the hill to the corral. They secured the mounts within and explored the property.

It was quiet with no other animals about—no milk cows in the barn, no oxen tethered to the plow, and no chickens underfoot. The old steps and porch planks groaned but bore their weight. Tired hinges creaked. Much of the furniture remained in the bedrooms upstairs and the parlor below, covered with canvas when Rook moved Aimee away. Dust had settled over everything. Footprints indicated recent intrusion and the kitchen table and chairs were uncovered. Ash in the stove showed they'd stayed a few days.

Both brothers breathed more easily back in the open air. The stalks of the last crop remained, unharvested, overrun by the tall grasses and wild flowers that needed no care to thrive.

"The fence will need repaired," said Tyler. "A new roof for that shed." He turned to consider the big old house. "Do you reckon Beth will like it?"

"Miss Cooper has had to make the best of worse," said Trace. "Sure, she will," he added, more definitively, when his brother remained solemn.

"I bet Holly would," said Tyler. "We always talked about settling back here together, you in charge of livestock, me in charge of the crop."

Trace shook his head. "If we're to have a future here, the Kellys will have to be dealt with first. After that, these parts will need an honest man to keep the peace." The disappointment in his brother's eyes was for both their sakes, Trace knew. But he wouldn't entrust it to anyone else. He said, "You and Beth will do fine running the place yourselves. Better when you have some boys to help you, like Pa had us." He expected that thought to please Tyler. Instead, his brother's eyes grew more troubled. "Prospect ain't far. I could still lend a hand at harvest time. And with the repairs."

"You got me thinking about children," said Tyler. He didn't know if they were even a possibility after what Beth had been though. "I don't even know if she'll have me."

"Sure, she will," Trace said again. But he'd never known his brother to doubt a good thing.

***

Beth Cooper was not sad to leave home. She knew she'd be back soon enough. Her father was to accompany Trace Malloy to Prescott, a trip that would take over a week not including their business with the governor. The brothers decided to first return to their own home, in hopes that their sister would be more comfortable in familiar surroundings. The younger woman had a delicate disposition that had been tried by her kidnapping and by her journey through the wilderness with Josiah Wyland.

Beth anticipated remaining alone to look after the cabin, since her father's resurgence of health negated the need for her to go along to Prescott. She hadn't relished the idea but wouldn't have complained. She'd gotten along by herself before. It surprised her when Tyler suggested she come with as a companion for Aimee. She suspected it was partly a chivalrous notion, for her benefit as much as his sister's. Certain there would be much to do at the abandoned farm, Beth was determined to reciprocate his kindness by making herself indispensable.

Trace and Tyler helped to pack the Coopers' wagon before riding ahead to ensure the homestead wasn't guarded by Kelly men or infested with squatters. The uncovered cart was crowded with hogs and the chickens in a crate, with the cow roped to the back of it. They'd loaded all the garden's ready produce and herbs, most of the canned goods, cook and tableware, the bedding, and as much feed for the animals as would fit. There was no knowing what remained or had been looted from the Malloy residence.

Trace purchased two mules to pull the wagon that Del drove. Aimee sat on the bench seat beside him. Beth walked. The pace was slow enough that she had no trouble keeping up, and she enjoyed the exercise despite the heat and the bag over her shoulders. In it, she carried her clothes and sewing kit, her father's most treasured books, soap and other necessities, and the frames off the mantle.

Four miles eastward progress put them halfway between the cabin and the remains of Promise. They veered northeast, following an old trail that led to a river crossing. The brothers met them at the south bank. Tyler waved from the saddle of his paint gelding. Beside him, Trace sat on her father's gray mare. Beth reached them ahead of the wagon, not realizing she'd picked up her step at the sight of them.

"Howdy." Tyler grinned. He appeared hale, in no need of her concern.

"Allow me," said Trace, leaning over to take her pack. He lifted it from her shoulders before she remembered to thank him, distracted as she was by Tyler still smiling down at her.

"We reckoned we'd help with the crossing," he said. "Come on up, so you don't get your feet wet." He offered his hand and she reached for it—too eagerly, she thought and hoped he attributed her blush to exertion. Beth realized, as soon as she was up on the horse, that she'd worn her split-skirt, as though she had a premonition—or a secret wish—that she would be riding.

Tyler directed his horse out into the center of the stream and turned to supervise the crossing, Trace on the other side of the cart, opposite him. The water was low, a couple of feet at the deepest spots. The mules splashed through as easily as on dry land.

"Hang on." Tyler steered his mount up a steeper section of embankment, laying a hand over the arm she wound around his middle as the animal bounded up the incline. He kept it in place once they gained even terrain. "You've walked a good distance." He peered at her over his shoulder. "You can ride the rest, if you like." Her nod was a tad too indifferent for Tyler's satisfaction. He leaned back toward her, lowered his voice and said, "It's good to see you." Her lashes lowered, and she chewed on her lip. There was no mistaking her blush.

They passed Promise and skirted the range of hills, leaving and coming back to the river. As Trace led the wagon around to avoid the softer soil of the fields, Tyler took an even wider circle back up to the small ridge. Together, he and Beth looked down on what was his. He'd wanted her to see it from that vantage point. When she didn't comment, he stole a glance at her. She'd raised her hand to rest lightly over her chest, and her expression pleased him more than any words. He scooped her other hand up from his waist and pressed his lips to the back of it, holding her palm over his heart when he was through.

It was perfectly situated, somehow both practical and romantic. The house was pale blue, the porch railings white. Beth knew her heart would break a little when it came time to go back to the lonely little cabin.

***

When Aimee sent her letters pleading for Trace and Tyler's return, it had been her wish that she and her brothers would come home together. Though their parents had died there, Rook had taken her to town that tragic day, so she had no sad memories to sully the sweet. But as the wagon brought her within sight of the Malloy house, all her expectations were overwhelmed by a singular sense of dissimilitude. She was a butterfly returning to the cocoon only to discover she no longer fit within the confines of her former existence.

Once she'd dreamed of joining her brothers in their adventures driving cattle and camping around the chuck wagon, watching the sun rise and set on new horizons each day.

Then she'd had adventures of her own. She'd been kidnapped and rescued, had escaped and been recaptured. She'd ridden a beastly horse, shot an outlaw's gun, drunk whiskey in a saloon, and made love under the stars. She'd gone into the desert wilds and emerged transformed—cured of invalid fears, unbound from the chains of propriety and unleashed of maidenly inhibitions. She'd found safety in the arms of a dangerous man, freedom in the untamed spaces outside civilization and beyond convention.

Now she was expected to forget him, to conform to an outgrown role, to return to which she no longer belonged and perhaps never truly had.

The sight of the corral was a comfort, a tangible link to a memory that had always been there for her. The blue-eyed boy and white horse had never returned—Aimee reckoned she knew the reason. For the first time since he'd taken her off the train, she faced Del Cooper. She asked, "Who was he, the first man Josiah killed?"

Del spoke only after bringing the mules to a halt. "He was an out-of-towner with no name that anyone knew, a man of little consequence, no better than Wyland himself."

"Why did he kill him?"

"Wyland caught him trying to steal his horse. Witnesses said the first shot might have been a warning, but it ricocheted off the rocky ground."

"And hit the man?"

"No," said Del. "It hit the horse. After that, Wyland emptied his gun into the man's chest. He had to load another round to put down the animal. By all accounts, he hasn't fired a warning shot since that day."

The world dimmed and smeared. Not waiting for assistance, Aimee staggered off the side of the cart. She stumbled toward the circular fence and sagged against it with her arms over the top rail and her cheek resting against a rough wooden post. Soundlessly, she wept.

Trace approached her first. He stood beside his sister, not sure he should touch her, certain there was nothing he could say. He knew what slow treatment time was. Eventually, Aimee released the post to lean against him instead.

"Is it to do with Ma and Pa?" Tyler had come up behind them. Del and his daughter stood by the wagon, looking on. Trace shook his head.

"Ask Beth to help ready her room. Show her which it is."

Trace hadn't told his brother or their parents about Aimee and Wyland's secret ride. Neither had he let on to Aimee that he'd seen them. The sight of his ten-year-old sister so innocently and blissfully oblivious to the harm a strange boy might inflict upon her had shaken Trace to his core. He'd put all that angst into the beating and banishment he'd bestowed upon Wyland the next day. The way things turned out, he needn't have bothered. Wyland found other trouble and fled Promise not long after. Trace never expected to have to contend with that fear again, seven years later.

20

Josiah Wyland bolted upright from the hard ground at his horse's hooves, awakened before dawn for a third day. Blood pounded in his head, thunderous in comparison to the dream's silent conclusion. There'd been the click of the hammer meeting an empty chamber and then nothing.

Nothing the first night, after the baying of Silas's dogs chased him through a canyon of jagged rock upon which he gashed himself at every turn, leaving a trail for the blood-crazed hounds to pursue. The winding chasm ended in a moonlit clearing with sheer walls that left no way out. A silver beam of light gleamed upon the ivory grips of his twin Colts. As he raised the weapons to meet snarling snouts, they'd felt too light.

Nothing the second night, after he trudged through a red-dirt wasteland dragging clanking, rusted chains fastened to his wrists and ankles by heavy iron manacles that chaffed his flesh to the bone. As the sun bore down, pink dust clogged his nose and throat, his sweat evaporated, his skin cracked and bled and crusted over. Carrion circled above his head as his wandering brought him closer to no place and no one. When he stumbled over the pistol, its plating blistered with corrosion, he wished for mercy. Neglected mechanisms screeched, the trigger resisted. And click.

Josiah thought the third night different. The dream began with Aimee's wide gray eyes as she looked at him over her shoulder while reaching to pet the white horse. Then they were on a black horse, riding fast, his heart beating faster. And faster as her arms tightened around him in the dark, as he slid between her thighs and was both lost and found. Then they were apart. She called for him, needing him to save her. He drew his guns, already knowing how it would end—forsaken by silence.

He pushed to his feet, limbs trembling, half-aroused by how the dream had begun and queasy by how it ended. For the third morning, he was awake to see first light breach the horizon and bring color to another river. Yesterday, it had been the San Pedro and the Santa Cruz the day before that. Now the sun shone on the waters of the Rio Grande.

He had only to follow the river into Old Mexico. Josiah knew he could disappear there, die some other way than a gunfighter's end by another man's bullet.

He took the tin from his pocket and ran his thumb over the top. He'd discovered she had kept the combs, replacing them with a token of her own. He took out the long lock of golden hair, felt it glide through his fingers, watched it shimmer in the sun. He stretched out his arm and a breeze caught the strands, making them dance. He told himself to let go, that she'd be better off. He reminded himself he had nothing to offer her, was nothing without her. He'd gotten her to Tucson. She was home by now. Back in the safety of family and good society, she wouldn't feel for him as she had when she'd been misplaced and afraid. She would forget him, and he'd be better off to let her. *Just let go*—he couldn't. His fingers curled and caught the tress against his palm. He wound it and tucked it back into the tin, replaced the lid, and slid it back into his pocket.

If he crossed the border, would it matter that he might live another twenty-some years? If he turned back, would it matter that he might live only a day? Everything he wanted but couldn't keep was behind him and only empty desert and empty years ahead. All his life, he'd wandered in and out of that nothing-land. He had survived to become as lonesome as the landscape. He was tired of fleeing his past, of meeting his reputation wherever he went. He knew what the dream meant—he was running out of time and his guns wouldn't save him.

The sweetest end he could imagine was to die in Aimee's arms. She'd give him that, he reckoned, but she'd suffer for it. Would she rather see him die than know he had left her? Or was it kinder to let her wonder what had become of him, where he'd gone to and why he hadn't returned? Maybe she'd think on it only when the wind blew a certain way, maybe it would be her first and last thought each day.

***

"Unspeakable." The headline was belied by a corresponding account of Silas Kelly's deeds in Tucson, which preceded him to Prospect. Rook surmised word of what transpired must have been scribbled down at the telegraph office sometime after he received Jerrod's message. The newspaperman had undoubtedly burned the midnight oil to feature the incident on the front page of the Arizona Weekly Enterprise. The damning specks of ink barely filled a column and were dwarfed by advertisements for mining supplies, hats and shoes, and "groceries of every description," yet Rook knew they would obscure more than the surveyor's maps laid out on his desk.

"Have you any conception of what you may have cost me?" he said when Silas strolled through the jailhouse door dusty and windblown from a hard ride.

Flashing a grin, his older brother raised his arms from his sides to display that he was unscathed. Silas said, "I appreciate the concern." He dropped into the chair across from Rook. "Posse chased us out of the city. I baked my horse by the time they turned back." Silas put his heel on Rook's desk and crossed one long leg over the over.

"You made the papers," said Rook. "The governor will be reading it this morning."

Silas yawned. "They have a high regard for their whores down in Tucson."

"Louanne Fitzgerald was respected as a business woman."

"More like them law dogs hump her working girls."

"Even so," said Rook. "They wouldn't stand to let an outlaw gang run her customers out into the street." He quoted the article, "Without a thread of dignity."

Silas threw back his head and laughed.

Rook slid Jerrod's telegram across the desk. "What's this mean?"

"Regarding Kelly business. To each his own. Tell Silas." He let the note slip from his fingers. "Little brother has washed his hands of us."

Rook fumed. "What did you do to bring that about?"

Silas said, "Relax, you won't need him if you've got Wyland."

"I don't have Wyland. We don't know where he is. Besides, I can't control him, not even with the threat of prison."

"That's because you never understood him," said Silas. "A man like that, you can't use his fears against him. He's survived prison already. And death is no deterrent when you consider the life he's led."

"Okay," said Rook. It was strange to hear Silas speak sense. He sat back and waited to have his hat knocked off.

"It's not what he stands to lose, it's what he stands to gain," said Silas. "As a boy, he learned to harden his heart against hardship. That's a stone no hammer can crack."

"What then?" Rook decided Silas was talking nonsense after all. His mind moved to reassuring the mayor that Prospect would not suffer in the way of Tucson from the Kelly gang's coming-and-goings.

"A woman," said Silas and Rook forgot the mayor. "He's mashed."

It was the perfect explanation. Wyland would never side with Malloy for either's sake. But for Trace's sister, he'd forsaken the only protection he had against a lifelong enemy. In Rook's own kitchen, sweet, simple Aimee unwittingly planted the seed of the gunfighter's downfall. Rook had his ace. He need only to decide how to play it.

Silas said, "I need a whore. And a nap."

"Pick a woman that won't be missed, go to a hotel, and let this blow over." Rook indicated the newspaper in front of him. "Or I'll have to arrest you." Silas smirked.

Once he left, Rook picked up Jerrod's telegram and read it anew. He got up and went to the doorway. Dawes had a chair tipped back against the building so its front legs were in the air. Rook told him to go and round up Silas's most-trusted. "Tell them I want to talk quietly and that I'll make it worth their while. And go pack your war bag. I'm sending you back to Tucson."

21

Trace and Del departed the morning after the move. Before they were a week gone, Beth came to realize the Malloy farm was only a larger, lovelier stage for the continuation of the quiet drama betwixt her and Tyler.

He thought he knew what had happened to her, what it had done to her. He thought he could accept it. He thought he knew how to handle her. While his gentle optimism protected him, it destroyed her. And this place of his bolstered him as it diminished her.

He no longer required her nursing and rejected her opinion that he pushed himself too hard. Her protests only prompted annoyance, so what could she do? They were in his territory now, on his terms. He claimed most of the work outdoors, leaving her to attend to his sister and the house. Aimee retired early and was late to rise yet fatigued easily when she attempted to help Beth with the chores. Since she had no treatment for what ailed the younger woman, Beth left Aimee to her solitude and occupied herself with the considerable work of restoring the home.

She worked tirelessly, and Tyler did as well. Beth reckoned they owed their comfortable companionship during meals and before bed to exhaustion.

Tyler busted his back and was getting stronger every day, but she wouldn't pause to take notice. The stubborn woman worked herself to the bone, undermining all his efforts to reciprocate her hospitality. At the cabin, Beth was a slave to her father's needs, competing with a ghost for his attention. But here, she toiled twice as hard, and Tyler had to work harder to show her there was no need. They spent so much time endeavoring at their respective tasks they only saw one another from a distance or in passing, except for meal times and evenings when they could hardly stay awake to converse politely about nothing.

Repairs to the homestead were accomplished daily but at the expense of a more personal agenda Tyler deemed far more important. He'd been in bad shape when first they met, but even then, he'd felt a spark. Damned if he could reproduce it. He hadn't managed to make her blush with pleasure since the day they arrived at the farm. But Trace had—what his brother said to her on the morning he and Del left, Tyler hadn't been in range to hear. He was sure of Trace's support. But the old lawman might prefer another man for his daughter, a protégé as opposed to a farmer. The thought that Beth might defer the matter of her heart to her father depressed Tyler. The idea that Del could neglect Beth and still demand such devotion pissed him off. He wanted to win her favor regardless of the judge's verdict.

Tyler ruminated on those frustrations as he hauled water up from the river to the corral where the mules rested when he wasn't working them. He weaved under the weight of the buckets dangling from the yoke across his shoulders. He'd lost count of how many times he'd made the trip to refill them, only glad that this final load would top-off the trough. He saw Beth step off the porch and move to intercept him.

She said, "Why don't you use one of the mules?"

"Trace and I always did it this way." He staggered the last few steps, stooped to lower the buckets, and shrugged off the yoke, leaning it against the fence. He turned to find her between him and the trough, hands propped on her hips.

"You were shot not two weeks ago." She waved a hand at the front of his shirt, spotted where his sweat had softened the scabs and made them stick and stain.

"Well, I'm done now," he said. "If you'll get out of my way."

"I'll do it," she said. They reached for the same handle, and the first bucket sloshed between them.

"I can finish it," said Tyler.

"You're spilling," said Beth.

"Then let go." He moved to step around her, she shifted to block his path, and he moved around her in the other direction. Tyler wasn't sure how it happened, if she slipped or bumped the edge of the trough. She lost her balance and let go of the bucket. He could only watch as she toppled into the water. She surfaced with a gasp and stared up at him, sitting in the trough, water dripping off her chin. Tyler knew better than to smile but damned if he could help it.

He saw mischief glint in her eyes before she kicked, splashing him. He dumped the bucket over her head. And relished her evil smile as she seized his shirtfront and hauled back, managing to tip him over the edge and squirm out of the path of his descent, rolling like an otter so his back went straight to the bottom.

He broke the surface laughing and scrambled out after her as she made for the other bucket. She heaved it and dropped it with a shriek when Tyler's arms snaked about her waist and swung her around. His boots slipped on the mud and they both went down.

Smeared with silt, Beth wiggled free. Tyler grabbed for her skirt to prevent her scuttling away and tried to pin her beneath his weight. Slick as hogs after a rain, they grappled. And froze when the shadow of two horses moved over them. Over the fence, a pair of riders stared down at the couple. One of them, a woman, burst into laughter.

"Holly?" Tyler recognized her bubbling giggle and felt a surge of gladness. He pushed to his feet and having lost his hat, raised a hand to shield his eyes against the bright sun.

The other rider was a man of roughly the same age and build as Tyler, with dark hair and green eyes that shifted in the direction of the house, watching Beth as she hurried toward it.

"Whoa," said Jerrod when Tyler pulled his revolver and pointed it at him. Though he was fairly certain the waterlogged gun wouldn't fire, he held up his hands. "I'm here as a friend, Malloy. Can we talk?"

Tyler ordered a wide-eyed Holly to take the gunfighter's pistol and hand it over. When she hesitated, Jerrod said, "Go on, Holly, do it." Tyler took it from her.

"Do you know Beth?"

"I do not know Beth," said Jerrod. "Can I put my hands down now?"

"Stay here," said Tyler. He took Jerrod Kelly's gun with him, into the house.

The door to her room was closed. Tyler paused outside to shore up the mess of feelings never consistent when it came to Beth. Days of thwarted effort had peaked in anger, only to be toppled by the most fun Tyler had had in a long while. But now he questioned whether he'd gotten carried away. Perhaps it was only the unexpected company that had unnerved her. But he worried that it was him, that she'd somehow sensed the miniscule—but infinitely significant—thrill of arousal he'd felt with her body sliding beneath his and was spooked by it.

Tyler took a deep breath, tapped on the door, and when no answer came, walked in. Beth was wringing out her hair into the wash basin and looking out the window. Tyler trudged over to stand beside her.

"Who are they?"

"Holly Watson, from Tucson. She's a friend of Trace," he said. "And Jerrod Kelly." He watched her nod. She seemed all right, but he had to be sure. Jerrod was known to ride with his brother's gang from time to time. "He wasn't there that day?" She shook her head. "He says he just wants to talk. I'll tell him to go, if you want."

Beth watched Jerrod assist Holly down from the horse. "I'm not the one you should be asking." Tyler followed her gaze. Jerrod took Holly's hand. With his free hand splayed over the small of her back, he guided her to sit upon one of the buckets which he overturned and brushed off for her. When she was seated, he remained close.

"Beth." Only when he looked at her and found her looking back, did he realize he'd actually spoken. "You're a guest, not a hired hand," he said.

"You don't want my help," she said.

"No. I mean yes. Just less of it," he said.

She gave a slight nod and a slighter smile. "I'm a guest." It was his word, but her soft voice changed it, somehow making it sound unwelcome.

"It's a pleasure having you here," he said.

"It's okay, I understand," she said.

Tyler frowned. "It's not okay. Tell me what I'm thinking, since you understand."

She knew him well enough now to recognize the indignation in his tone. He scowled at her and she scowled back. "I think we should speak plainly," she said.

"You are maddening," he said and took a step closer to her. He raised his hand beneath her chin and used the knuckle of his thumb to keep her eyes level with his. "Have I been too polite with you, Beth?" He reckoned she could retreat if she wanted to. One finger was hardly overpowering. "As plainly as I can," Tyler said and kissed her. The kiss tasted of mud and was better than anything. He couldn't afford to make it gentle—he feared her doubting his desire more than he feared offending her with it. They were both breathless by the time he ended it. He said, "I want you here. I want you to want to be here." *I want you to want me back.*

"Then you'll let me use the swimming hole down by the river to bathe?"

Tyler blinked at her. He and Trace had dug out the spot to cool off during their breaks from working the fields. "If you like," he said. She left him standing there and moved to take a fresh skirt and blouse from the dresser. She came back to collect a bar of soap from the wash stand. He said, "How did you know about that?" After working outdoors each day, he used the pool to rinse off sweat and dirt.

"By accident, since you didn't bother to tell me," she said. "I made the new curtains for your room, you know."

"You saw me?" Her only response was the telltale blush that had a grin spreading across his face and heat spreading through his body. "Did you watch?"

Beth's cheeks were stained a becoming pink. There was a wicked gleam in her eyes when she said, "If I see them stir, you're not getting supper."

He followed her out of the room and paused at the stairs, gaze drifting down the hall to the door at the house's southeast corner. A few steps down, Beth turned to look up at him.

"Right behind you," he said.

She walked over and introduced herself to Holly and Jerrod, apologizing for her appearance and inviting them to supper. To Holly, she said, "You should go up and visit Aimee. It will do her good." She excused herself and headed around the house toward the fields and the river beyond. Through it all, Tyler hadn't managed to tear his eyes off her.

***

Tyler determined Holly Watson was not quite herself. Her smile was bright but fleeting, and there were shadows under her eyes. He drew her aside while Jerrod moved their horses — his and the

217

one he'd bought outside of Tucson for Holly—into the corral. Tyler asked if she was well. She nodded and kissed his cheek. "Trace is away for a little while," he told her, not wanting to say too much with Kelly in earshot. "He'll be glad to see you."

Holly said, "Will he?"

"Of course," said Tyler. "Are you sure you're all right?"

"Thanks to him." She cast a solemn glance in Jerrod Kelly's direction. Tyler pointed out the room and Holly went up to see Aimee, leaving him and the gunfighter to talk.

Jerrod fished Tyler's hat out of the trough. Though Malloy thanked him, Jerrod reckoned the other man would rather him have let it float. He sensed Tyler was sore over more than the interruption of his wrestling match with the feisty brunette. He knew it probably had as much to do with his last name as his showing up with Trace's gal. He pretended not to notice the way Tyler straightened to emphasize every fraction of their one-inch difference in height. They were the same age and would be well-matched for a tussle, except Tyler had Jerrod's firearm and Jerrod knew Tyler was still recovering from the gunfight in Promise.

"Funny how you can grow up a few miles from a person and never have chanced to meet her," said Jerrod. One glance in the direction Beth had gone was enough to earn him a glower from Tyler. Diverting his gaze toward the window Tyler pointed out to Holly was no good either. Jerrod sighed. "I didn't come looking for trouble," he said. "And I'm not reporting back to my brothers, if that's what you're thinking."

Tyler said, "You expect me to take you at your word, Kelly?"

"I do," said Jerrod with a glower of his own. "Listen, with Trace away, seems like you could use some help around here. I'd like to stay and lend a hand."

Tyler reckoned he could use one, but he wasn't keen to make friends with his brother's rival. He said, "Don't tell me you're looking to change professions."

"No," Jerrod admitted. "I just want my chance to win her fair."

Green eyes dared Tyler to deny him. Tyler found himself considering—he really could use the help, and so could Beth. And if he turned Jerrod away, the gunman might take Holly with him. Tyler reckoned seeing her apart from The Wishing Well might be what Trace needed to accept the possibility he could have Holly in his life. His brother would be madder than an old wet hen to find a Kelly under his roof, but Tyler reckoned Jerrod deserved his shot. Personally, he didn't think the other man stood a chance. It occurred to Tyler that he might have some success courting Beth if they each weren't so dragged out by day's end. He said, "Ever done any farm work?"

Jerrod laughed and shook his head. "I know horses and I know guns. The rest I'm willing to learn. And I can help protect the women."

"Against your brothers?"

"If need be," said Jerrod.

Tyler said, "If the girls agree, you can stay until Trace gets back." He returned the revolver and Jerrod holstered it. It was as good as a handshake.

***

With her first glimpse of the farmhouse, Holly realized she'd longed for the place for years, more than she'd ever wished to be back in Chicago.

Standing just within the front door, her heart swelled with all her eyes absorbed and more. There was a large parlor to her right, furnished to accommodate a big party—specifically, an extended family. Less formal and even more inviting was the kitchen to her left, with its massive table and light from multiple windows. Holly could almost see the rooms peopled—children laid out on their bellies on the parlor rug, playing with toys while the adults sat contentedly looking on, reading, or talking—folk lining the table at breakfast or supper, passing around dishes laden with the fruits of their labors.

Her home in Chicago had been smaller, but Holly remembered it filled with joy even in the hard times. She imagined Trace and Tyler would fill theirs likewise—with children, love, and laughter—and her heart ached to be part of it. Whenever Holly had imagined visiting the Malloy home, she envisioned it with Trace beside her, showing her around, welcoming her. How would he feel when he returned to find her there? Would he really be glad to see her?

A section of wall shielded the parlor from the heat of the kitchen. Holly passed framed pictures, paintings, and needlework. It ended with a second opening connecting the kitchen to a staircase that led to the second-floor bedrooms. A backdoor looked out upon the fields.

At the top of the stairs, Holly counted six doors—there were three bedrooms at the front of the house and three at the back. She wondered which belonged to Trace. A trail of dripped water and wet prints led into the middle front one. Holly smiled to recall the playful skirmish between Tyler and Beth Cooper, with whom he was so obviously smitten.

Aimee's door was left cracked, so Holly's gentle knock pushed it open. It was a girlhood room, papered in pretty blue with matching curtains. A small dresser, bench seat under the window, and bed frame were all painted white. A love-worn doll sat on a chair in one corner.

The bed wasn't big but still dwarfed the young woman curled on top of it. She was dressed, and the bed was made, but it seemed as if that was all she'd had the energy for that day. Her hair was fanned out over the pillow, still mussed from sleep. Though she faced the door, Aimee hadn't noticed it open or Holly standing within its frame.

When they met in Tucson, Aimee had been a delicate and timid creature, battered and fatigued by the events that brought her there, but with a soft glow of life, of hope and curiosity, about her. Holly was shocked to see that being home had done nothing to restore her bloom. She'd paled as though she hadn't seen the sun since her return, her gray eyes had dulled, and even the golden hair had lost its luster. Neither Tyler nor Beth had mentioned Aimee being ill, but she lay upon the quilt like a dying flower.

Holly approached and saw Aimee's eyes were focused on the pair of combs in her open hand. She finally noticed her visitor when Holly knelt in front of her. She blinked at her then looked confusedly about, as if uncertain where she was.

A light flickered in gray eyes. "Have you news of Josiah?"

Holly shook her head and watched the glimmer dim. She said, "Why don't I brush your hair, and we can put the combs in?" Aimee nodded and sat up. She followed Holly to the window seat. Eventually, she asked what Holly was doing there. "Some bad men came to Tucson," said Holly. "I had to get away."

"Worse than Jerrod Kelly?"

"His brother Silas. It was Jerrod who brought me here."

Aimee nodded. Holly wasn't sure she understood. She wasn't sure she did either. When she'd fixed Aimee's hair, she put down the brush and folded her arms around the other woman. She couldn't help but wonder if she'd been wrong to encourage her romance with Wyland. Hope for Aimee and Josiah had given Holly hope for herself and Trace. But she hadn't thought through the difficulties, the opposition and subsequent suffering the couple might face. She didn't know if Wyland would come back, but she was certain Trace would never welcome the gunslinger under his roof. He might not even welcome Holly.

Later, they went downstairs for the supper Beth had cooked. Though she couldn't have said why, Holly was relieved to hear Jerrod would be staying for a time. She was offered one of the spare rooms but elected to sleep in the same bed as Aimee that first night.

When her friend was asleep, Holly tiptoed across the hall and tapped on the opposite door, beneath which she could still see candlelight. Jerrod opened it.

"Holly." He glanced down the hall at the other closed doors then over her shoulder. "Is she well?" Holly nodded. His eyes focused on her. "Are you?" She nodded again. Jerrod said, "It's odd seeing you like this." He gestured to the full-length, long-sleeved dressing gown she'd borrowed from Beth. Holly gave a soft laugh.

She said, "I wanted to thank you for bringing me here."

"Don't mention it," he said. He started to shut the door, but she stopped him, raising her hand and placing it upon his chest.

"If there's something you wanted from me," she said, pausing to wet her lips.

Jerrod glanced down the hall once more then down at her hand over his shirt before meeting her eyes. "I want something to be clear," he said. "To you. To me." His voice had risen above a whisper. He lowered it. "To Malloy when he gets back." He paused, knowing it was important she understand most of all. "You ain't a whore no more, Holly," he said. She lowered her hand. He bid her goodnight and shut the door.

Holly crept back across the hall and eased onto the bed beside Aimee. Not a whore. Not a wife. Holly stared up at the ceiling and wondered who she was now.

22

Only when he was standing in the parlor of the governor's home did Trace consider he ought to have invested in a new suit or at least gotten a haircut. His coarse clothes and dusty boots presented him as a working man, more of the country than the town.

While Del sat in one of the meticulously-carved and finely-upholstered chairs, awaiting their meeting, Trace opted to stand. He held his hat, noted the sweat-stained band and how stiff wool scratched when cracked and calloused fingers skimmed over the brim.

When a calamity of canines bounded into the room, Trace forgot his jitters. The motley pack danced around him before homing in on Del's lap. A spotted straggler skidded around the door jamb and made straight for Trace, rearing up to plant its paws above his knees. He was stooping to scratch its floppy ears when Arizona Territory Governor Frederick Augustus Tritle stepped into the room. He clapped his hands and the pack dispersed to sniff about, except for the hound standing up against Trace.

The governor and old judge greeted one another with first names and an exuberant handshake. Fred offered condolences for Del's son and asked after Beth. Then he turned and gave Trace an evaluating look. He said, "You should take him with you. He likes you." He offered his hand and Trace was surprised by its strength.

Though his chosen profession was that of attorney, Tritle was no dandy. Conservative grooming barely tamed his full beard and bushy mustache. His suit did nothing to soften blocky shoulders. His caramel-colored hair was combed back from a sharpening widow's peak. Mild blue-gray eyes were warm, but Trace imagined them hardening to steel when the occasion called for it. In a gruff voice, he said, "Would you call yourself a cowboy, Mr. Malloy?"

"My brother and I grew up farming before going to Texas to work as drovers," said Trace. "I wouldn't call myself either."

Tritle nodded. "That band of rustlers in Cochise County perverted the epitaph, a misfortune for all true cattlemen. We about had to call in the Army to subdue them."

Del spoke up. "Left unchecked, the Kelly gang will succeed them. Their numbers aren't as great, but they have a stronghold in Canyon Diablo in the north and a whole county as sanctuary in the south."

"Prospect's mayor was convinced making Rook Kelly sheriff would temper his brother's outlawry," said the governor. "With no better candidates stepping up, I was persuaded to appoint him."

Trace said, "Since we were kids, Rook and Silas have always protected each other."

"One with cunning, the other with coercion," said Del. "That alliance, across the line of the law, might have been their design from the beginning. Rook is credited with keeping the violence out of Prospect, while Silas engenders turmoil in surrounding counties, giving people incentive to keep his brother in office. Rook marries into further favor with the town by choosing a local bride. And he hires Josiah Wyland as a guard dog against rivals for authority."

"But now he's lost both Aimee and Wyland," said Trace.

"And," said Tritle, "Silas might have gone too far with his recent barbarity in Tucson. The bond between brothers might not be as ironclad as it once was."

Del and Trace shared a look. The older man said, "I'm afraid we've been traveling and haven't been apprised of the goings-on in Tucson."

The governor told them the Kelly gang shot up a saloon and took over a brothel for a night before a posse ran them out. "Their violence put the owner in the hospital." Trace asked if anyone else was hurt. Tritle said, "That's as much as I know. The Kelly brothers threaten the future of all Arizona. Prospect is the heart of the problem. We must end the corruption there before we can quell the reign of lawlessness and fear. Prospect needs a morally impregnable sheriff to serve his community, a hard-working man to provide protection of life and property and to reinstate justice in the land. I like you for the job, Malloy. What do you say?"

***

As they left the governor's house, Del clapped his hand down on Trace's shoulder and gave it a squeeze. The gesture felt like congratulations, reassurance, and comradery all rolled into one.

226

Trace felt a pinch in his heart that his father had passed. He asked what happened to Del's son.

"That's a drinking question," said Del. "Let's buy each other a whiskey."

They found a saloon where they could have a table to themselves. Trace waited as Del tasted his liquor and contemplated where to begin. The old man didn't speak until they ordered their second round.

He said, "A man's cause will ask of him his life—his time, his energy, everything. He starts with his principles and integrity, and in the end, they are all he can expect to keep."

Trace nodded, solemnly, as if he understood. Del knew he did not. There was still too much light in hazel eyes. Del wanted to prepare the young man. He knew he could not.

"Most men would not commit themselves to the preservation of others. It is for those with a sense of right they cannot turn their backs on," said Del. "You will not be rewarded for taking up this charge. For your sacrifices, you'll have the honor of serving the greater good. That is all."

"But it's worth it," said Trace. Del saw the asking in his expression. At countless points throughout his career, he would have answered with a definitive affirmation. Alas, he'd outlived that ability.

"You must make that determination for yourself and be willing to risk everything to uphold it. It was to the cause that I lost my son," said Del. "The wicked do not revere innocence. The worst among them destroy it for their own amusement. I chased one such blackguard from Missouri to Promise, Arizona where his final transgression was to defile a young woman and sire a child."

"Wyland," said Trace. He hadn't known the orphan's origins to be as unfortunate as that.

Del nodded. For his failures, he'd been made to watch the son grow as rotten as the father. "It was the spawn of my enemy that killed my boy."

Trace swallowed. "I'll help you bring him to justice."

"There's none to be had in this case," said Del. "You need to focus on making things right in Prospect. Decent folk are depending on you." He finished his drink and said, "These feelings your sister has for Wyland will bring her to harm."

"I know," said Trace, bowing his head.

"Tyler had the right idea bringing her home and asking Beth to come along," said Del. "Aimee could benefit from the example of a practical woman."

Trace smiled to recall his brother's real motive for inviting Cooper's daughter to stay at the farm. His smile vanished with Del's next comment.

"You'd do well to look for those same sensibilities in the woman you marry."

"Sorry?" Trace wondered if the man was recommending Beth for him.

"The job requires long hours and frequent travel," said Del. "You'll need a self-sufficient wife able to carry on in your absence."

Trace nodded, but his thoughts were suddenly flooded with worries he'd damned up in the back of his mind after hearing what happened in Tucson. He could think only of one woman.

But the oath he took before the governor left no place in his life for Holly Watson. If she were an acceptable match, she'd lighten his burden just with her laughter. Trace ached for her laughter. But he'd made his decision, had chosen his course. Trace Malloy had found his purpose. But he could find no peace in the resolution without first knowing Holly was safe. He said, "Before we head home, I'd like to go back to Tucson."

"I'll go to Tucson," said Del. "You go home. See that all's well with your brother and sister. And Beth, would you look after her for me?"

"Of course," said Trace. "But there's time. I can accompany you." The governor wanted to contact Prospect's mayor and arrange for Trace to have backup before venturing into town to claim his office.

"Better spent in preparation," said Del. "Read my law books. Practice your firearm. Remember to check in weekly at the telegraph office in Phoenix."

Trace shook his head. "How long will you stay in Tucson? I can't do this alone. I've still so much to learn."

"Keep to your principles. Recruit like-minded men to aid you." Del gripped Trace's shoulder once more. "You'll do fine, son."

***

Evelyn Deveraux rested on the bed in a room she hadn't left for days. The outlaw Silas Kelly lie stretched out on his stomach beside her. They'd subsisted on room service and booze and had passed the time dozing between bouts of physical exertion too debaucherous and debilitating to be deemed mere sex.

Almost a week earlier, The Treasure Room's madam had brought in fresher, younger talent and Evelyn had been turned out. She found herself at The Old Mare, standing on a horseshoe-shaped balcony, gazing blurry-eyed upon her diminished prospects. She was amazed to see the bandit prince stroll into the den of peasants as proudly and arrogantly as he'd bought his way into the parlor house. Emerald eyes had homed in on her in an instant, and Evelyn was lured downstairs by their beauty alone, willing to sell her soul if that dapper devil would make her glitter once more.

Her body felt tender from rough use bordering on brutal, her mind stuporous after all she'd endured. The first time he needed sleep, he'd tied her to a chair so tightly that her arms cramped and her hands went numb. But as her flesh became accustomed to the pains of pleasing him and the initial, overwhelming fright subsided, her knowledge of Silas Kelly grew into something like understanding.

She learned the insatiable sexual appetite worked to compensate for some deficiency and that the depraved preferences were akin to needs. Beneath his oft times vacant or incongruent expressions, Evelyn sensed other, honest emotions and seeking them helped her survive him.

She discovered a kind of receptiveness in his cruelty. He liked to take her when she was swollen from prior abuse and he was at his fullest, not because he wanted to injure her, she believed, but because the pinch of penetration brought tears to her eyes and her pain reached him on a level nothing else could. Something had taught Silas Kelly to be indifferent to the world, had remade him so comfortable in his own skin as to be an enigma to everyone he met. Evelyn found distraction in the mystery she never expected to solve.

"Do you know why I chose you?" His question shocked her into lucidity. For days, the only spoken communication between them had been his commands. She turned her head and found him studying her. He said, "There's a sadness in your eyes that has naught to do with me." His voice softened to become almost reverent. "There it is—part shame, part fear."

"I broke my mother's heart." She told him only to see how he would react. One eyebrow rose slightly, and he looked forward, resting his chin on the back of his hand.

"I killed my father," he said.

Evelyn shifted onto her side. "Because of the scars on your back?" Her eyes wandered over them.

"Sir was town marshal of Promise. Do you know it?" Evelyn shook her head. "It's gone now. He felt his sons reflected badly on his abilities as a peace officer."

"How could he keep order in town when he couldn't keep it under his own roof?"

He nodded. "The more we misbehaved, the more he punished us, the more we misbehaved. We made brass knuckles out of cabinet handles to give us an edge over some bigger boys in town."

Evelyn swallowed. "He used them on you?"

"We concluded that eventually he was going to kill one of us. Rook and I reckoned it would be our younger brother Jerrod," said Silas. It had been Rook's idea to make it look like an Apache attack. He'd gotten Jerrod away from the house and made it back in time to get Silas all cleaned up. "I loved my father, but I love my brothers more."

Evelyn said, "I left my mother to save myself, to change my fate." She still ended up at The Mare, then in the clutches of Silas Kelly. If he let her live, by the time he was done with her, she'd be ruined for even the most indiscriminate of men. She'd be sewing shirts and washing laundry after all. That was the conclusion she came to when he got up to take a piss and a swig of whiskey and returned to the bed with a knife. She'd fallen so far, Evelyn found she was no longer afraid. He ordered her onto her belly, tossed the blade among the sheets, and climbed over her.

Silas contemplated her skin, flawless as a blank canvas. Evelyn Deveraux was a beautiful woman. She said something that was muffled by the linens. He jerked her over onto her back and told her to repeat it.

Hesitant to say it to his face, she closed her eyes and missed his reaction. "If you need to strike me…" was what she said, once more letting the offer hang. For a moment, Silas went slack-jawed. Then he instructed her to draw her knees up. He pressed into her, gentler than all the times before. His gaze moved over her, from the point of their juncture to her closed lids. He grabbed up the knife and buried it in the mattress, to the hilt. Then he hit her, open-handed but with the force of a punch. They both moaned.

Evelyn tasted blood and wasn't sure if he'd split her lip or cut his palm on her teeth. He raised his hand again, changed his mind, and put his mouth to hers instead. When he reared up, his lips were smeared red. She watched the veins stick out in his neck and felt him pulse inside her. He rolled off her, missed the edge of the bed, and crashed to the floor.

Silas looked up at auburn hair cascading over the side and her arm hanging limp in the air. He reached up and hooked his fingers with hers. Her thumb skimmed over his knuckles.

When Evelyn awoke the next morning, Silas stood at the window, leaning his shoulder against the wall, squinting out through the curtain. He was dressed.

"I had a thought," he said as she sat up and swung her legs over the side of the bed. "Maybe you went about your salvation all wrong. You ought to have attached yourself to a gambler rather than go after a man of importance."

Evelyn said, "A gambler might be wealthy one day and penniless the next."

Silas shrugged. "Uncertainty is freedom. It's why men give up their fortunes to become cowboys or continually test convention. If not a gambler, would you consider a highwayman?"

"With a cave full of treasure and guns to protect me from danger?"

He snorted. "You can have your own gun, Evelyn. But it won't protect you from me." He said, "Your fate would be different than any other woman's and most men. Beholden to none."

"Can I think about it?" she said.

Silas pursed his lips. He toyed with the butt of one of the cartridges protruding from his belt. "Yes."

***

Though Trace tried to persuade him, Del Cooper declined to detour back to the Malloy farm for even one night. Forty miles south of Phoenix, they parted ways. Del continued on to Tucson and Trace turned east toward Prospect. As he rode the last twenty miles alone, Trace tried to think on the challenges that lie ahead of him but found he couldn't banish Holly from his mind.

As home came into sight, Trace reckoned he ought to feel lighter of heart. The trip to Prescott had been every bit a success. The Malloy brothers were pardoned of Rook's false charges, and the governor had contacted Judge Foster to annul Aimee's marriage. Trace saw Tyler was well enough to have made significant progress to the homestead. Aimee was safe, and with weeks separating her and Wyland, Trace imagined her infatuation faded. Rather than satisfied, he felt melancholy.

The spotted hound Tritle had gifted him led the way across the yard, yipping happily. Trace saw Tyler step out onto the porch, shielding his eyes against the late sun's glare. He spied Aimee and Beth on the other side of the corral, walking arm-in-arm from the barn. Not Beth, Trace realized, sitting taller in the saddle. She was closer to Aimee's height and had too light of hair. He dismounted, tossed his reins over a post, and rounded the fence to meet them out front of the house. Hazel eyes locked with cornflower blue over the top rail. His sister crouched down to pet the dog. But Holly stood stock-still as Trace strode toward her.

She seemed nervous, as if he wouldn't be pleased to see her. But his depression vanished. He was awash with relief at the sight of her. He said, "How did you come here?"

"I brought her." Trace's head snapped in the direction of the porch, to where Jerrod Kelly emerged to stand beside Tyler. His green eyes were wary, his chin up as if expecting a challenge or issuing one. Trace felt sucker-punched.

Holly watched in fearful fascination as Trace transformed from welcoming to defensive, as the hand he'd been reaching out to touch her closed and lowered to his side, as the curving of lips into a bemused smile flattened into a grim line. Golden eyes shifted from emitting light to reflecting it, with a brief flash to mark the transition. Holly knew she would be eternally grateful to Aimee for taking her hand and leading her into the house, mumbling the excuse that Beth had called them in to supper.

The youngest Kelly stepped off the porch. He kept his eyes on Trace as he moved. The two men pivoted to face one another. Jerrod said, "Well, Malloy?" And Trace said, "Well, what?"

"How's this going to play out?" The gunfighter spoke calmly—this was a game he was proficient at.

Trace glanced at the pistol at the younger man's side. "You think I'm fool enough to draw against you?"

"Fists then," said Jerrod. His hands moved center, he unfastened his gun-belt and tossed it to Tyler.

Trace had inches and weight on the other man. He saw enough resentment in Jerrod to know he'd put up resistance adequate for Trace to beat out considerable frustration. Trace wanted a good, bloody brawl. Instead, he said, "I don't fight over women."

Jerrod huffed. Trace reckoned the other man could use a row as much as he. It brought a victorious hint of satisfaction to turn his back. The feeling was short-lived. "Malloy," Jerrod called after him. "She deserves more." Trace collected his reins and led his horse to the barn.

Tyler handed Jerrod back his gun and followed his brother.

"How long they been here?" Trace noticed two new horses in the barn.

"A few weeks," said Tyler. "She's been a great comfort to Aimee. And Jerrod's been helping me with the repairs. How was Prescott?"

"The governor will be demanding Rook's resignation and that of his deputies. He's designated me his replacement. Del went back to Tucson."

So, they'd heard about The Wishing Well, thought Tyler. He reckoned his brother knew the harm that might have befallen Holly. He wondered how it would have gone if Jerrod hadn't inserted himself into Trace and Holly's reunion. "He's right, you know," said Tyler. She deserved a man willing to fight for her, willing to admit he cared. "He doesn't really want to slug it out with you."

"Yeh, he does," said Trace. "But I forfeited when I left her there." Once again, they worked together to untack the paint horse. "Is Aimee over that business about Wyland?"

Tyler shook his head. Trace said, "You know, it was him that killed Beth's brother."

***

Trace told Beth her father had gone to inquire after the incident in Tucson and look in on an old friend. He didn't go into further detail for Holly's sake. After that, supper was a silent affair. Jerrod was absent. Holly only picked up her fork to poke at her food. Aimee nibbled for a few minutes then the two went upstairs together. Trace made himself clean his plate before announcing he was going to bed.

Beth filled a dish for Tyler to take to Jerrod. He set it down on the table and took a deep breath before asking, "Was Wyland there that day?"

Beth reckoned he already knew the answer. "I was scared of him most of all," she said. She paused, remembering how Silas had used that fear against her. "But he was the only one that didn't touch me." Tyler nodded and picked up the plate.

He found Jerrod seated on a stump in the far corner of the recently cleared field. He had his boot across the opposite knee and was flicking the spur with his finger. He took the plate and thanked Tyler. "I suppose it's time for me to move on."

"I could still use the help, if you want to stick around awhile longer," said Tyler.

***

Jerrod Kelly stuck around. He was learning the farm, helping with the work, and seeming to enjoy it as much as Tyler. Of course, Trace knew the real reason he was still there. They hadn't fought, but the younger man was waging a battle none the less. Holly was warming to him. And unless he claimed her, Trace had no right to protest it.

He recalled a sermon from his youth on the virtue of patience. It had cited waiting in life as a prelude to purgatory. But for a boy or a man of action, such is hell. Trace made his first trip back to Phoenix only to receive instruction via telegram to check in again after another week. He was in limbo, unable to move forward with his life's plan, surrounded by his past. Though she kept her distance, Holly was a constant temptation. In his bed at night, Trace ached for her. And seeing her smile and hearing her laughter throughout the day was like rubbing salt in the wound. The worst of it was how well she seemed to belong.

Then there was Aimee, also waiting, recently convinced the scamp Wyland was on his way back to her. The sole voice of reason in the entire household, Trace didn't have the heart to crush her illusions when they bolstered her spirits. He could only hope she would accept the truth in time and that time would lessen her disappointment.

He was up early one morning, straining his eyes and mind with books as Del had recommended, while the spotted hound snoozed nearby. He overheard whispering in the stairwell—it was Holly and Beth. He met them at the landing, in time to hear Holly say, "I don't think we should tell the men."

"Tell us what?" Both women startled at his voice.

While Holly only gaped at him, Beth said, "Aimee isn't feeling well again this morning." She moved into the kitchen to start breakfast and Trace let her go. He took Holly's arm and drew her into the parlor where he'd been reading.

"It's nothing serious," she said.

Trace's eyes narrowed. "You don't think it's time we sent for the doctor?"

Holly shook her head. "It wouldn't help. I've seen the symptoms before, many times."

Though she trembled beneath his hand, Trace didn't release her. He heard someone else coming down the stairs but ignored it. He held her in place and stepped closer. "Tell me," he said. Holly bit her lip and raised wide violet-blue eyes.

Jerrod reached the bottom of the stairs. His gaze moved from Trace down to Holly and back up. Without a word, he continued into the kitchen.

23

In the West, a drifter could tell a town's temperament by the absence or abundance of its saloons and brothels. The greater the sin, the more volatile, but also the more tolerant of a man like Josiah Wyland. He'd learned to approach a settlement as he would a fight, with guns and instincts ready. Some communities looked suspiciously at any stranger and twice at one uncommonly tall and curiously scarred, with a need to carry more than one pistol. Others didn't care if an outlaw had his likeness plastered on every bulletin—if he didn't bother folk, they didn't bother him. Some towns revered notoriety, others reviled it, and the former could be just as dangerous as the latter. A lone fifteen-year-old boy with first blood on his hands learned quickly or died quicker.

That first year away from Promise had been the hardest. Josiah found it was less trouble to face a fight than flee it, that meeting one challenger made the next think twice. He discovered the name Wyland was known all over Arizona, that people recognized his daddy's blue eyes and rangy form, that a reputation could be inherited. He was never certain whether folk feared and hated him for what his father had done or for what he had done, and after a time, it ceased to matter.

Josiah learned that though small settlements had less law or none at all, bigger towns were easier to get lost in. He could sneak in for supplies or a half-hour with a whore and sneak out again before trouble could find him. One day, he found himself in the same saloon as Silas Kelly and for a few years, his days of solitude and subtlety were over.

Silas recognized Josiah as the Promise orphan who'd often tagged along with the Kelly and Malloy brothers. He also remembered him as a crack-shot and recruited him on the spot to ride with his gang. It didn't matter the town, they rode in down the main drag in broad daylight and often rode out shooting.

Rather than a band of brothers-in-arms, the Kelly bunch was an ever-shifting assortment of cutthroats and thieves tenuously united by common greed and bloodlust. They rustled cattle, robbed stages, and shot-up saloons. They battled rival bandits and went to war with lawmen. At the gang's core was the Kelly trio with Silas more of a driving force than a leader, Rook bringing focus to his ruthlessness, and Jerrod instilling enough order in the ranks to keep members from killing each other, for the most part. Josiah became Silas's shadow—sometimes bodyguard, sometimes enforcer. It was a role both integral and separate, and more than he'd ever had before. For his participation in their exploits, Josiah shared in the spoils and the security that came with numbers. He also shot many men and was shot plenty himself.

Josiah never examined his reasons for joining Kelly, never questioned whether it was merely a means to survive or if he'd been seeking anonymity among men as bad as he. But the contrast of Silas's hot-blooded and chaotic nature with his own brought

Josiah only further distinction as a cold and careful killer. Eventually, Silas discovered Josiah's name was as useful as his dual revolvers, and Josiah finally understood what vileness he'd been born from, that his daddy's evil could still work through him.

She was a shopkeeper's daughter in a town Josiah didn't care to recall the name of—where his father's face still hung in the general store, and the rape and murder of another young woman was still an open wound. It didn't matter that Josiah was too young to be that Wyland or that the atrocity had occurred before he was conceived. The truth wouldn't stand up to the threat of his reputation and appearance. Given the choice between them, the girl had submitted willingly, even gratefully, to Silas's violation. She set another precedent—the first of many to accept pain from a pretty serpent rather than chance the blue-eyed son of a devil. Cooper's daughter had been the last.

Josiah had been aware—as he raised the rifle and took aim on Cooper's son—that it might cost him his life, by the old judge if not Silas. He hadn't cared. And only a quirk of fate had spared it, sending him to Yuma instead.

Upon his release, Rook offered him a chance to work on the other side, which Josiah found much the same. He'd gone from killing for one Kelly brother to killing for another, from murderer to executioner, a distinction too subtle to improve his reputation or his reception in any town.

Now, he was independent again, with neither Rook's authority nor Silas's audacity to dictate his actions or detract from his identity. He kept to the wilderness for weeks, knowing that to show his face in any town might attract trouble and force him to cross the border that much sooner. Somehow, he felt Old Mexico was an irreversible decision, that returning would be like stopping a bullet once the trigger was pulled. Leaving would sever him and Aimee, and he still wasn't ready to let go.

He began slinking through the border towns, making his way west back into Arizona. He dallied in Bisbee, loitering in one of the less savory saloons and listening in on the local gossip, loafing about a rented room and picking through the papers for word of what progressed in Prospect. Every thought he had eventually connected itself to Aimee, even though the few days they'd been together were outnumbered by the weeks since. When he slept, his dream awakened him. Restless, he headed northwest from one mining town to the next.

With its three hotels, four saloons, shops, and a livery, Dereliction wasn't the total wreck its name implied. Only five hours from Tucson, it wasn't long before Josiah heard tell of what had transpired at The Wishing Well. Updates said that Lou was still in the hospital, her businesses were closed, and her girls had moved on to work in other establishments. Josiah reckoned it would only bring them both trouble if he visited her, so he waited for news to drift south with travelers. A liquor supplier brought word of a man loitering about the empty saloon waiting to meet a gunfighter.

Josiah made the trip during the night, coming into the city in the pre-dawn hours. He hitched his stallion to an outside staircase in an alley between two shops, both closed. He approached The Wishing Well by way of the alley, passing the stable which housed a single horse. Lamplight from within illuminated a splintered hole in the saloon's side door about even with Josiah's chin. He stooped and peered through it, detecting no movement. Standing to the side, he drew a revolver and held it in his right hand while slowly opening the door with his left. When a quick glance revealed no one, Josiah slipped inside. Broken glass crunched beneath his boots. The saloon had been left in disarray, the stock of liquor on the shelves behind the bar sorely depleted, bottles and glasses on tables throughout the room. Josiah followed the dim light to where a man lounged with his feet up on a table and a low-burning lantern beside his boots.

***

Thurman Dawes wasn't much of a gambler, but he knew when to ante up and when to fold. There'd been a time when working for a sheriff—even a crooked one—was the safer bet. Dawes might earn his buck slower than when he rode with rustlers, but he was more apt to keep it and his life. Now that Rook Kelly had sent him out of their jurisdiction, without backup, to rendezvous with a man more prone to shooting than listening, Dawes reckoned his current hand had run its course. The periodic encounter with Josiah Wyland when they were on the same side was a bit of bad luck. Facing the gunslinger when he was locked up and relieved of his firearms was a hazard of the job. But to go seeking the killer was more than he'd signed on for. With a power struggle between his employer and Trace Malloy imminent, Dawes decided it was time to find another game.

He had a legitimate skill, good for more than framing Rook's enemies. He'd learned it working for and then against cattle barons in Colorado. He reckoned he knew enough of brands and their forgery to get a gig consulting for one of the stockman's associations or even the federal government. Dawes planned to turn in his deputy's badge as soon as his duty in Tucson was done. If he was lucky, Wyland wouldn't even show up. Dawes had put his feet up, prepared for another idle night, when the world went topsy on him.

His seat tipped and he plummeted backward. He flung out his arms, attempting to avert his fall, and watched his boots arc over his head. The impact with the floor knocked the wind out of him. The chairback surely bruised his spine. He faced the ceiling and was either seeing double or looking into the barrels of twin pistols. The latter, he realized, recognizing the cold blues sighting down at him. Wyland had come after all.

"Message," wheezed Dawes.

"Talk," said Wyland.

When he could draw enough breath to speak, Dawes told him that Rook Kelly was offering to revoke the warrant on his head if he would come back to Prospect.

"I'm done killing for Kelly," said Wyland.

"Rook will give you the woman," said Dawes.

"He doesn't have her." Josiah hoped it was still true.

"He has his brothers and a boarding house full of mercenaries. Malloy has an old man," said Dawes. "Rook said to give you this note." He was careful to draw it slowly from his vest pocket. His arm trembled as he held up the paper. "One more job."

He thought Wyland might leave without it or shoot him for delivering it. But the gunman holstered one weapon then the other. Long fingers plucked the note from Dawes's clammy grip. When he was gone, Dawes squirmed off the fallen chair and staggered to his feet. He had one more message to deliver. Then he was out of the game.

***

Josiah left Tucson before the break of dawn, before he could be sighted and word of his presence there passed along. It meant he couldn't say a final farewell to Lou, but he reckoned he already knew what her last bit of advice would be.

He needed time and distance and to think. He rode hard, as if he could speed along revelation and leave conundrum in his dust. But the pounding of his horse's hooves couldn't shake apart the tension in his chest. And the wind wasn't strong enough to clear his mind. Man and mount were both slick with sweat by the time Josiah eased up. He let the stallion choose the pace and their course.

All his life, Josiah had done what he must to survive. With death as the alternative, all his decisions came easy, he realized. Until Aimee, he'd never had to consider another person's welfare or how what he did might affect her. She'd given him her trust, had chosen him at her peril. She was his to claim, his to protect, except Trace Malloy would probably see him dead first. He reckoned Rook's offer gave him a chance to get close enough to find out. So long as it wasn't Malloy's name on that paper, all Josiah had to do was what he did best and add one more kill to his own. Odd that now, when he stood to improve and not just prolong his life, his profession would seem so wrong. But if he didn't accept the deal, he might as well follow one of those rivers south.

Josiah took out the note and read it. There was only the name, impossible to misinterpret, impossible to make sense of. *Silas*

Kelly. Josiah crumpled the paper and tossed it amongst the sagebrush. He looked up and recognized the sloping landscape and sporadic placement of buildings. His horse had brought him back to Dereliction.

Close to Tucson, the town was often a stopover for folk traveling to and from the Pueblo. It welcomed and promptly forgot countless strangers. Even Josiah Wyland could enjoy some degree of anonymity. He checked into the same hotel and was given the same room. It overlooked the livery where a horse trader did his business. Josiah saw the corral was packed with a new herd. There was a horse of every color, including a small white filly that evoked yet another memory of Aimee to muddle his mind.

He decided to go out to a saloon and muddle it further, with whiskey. He chose the same tent, a short walk from the hotel, he'd frequented before. A few men stood outside it, watching an altercation between the horse trader and another man. As he passed, Josiah caught enough of the argument to gather that the other man was a mine foreman who'd worked several horses to death and was demanding replacements which the horse trader refused.

Josiah found a stool without a glass in front of it. About the time he was paying for his second drink, a single shot rang out. The crowd of spectators shuffled in, back to their seats and their cups. It was reported that the horse trader had lost the shootout.

Josiah was about to toss back his third round when a fellow drifted through the canvas-lined entrance. The whole saloon watched him wander up to the bar and claim his seat beside Josiah. It was the horse trader, a bit pale, with a hole in his jacket.

He seemed to notice the silence and glanced around at the other patrons, finding all eyes on him. Josiah watched with the rest as he reached under his coat, removed something from an inside pocket, and set it on the counter. It was a stack of letters, tied with twine. Embedded in the paper brick was the bullet meant to kill him.

The saloon erupted in cheers. The horse trader accepted handshakes and backslaps. The bartender poured a round on the house and drinking commenced with uncommon joviality.

"A miracle," said the barkeep.

The horse trader shook his head. "Wasn't luck or God's grace that saved me." He patted the bundle that still lay between them and Josiah noticed the elegantly flowing script. "It was a good woman's love."

It was the story of the night. Word traveled and drew a crowd. Pretty soon, the tent was full of men reminiscing and poeticizing. All seemed to have a sweetheart waiting on them or women they'd either lost or hoped to win. As the night waned, men waxed on of beauty, constancy, and gentleness. They marveled at the mystery of what inspired the return of their affections.

The next morning, the horse trader rose at his usual time. He dressed and fitted his stack of letters into the inside pocket positioned over his heart. As he came to his place of business, he noticed a gun-belt looped over one of the corral's posts. Sticking up out of the holsters were the ivory handles of two scroll-engraved Colt Peacemakers. And a note.

The crude scrawl read: *trade for filly*.

***

Lou knew without opening her eyes that he was back. She recognized his scent—coffee with undercurrents of whiskey, oiled leather, and shaving cream. Del Cooper had been at the hospital two days that she was aware of, sitting at her bedside all through visiting hours.

"You'd see more action if I were pushing daisies." Lou cracked open her good eye to look at him and light speared her head.

"They wouldn't be near so colorful," said Del.

Though her smile was slight, her whole face ached with it. She wondered how many days he must have waited for her to first awake, becoming accustomed to her altered appearance, to be able to joke with her now.

"Did you bring what I asked?"

He shifted his jaw and dragged his bottom teeth down his upper lip, combing the hairs of his mustache. He picked an object up off the bedside table and placed it beside her hand.

Lou doubted he could have found a smaller mirror. It was the type a man used to shave by whilst traveling. But as she lifted the glass—set in cold metal—and held it aloft, she was relieved it was no bigger. She had to examine her battered reflection in portions as her whole face wouldn't fit within the frame. Her good eye was dilated, the tender skin beneath speckled with burst capillaries. The other lid was forced shut by swelling. Her skin was split over one cheekbone and colored everywhere with bruises. Her mouth was puffy but her teeth unbroken. It would all heal—the flesh and fractures beneath. She tilted the mirror to view her throat where a man's hands were imprinted in shades of red and purple, and the frame dropped from fingers gone numb.

Del put his elbows on the bed and pressed his palms to either side of her hand. She asked when she could go home. She'd already had him visit her room on the first floor of the parlor house to make sure it hadn't been disturbed by the bandits or by burglars.

He stared down at the blankets that hid the more serious of her hurts. He told her the doctors had decreed she must stay until internal injuries healed and the risk of infection passed. To distract them both, she asked if he'd found Holly.

"None of the other girls have seen her, and she wasn't at any of the other watering holes or brothels," said Del.

Lou nodded. She knew Holly had escaped or Silas Kelly wouldn't have gone so far in taking his frustrations out on her. Even in the midst of it, Lou took solace in knowing Holly was safe.

Into the quiet hospital came the sound of footsteps. As they approached, Lou watched Del's eyes slant away from her and sharpen. A man appeared at the foot of her bed. He grimaced at the sight of her but couldn't seem to tear his wide eyes away.

Del growled at him. "Can I help you, Deputy?"

"Dawes. Sorry to disturb." The man fidgeted as he told them he had a message for Mr. Cooper from Sheriff Kelly.

"You're a long way from home, Deputy Dawes," said Del. "You might want to check in with your boss, see if you still got a job."

"Yes, Sir," said Dawes. "But the message, I'd like to have it out, if you'll hear me."

"I'm listening," said Del.

With a nervous glance at Lou, Dawes began. "As a show of good will, uh, for the sake of justice—"

"Justice is no longer Rook Kelly's concern," said Del. "Get to the point."

"Rook wants you to know Silas Kelly and Josiah Wyland will return to Prospect this coming week. He knows you got a score to settle with them and pledges his cooperation."

"How does he know Wyland will be there?"

"He'll come for the lady," said Dawes. "Rook's certain of it."

"You can leave that badge. I'll make sure the new sheriff gets it."

Lou watched Del's face as the footsteps retreated and the hospital grew quiet again. He wore the same look she'd seen on him at The Wishing Well weeks before.

She said, "You'll kill a man for me, but you won't spare one." She meant it as an accusation and hated that it sounded pleading. "I don't need your justice, Del Cooper," she said. "I never did."

24

Trace sat in the parlor with his elbows on his knees, his hands fisted in his hair, and an open book on the rug between his feet. For two weeks, he'd waited for a call to action, making a lead mine of a nearby hillside and poring over Del's law library to pass the time. He even returned to Cooper's cabin for additional volumes. He planned to head back to Phoenix the next day and stay if Tritle's telegram told him to wait another week.

Outside, a woman squealed, not for the first time. No longer able to ignore it, Trace wandered out onto the porch to see what was amiss. He knew it was Holly. Aimee was upstairs taking a nap before supper and Beth wasn't the squealing type. Besides, he'd heard the sound before.

Tyler stood outside the corral, close to Beth, his arms folded over the top rail. They were watching the antics of the two within. What had begun as lariat practice had dissolved into horseplay, with Jerrod in the pen's center attempting to lasso Holly as she danced in erratic circles about the perimeter squealing each time she dodged the sailing loop. Trace watched Jerrod rope and reel her in as she wiggled at the end of his line.

Holly was caught, as much by glimmering green eyes as by the lariat. As she'd darted around the dusty corral, her attention split between randomizing her flight, the whoosh of the lasso, and the cheers of the couple looking on, Jerrod's focus had been entirely on her. He seemed to disconnect from even the motion of wrist whirling rope, attuned to anticipate her every move. Holly had seen that patient, evaluating look in his eyes time and again. She was struck by the inevitability that he would have her. As the rope tightened, she teetered between acceptance and panic.

Holly knew what it was to be desired. But the infatuation of men she'd entertained had been temporary, sometimes lasting only until a man left her bed and usually fading by the time he sobered up. They made besotted declarations and impulsive proposals, but always returned to their regular lives and left her to hers. She tried to ignore the fact that Jerrod was different, that he wanted more from her than he could buy. She hadn't wanted to believe he might feel for her what she felt for Trace.

When she ceased to struggle, Jerrod understood the game was up. He stepped toward her, allowing the line to slacken. The loop fell to the ground, around the hem of her dress. Jerrod asked if she was all right, and Holly noticed the pink marks below her rolled-up sleeves, where her arms had been kissed by the rope, trapped when it tightened around her hips. She knew the rawhide burn was more likely due to her resistance than any of his doing. She said that she was fine and allowed him to inspect the abrasions as proof. She shivered when his thumbs grazed sensitive skin, but the intensity in eyes like smoky emeralds caused her the most discomfort. She glanced away, up toward the ridge, and was the first to spot Wyland.

She thrust her hand into the air and waved. Tyler and Beth turned to look, and the gunslinger started down the hill toward them. At the flank of the big black stallion trotted a small white filly. As man and horses drew nearer, Jerrod muttered, "Josiah Wyland is unheeled."

He stopped a few yards from the group and dismounted. Jerrod stepped forward and offered to see to the horses. Josiah nodded his thanks, handed over the reins, and turned toward the house. Holly led the way, calling out for Aimee to come to the window. Tyler and Beth followed.

When Aimee swept aside the blue curtain and he watched the smile blossom upon her face, Josiah felt cleansed. He was watching her, as were the others. None noticed Trace step off the porch. Josiah never saw the punch coming—he hit the dirt as half his face went numb.

"Don't got to tell you what you already know," said Trace. "That so, Wyland?"

Holly stepped in front of him, put both hands on his chest to stop him, but Trace swatted her aside. Josiah was on his feet in time to dodge the second swing which glanced off his shoulder. He had enough reach to get in a quick jab that clipped Trace's chin. Then Trace landed a blow to the gut that Josiah felt punched right through him. He was on his hands and knees, relearning how to breathe, vaguely aware of Aimee hovering at his side and of Tyler battling to keep his brother at bay, while his blood and Trace's shouting flooded his head.

"She's been sick each morning for weeks," said Trace. "And she's only begun to suffer for what you've done." He said, "If she survives bringing your bastard into this world, she'll pay for it, once folks find out. You should have stayed away."

Words were as punishing as fists. As Josiah started to make sense of them, he found they hit twice as hard. He lifted his head and faced the rage blazing in Trace's eyes, cold hatred in his own. He pushed to his feet and wiped blood from his nose. He glanced at Aimee, with her gray eyes wide and hands splayed over her belly, and knew the truth of what Trace said.

Finally losing steam, Trace uttered, "She'd be better off if it were Rook Kelly's."

"Say something," said Aimee, afraid to touch him. Sapphire eyes had turned to mirrors.

"Trace is right," he said. "Better it were Rook's." As she backed away from him, Josiah reckoned it was the wrong thing to say. But it was the truth, with his whole life as proof.

Aimee took small steps toward the house, fearing she would fall to pieces before she reached it. Josiah watched her go. Then he turned and started walking.

Trace and Holly stood face-to-face. Her expression was the same shattered look that had come over Aimee. "He's a killer," said Trace.

"And I'm a whore," said Holly. She spun and stalked off in the direction of the barn. Trace headed for the house with Tyler on his heels.

Beth saw Wyland reach the east fence and change course to wander along it. His hands went to his hips, hesitating where his guns used to be, then dropped to his sides. She took a deep breath and before she could change her mind, followed. He looked over his shoulder when he heard her coming up behind him. He stopped and faced her, wary eyes expecting more condemnation. For the first time, Beth questioned her father's judgement. She reckoned a person had to be shown mercy to give mercy, had to be loved to be able to recognize and return it. This man knew only persecution and rejection.

Josiah said, "I reckon I ought to have known what it would come to. People been telling me all my life. I'm just like him."

"She wants the baby," said Beth. She decided he'd have to come to the rest on his own. "There's a hole in the river," she said, "and a bar of soap on a rock near it, if you want to clean up before you see her again." She left him to go check on supper.

***

The parlor was too quiet, the kitchen too hot. Trace moved through the house, aware of Tyler shadowing him. He stepped through the back door and stood looking over the freshly tilled field. Tyler stopped beside him.

"He didn't have his guns," said Tyler.

"I noticed," said Trace.

"He saved her, and he came back for her," said Tyler.

"You reckon he's reformed." Trace knew better. Men didn't change, they only hid or revealed their true selves.

"She loves him. I reckon he loves her back." Tyler wished it could be as simple as that.

"I love Holly," said Trace. "It didn't keep me from hurting her."

"You can't always protect us, Trace. You got to let us choose for ourselves, even if we choose wrongly."

"*You* won't choose wrongly," said Trace.

Tyler smiled. "When her father returns, I'm going to ask for his blessing." His smile dimmed. "Though I think he had a different Malloy in mind for a son-in-law."

Trace shook his head. "You know I wouldn't infringe on your happiness." He looked back across the field and sighed. "Aimee's neither."

Tyler swallowed. "What about you, Trace? Do you really want to be sheriff?"

"I got to do what's right."

"According to who? The governor? He made the mistake of appointing Rook. Del Cooper? He hardly knows he's still got a daughter. I never needed you to be more than my big brother. Ma and Pa were proud of you for just being their son. She'd have you, Trace, it ain't too late." Tyler hoped Trace's silence meant he was considering it.

"Did Beth tell you what I said to her the morning Del and I left for Prescott?" Tyler shook his head. Trace said, "I told her I was sure glad she came with us, because wild horses weren't going to drag you away from her." Tyler smiled again. Trace remained solemn. He said, "That's the sort of devotion Holly deserves."

***

After leading Wyland's horses into the barn, Jerrod bribed the stallion into a corner stall with food and water. Ready for rest, it tolerated being untacked, but Jerrod suspected he'd have a harder time were he attempting the process in reverse. The black had a spirit that would never extinguish. The filly was of a gentler nature and went where Jerrod directed it. He put it in another stall and was running a brush over its hide, using short, fluid strokes to disperse some of the desert dust, when he noticed Holly.

She stood just within the doorway, backlit by the white of a blinding sun, watching him. He paused grooming as she crept further into the barn.

"Where would we go?" Her question caused his heart to knock in his chest. He'd been waiting for it for weeks. With Trace's return, he reckoned he'd have to be patient awhile longer. She caught him off guard.

"I had a couple ideas," he said and resumed brushing, needing the activity. "I thought I'd take you to Chicago to visit your family. If there was someplace you saw you liked along the way, we could go back to it." She seemed surprised, but he couldn't tell if she liked the idea. "Or," he said, "we could find our own plot of land around here, close enough for you to see Aimee on occasion." He shrugged and added, "Lou too." He put up the brush and exited the stall. She looked at him like she was seeing him for the first time. He said, "Do you reckon you'd like to see California? Or Alaska? We can go anywhere you want."

"Why me?" It was a question he hadn't anticipated. He opened his mouth only to find he couldn't articulate a response.

Why her? Because there was no other woman. None with her laughter, her joy. Even in sorrow, Holly radiated life. He hadn't realized until he met her that he'd been living at the opposite end of the spectrum. He started to tell her but couldn't translate his feelings. Jerrod reckoned there were a hundred reasons, but he couldn't settle on a single one.

Holly watched him scowl and listened to him stammer, and her eyes started to shine.

It ambushed him when she seized his shirt in her fists, pulled herself up onto her toes, and kissed him. When her lips broke with his, she whined his name and Jerrod realized he'd been hesitating. He kissed her back.

She met his weeks of pent-up passion. He found himself taking her up against a barn wall with bridles swaying alongside them. When his legs began to shake, they collapsed into the hay and she rode him. When her strength flagged, he rolled her beneath him. Afterward, they lay together dazed. She pecked kisses along his collarbone and he combed the tangles from her hair with his fingers.

***

Beth considered ringing the supper bell but didn't want to disrupt the hush that had befallen the farm. She let the cook-fire die out and night stole some of the heat from the kitchen. She sat alone at the big table thinking of her brother and trying to imagine him growing up—would he have strived to meet with their father's expectations or struggled to forge his own way? If his son were alive, would Del Cooper see his daughter as a woman needing a life of her own, or would she always be a reminder of the people he'd lost—a walking, breathing picture framed in a one-room cabin?

Beth heard the scuff of boots in the foyer before Wyland edged into sight, keeping to the other side of the doorway. His face was washed of dirt and blood, blotchy with the beginnings of a bruise. His hair was still wet.

"First door you see, top of the stairs," said Beth.

He looked in that direction but didn't move. Blue eyes focused on her and he said, "Holly would tell me what I ought to say."

Because she could imagine it, Beth almost smiled. "She'll want to hear you'll make everything right." He nodded, gaze drifting toward the floor. She said, "But you can't."

"I know." He looked at her once more. "I know that," he said, and Beth wondered if it was an apology. She didn't have a reply and he didn't wait for one. He moved out of view and she heard the stairs creak under his step.

A few minutes later, Tyler came through the back door. "Was that Wyland come in?"

"He went up to see Aimee," said Beth.

"Good." Tyler pulled up a chair beside hers, turning it toward her before sitting down. Then he simply stared at her, his lips formed into a gentle, happy smile and his green-flecked eyes beaming. She asked if he wanted something to eat, but he only shrugged. Beth shifted sideways so that she faced him and tried to calmly meet his gaze. He lifted his hands. She clasped hers together in her lap. He touched his fingertips to each side of her jaw, beneath her ears. He didn't kiss her so much as taste, taking his time with it while she breathed in hitches and ending it with a little nip that made her jolt. He leaned back to study her, a satisfied sparkle in hazel eyes.

They heard Holly and Jerrod come in by way of the porch, heralded by her customary giggle. She was flushed, her eyes as bright as sky, and there were pieces of straw caught in mussed curls. Jerrod too had bits stuck in his hair and clinging to his clothes.

Tyler asked if they were hungry, dished up and passed them each a bowl of corn chowder. He plopped one down in front of Beth, giving her an amused look, before serving himself. She'd been staring at the couple—every time she managed to tear her eyes away, they wandered back. Jerrod and Holly were oblivious to her attention. He looked at Holly like Tyler had been looking at her a moment ago. Beth wondered if it were possibly for her to glow like Holly seemed to.

Tyler warned them that Wyland was upstairs with Aimee, but they both headed up anyway, and Beth realized they would not be going to separate rooms.

***

Josiah tapped on the door and listened. He remembered standing outside Rook Kelly's house, waiting for her to answer, not knowing the woman on the other side would remake his world. His fingers ran over the knob as he was met with only silence.

Aimee felt a lifetime had passed since she'd first heard his steps beyond her door. Now hope had much the same effect on her as fear. But fear at least could be faced with courage—she had no defense against hope. She pushed up from the bed to sit on her hip, eyes fixated on the door, willing the knob to turn.

He opened it and stepped inside, watched gray eyes warm and alight. The love in them amazed him and always would, but the trust terrified. It was as Beth had said—she was waiting to hear that he would make it all right.

Aimee once thought Josiah Wyland void of kindness, incapable of mercy, insensitive to love. Now she saw a reluctance to hurt as he knelt at her bedside.

"It's no good," he said.

Aimee shook her head and opened her mouth to argue, but Josiah put his hand over hers, giving a squeeze that was both gentle and firm.

"My name, Wyland, I can't change it," he said. "I've done things I can't take back."

Aimee fought not to cry. In his voice was the same roughness she heard at The Wishing Well when he told her he'd never had a woman of his own and outside, when he'd agreed she would be better off if her baby wasn't his. It hurt him far more than her, she realized. Aimee placed her other hand over his.

Josiah said, "Will you take my name, make it good?"

Aimee's tears overflowed. He was asking her to make everything right. She accepted him and felt that, when he pulled her into his embrace, it was she holding him. She told him to stay and he moved to the quilt beside her, drawing her back against his chest. They slept.

25

Josiah awoke to Aimee's hair tickling his lips, his every breath infused with her scent like the night air when the cactus flower blooms. Her soft body yielded to his form, as supple as his heart to her. With that dawn, Josiah felt a sense of belonging he'd searched for all his life. But also came the understanding he couldn't stay.

He'd had the dream, sometime in the night so now it was faded, almost forgotten. Still, the chill at his back seemed to warn that his past would not let them be. It wasn't enough that he'd laid down his guns. There was a greater price to pay for his crimes, and he'd have to settle it to keep the debt from passing to Aimee and the child. Maybe he'd be allowed to return to her when it was done.

He eased away before his stirring woke her, before he gave in to the temptation to remain, come what may. He sat up slowly, belly sore from Trace's punch, leveraging his legs over the side of the bed and placing his feet soundlessly on the floor. But Aimee shivered and shifted toward where he'd been. Gray eyes opened and looked at him, into him. "Must you go," she said, "so soon?"

There came a high whinny from out the window. Aimee got up and Josiah watched her round the bed barefoot. He moved with her to the window and held the curtain as she looked out. Someone had put the filly in the corral. Red dawn reflected pink on its white coat. He told her it was for her and watched pleasure glitter in her eyes. He brought it to resurrect a memory, he realized, of how he wanted her to remember him. Josiah slipped his arms around Aimee and brought her back against him once more.

"I'll come back," he said, the words slipping out before he knew he would say them, before he knew he needed to. "I will always come back to you."

***

Jerrod slid his hand over cool sheets, searching for Holly. He raised his head and saw her standing at the door, peering out. She'd dressed and gathered back her curls.

"What are you doing?"

She shushed him over her shoulder then poked her nose back out into the hall. Jerrod rose and moved up behind her, clad in the gray flannel union suit he slept in. Holly watched Aimee's closed door. "I'm waiting for him to go down," she said. "I want to make sure she's all right."

Jerrod wondered how long Holly had been awake. He was amused to catch her eavesdropping but disappointed she'd left him sleeping. He said, "Are *you* all right?" Her coming to him in the barn had been an impulse, he reckoned, prompted by Aimee's reunion with Wyland and by whatever drama had played out between the unlikely lovers and Trace. Jerrod's ignorance of it might have been why she turned to him. She'd been brimming with suppressed emotions but had chosen lust to give in to. Jerrod was gratified to finally have her snuggled up beside him, but as she slept, it occurred to him that Holly might awake with regrets. He was prepared to take a step back and give her more time, but he needed to know where he stood with her. He started to ask, but she shushed him again.

When the door across the hall opened, Holly ducked back inside, bumping into him. Jerrod grasped the edge of the door and widened the gap, lifting his chin in salutation when Wyland's eyes moved to him from Holly. The tall man donned his hat and returned the nod. His boots fell heavily on each step and only marginally quieter when he reached the base of the stairs.

Holly scurried across the corridor, tapped on Aimee's door, and slipped inside. Jerrod heard her sing out a greeting. Her voice bubbling beyond the wall made him smile, but once again she'd left before he could confirm the significance of their night together.

The smell of bacon wafted up the stairwell signaling breakfast—Beth was up. Jerrod dressed and stepped out, meeting Tyler in the hall. Together, they headed down.

***

Josiah slunk into dives in Tombstone feeling less apprehensive than he did hovering outside the farmhouse kitchen. Trace sat alone at a table that looked solid as a butcher block, an untouched cup of coffee cooling in front of him. Beth tended a big cast-iron skillet spitting grease.

"Take a chair, Wyland," said Trace. It was more command than invitation. Beth glanced nervously from one man to the other. Josiah shuffled in and sat across from Trace who studied his battered face. "If you're done shooting irons, you really ought to learn how to use your fists," he said.

Beth plucked the last strip of bacon from the grease and wrapping her apron around the handle, moved the heavy, blackened pan from the fire. She mumbled that she needed eggs, grabbed a basket, and exited through the back door.

"Reckon it was you put the filly in the corral," said Josiah.

"I ain't giving you my blessing." Trace shifted his shoulders and raised golden eyes to blue. "But I won't stand in your way if your intentions are true."

"I asked her to take my name." Josiah paused. "She said yes."

Trace gave a slow nod.

"I'll be going to Prospect to make it known and to break with Rook and Silas."

"Why not go to town after?" Trace and Josiah both looked up as Jerrod entered the room followed by Tyler. The younger Malloy took a seat next to his brother, and Jerrod dropped into a chair at the end of the table. "Make her your wife before you go." Tyler seconded the notion, and Jerrod offered to ride into town and fetch the pastor.

"I'm going with you," said Holly, chiming into the conversation as she danced though the doorway ahead of Aimee. She said that a bride needed a fine dress and she ought to come along to pick one out, being that they were the same size.

Josiah watched Aimee step around Holly and skirt the table, moving toward him with a soft smile. He knew she was pleased with the new filly, had come to believe her glad about the baby, but he wondered if some of her joy might be just for him. As she slipped into the chair beside his, he found himself reaching for her hand under the table.

Tyler suggested they might persuade Beth to make a special supper.

"A cake!" said Holly.

"What's the occasion?" Beth returned to the back door, surprised to find the kitchen crowded. Tyler jumped to his feet to relieve her of the basket of eggs.

"A wedding." He winked at her.

26

While Holly changed for the trip to town, Jerrod saddled the horses they'd ridden from Tucson and questioned his decision to bring her to the farm. It had been the considerate choice, to place her among friends who would comfort and distract her after the trauma she'd endured at The Wishing Well, and a way for him to make amends for his role in the ordeal. But Jerrod was forced to admit his motives had been partly influenced by pride—he'd wanted to stand side-by-side with Trace Malloy and have her choose him. The previous night had been a victory but come dawn, Jerrod wasn't certain anything had been won, especially when he emerged from the barn and saw Holly and Trace together.

Trace had prepared the paint horse earlier that morning, before anyone else but Beth had risen. It was hitched to the porch railing, ready to take him to Phoenix. He and Holly stood together watching Aimee and Wyland in the corral with the filly.

The split skirt Holly borrowed from Beth was brown canvas, drab and coarse compared to the yellow cotton blouse she'd coupled it with. She wore a straw bonnet and held thin riding gloves. She wrung the soft leather in her hands and stole glances at Trace. He studied Josiah and his sister, his expression one of perpetual brotherly concern she'd tried countless times to smooth away.

"Won't you stay to see them wed?" said Holly.

"I reckon we'd all be more comfortable if I didn't," said Trace. He watched the brim of her bonnet dip. His fingers found hers. "In my heart, I always thought of you as more than a saloon girl."

His hand was warm and dry, gentle despite his strength, and too familiar. Holly nodded since she wasn't sure she could speak. They watched Jerrod lead the horses from the barn.

"He's a fool for you," said Trace. "I couldn't bear the thought of him having you otherwise." He released her hand and stepped down from the porch to untie and mount his horse. He turned golden-hazel eyes on her and said, "Be happy, Holly." Then he rode around the side of the house to find Tyler.

Jerrod brought Holly's horse alongside the porch so she could mount from the steps. He handed her the reins and she thanked him. He got up on his horse and glanced toward the corral. "She glows," he said about Aimee.

"She's in love."

Jerrod nodded. He recalled Holly had the same luster when first he laid eyes on her. He soon discovered he'd been enticed by the effects evoked by another man. Approaching her and Trace, he'd been afraid to really look at her, fearing he would see that shine returned.

"It's a good thing you're doing for them," said Holly. "I'm glad they won't have to wait." She had a smile ready for him, but he barely glanced at her. He nodded and made a clucking sound to his horse. Holly followed suit, lest she be left behind.

***

Beth was gathering up the last of the dishes and Tyler was finishing a cup of coffee, standing in the back doorway, when Trace trotted up on Tyler's paint. He announced he was off to Phoenix and told them Jerrod and Holly were heading out as well.

"I reckon that leaves us to do the work today," said Tyler. Though he was thinking were Beth already his, he'd drag her back upstairs with him and dilly in bed until noon. But she was already up to her elbows in dishwater, her thoughts obviously far from his.

They went about their respective chores, finding the homestead quieter and the work lonelier. Tyler saw to his tasks, occasionally catching sight of Beth sweeping dust out one of the doors, carrying a milk pail from the barn, hauling laundry down to the riverbank and back up again. By afternoon, the filly had been returned to its stall and the stallion turned out to graze along the hillside. Josiah and Aimee had quietly disappeared. Tyler and Beth were all but alone, reminding him of the days they'd spent at the cabin.

Tyler stopped at the corral to secure the gate should the wind pick up. Beth worked the butter churn in the shade of the porch. He saw her wipe her brow with the sleeve of her dress. Deft fingers loosened the silk scarf tied round her throat. She looked up and caught him watching her. He noticed her gaze was no longer quick to dart away. She waved him over and brown eyes boldly assessed his approach. She was rosy-cheeked from operating the churn. Her bun had relaxed to release wisps of hair that clung to her damp neck. Again, he imagined her in his bed, knowing that he was torturing himself.

"You need a haircut," said Beth. She told him to bring a chair from the kitchen and went to fetch her scissors.

When Beth's fingers combed through his hair, sinking to his scalp, Tyler's eyes rolled closed. He listened to the snip of the scissors, felt her arm brush his shoulder and her nails graze his skin. There was a swish of skirt as she moved in front of him. He felt the warm touch of skin and cool touch of metal as she trimmed his bangs and around his ears. She set down the scissors and ran both hands through shortened, sun-kissed strands. Tyler wondered, was it his imagination or did she linger?

Beth told him to keep his eyes closed. She blew clippings from his forehead and cheeks. Tyler raised his hands and found her waist. When his touch settled on her hips, she lowered herself to sit upon his knees. Tyler planted soft kisses under her jaw, from ear to chin, and used his teeth to draw the silk scarf from her collar. She gave a small moan when he put his lips to the hollow of her throat.

Slowly, he raised his hands to the front of her dress. He told himself he would only loosen two buttons but got greedy and took three. She tensed, but only a little, so he dipped a finger into the gap and stroked her breastbone. Then he opened his eyes.

Beth sprung to her feet and whirled away from him. She stood there for a few seconds, him gaping at her back, before she rushed inside, saying she had to start the cake.

She wasn't in the kitchen though, when Tyler finally ventured in. He'd sat outside at least ten minutes. Once the shock had passed, he'd begun to shake. He didn't recognize it as rage until the idea of facing Silas Kelly with a gun in his hand formed in Tyler's mind. Once the shaking passed, Tyler felt drained. He also felt gritty from sweat drying on his skin and itchy from loose hairs. He went to the corral and dunked his head in the trough, partly to clear it. He hung his shirt on the fence, pulled his arms out of long underwear, and washed his upper body with cool water. Then he trudged inside.

The door to Beth's room was closed. He moved past it to his own. He decided, since he'd had a haircut, he ought to shave. After, he sat at the foot of his bed, running a hand over the scars on his chest, trying to imagine how he'd feel revealing them to Beth if she hadn't seen the wounds they'd come from, if she hadn't been the one to make sure those wounds hadn't festered. But he couldn't imagine being afraid to show himself to her, not his body nor his heart. He was roused from his thoughts by a soft tapping on his door.

"May I come in?" It was Beth.

Tyler reckoned he was decent enough. She opened the door and hesitated, not expecting to find him half-dressed, but entered his room. She had washed and changed. She was tidy. She was composed.

She said, "I wish to ask you something."

"Ask," he said.

She moved to stand in front of him first, her hands clasped in front of her, very proper.

"Will you close your eyes?"

"You need me to close my eyes to ask me a question?"

"No," said Beth. "Will you close your eyes when we go to bed?"

"You want me to close my eyes when we…" He trailed off, thinking he hadn't heard her correctly, knowing that he had.

"Only the first time," she amended.

"Are you going to close yours?"

"If you like," she said. He told her she didn't have to. She said that it was only fair.

For a time, they both were silent. She said, "Your eyes are open."

"Now?" They opened further. She glanced around. He did too. She'd closed the door. The curtain covered the window. They were shrouded in the silence of an empty house. Tyler said, "Don't you want to wait for—" He swallowed the next word. He hadn't asked her father yet. He certainly hadn't asked her.

Her smile was sweet and vulnerable. "I want you to be sure of me."

"Beth," he said. "I'm sure." He saw in her eyes that she didn't believe him. He didn't know if he could prove it to her, but he'd try. He closed his eyes.

***

Jerrod and Holly traveled at a canter until the sun started to get hot then slowed the horses to a walk. Jerrod hadn't looked back at or said a word to her since they left the farm, so when Holly stopped it surprised her that he immediately circled round.

"What's the matter?"

"You tell me, Jerrod Kelly."

He reckoned she saw straight through him, knew he was seething. There was a defiant flash in her eyes he'd seen before, at The Wishing Well when she stormed out of her room after Trace.

Jerrod was about to see that wrath turned on him. He was past ready for it.

Holly held her head high, kept her spine rigid, and clenched her teeth to keep from trembling as Jerrod sidled his horse up to hers. He tipped his hat back, grabbed Holly, and planted a kiss on her, quick and hard.

The glove she wore took the sting out of the slap, but it was enough to startle the horses and have them dancing apart. Man and woman eyed one another from their respective saddles. Jerrod's pulse was loping. Holly could no longer conceal her shaking.

"What were you and Trace talking about?"

"That's no concern of yours."

"I say it is."

He swung his leg over his horse and dropped to the ground. He stalked toward her, noticing both woman and horse were nervous. When he was close enough, he took hold of the bridle and ran his hand down the animal's neck, soothing it. He made his tone likewise soothing, and Holly didn't know if it was for her sake or that of the horse.

"Do I frighten you?"

"Yes." She saw that it surprised him.

"Come down from there." Because it was more request than order, Holly dismounted. "I can't see your eyes. Take that off, please." She removed her bonnet.

"It's the way you are," she said. "I noticed it the first time."

"You remember the first time?"

She nodded. "You took your time with me, like it meant something."

"That frightened you?" She nodded. Jerrod thought about that. "Because of the way I make you feel." She nodded again.

Jerrod took her hands in each of his. "When you're picking out a dress for Aimee, why don't you choose one for yourself? I reckon if the preacher will come all this way to marry one couple, he'll marry two. I'm not going to make you wait," he said.

He thought she would be pleased at the notion of a double wedding. He thought she might chastise him for proposing wrong, for not saying the right things. He didn't expect her to cry, but she did. He had to hold her until she stopped. She nuzzled against his shoulder, and he kissed her wet face. When she calmed, he asked her proper, just to be clear.

***

Tyler closed his eyes and a velvet curtain fell between him and the world. A momentary deafness accompanied his blindness then he heard the whisper of clothing that told him Beth was undressing. His mouth went dry and his loins grew hot.

When his straining ears could catch naught but the chirping of crickets out the window, he realized she was done. He took off his boots, grimacing when he fumbled one and it knocked loudly against the floorboards. He stood and peeled the rest of his clothing, now damp, from his body. He felt more than a little lewd standing naked before a woman in the middle of the day, his cock jutting out into the open air.

"Are you certain you want to do this?" He had to ask.

"Aren't you?"

"Hold out your hand," he said. He reached out, found it, and guided her to his side.

They sat, and Tyler trapped himself between his thighs to prevent touching her before he—or she—was ready. He shifted, twisting toward her, and their knees bumped. He laid her hand upon his chest and she raised the other to rest beside it. With his fingertips, Tyler traced her skin from wrist to elbow, up to her shoulders. He discovered she'd let down her hair. He gathered it in his hands, followed the length of it down to the linens. His touch skimmed over her buttocks before slipping beneath the veil of hair and moving up her back, drawing her as close as he could with her arms still folded between them. Tyler felt her breath gust against his ear, turned his head and kissed her.

It was easier after that, almost natural, to keep his eyes shut and discover Beth with his remaining senses. He found scars and he found curves, places soft and sensitive. He let the sounds and feeling of her guide him as they inched further up the mattress.

Countless times, he whispered that she was beautiful, his voice full of awe and certainty, though he kept his eyes closed. Beth knew—she'd had to see him. When he was positioned over her, poised to enter her, he hesitated. She watched the struggle on his face.

Tyler knew he was where he needed to be. Beth's knees were drawn up to his sides. His hips were nestled between her thighs. The dewy warmth at the tip of his cock told him he was pointed straight for heaven. He couldn't move. It no longer felt right. But to pull back now might wound her. It would surely kill him.

"It's okay," she said. "You can open them."

Tyler took in her passion-rouged face, her soft eyes on his, her hair fanned out over his pillow. He placed a gentle kiss to her lips and with that same gentleness, made Beth his.

27

As he and Holly came within sight of Prospect, Jerrod's senses began to stir. Instincts that had been dormant, unneeded for weeks, awakened. He ran his thumb over the grip of his revolver and felt his fingers tingle in anticipation. For a moment, he wondered if he would miss that thrill, the ready power of a skill well-honed and deadly. But he had only to glance at Holly for the sensation to evaporate.

They drifted into town with the current of Main Street congestion, emerging from horse-drawn traffic in front of the dressmaker's shop. Jerrod hitched their horses and helped Holly dismount. He told her to take her time and waited until she was inside before he crossed the busy dirt corridor to where a man leaned against a post outside a gunsmith's store. Only the brim of his hat and the knee of one cocked leg were visible, but Jerrod had recognized him.

Silas waited for him to step up onto the boardwalk. He said, "I missed you that morning in Tucson, little brother."

Jerrod said, "I wanted no part of it."

"You stole away with the part you wanted." Silas pointed his chin back across the street.

Jerrod met green eyes so alike yet so different from his own. "She's nothing to you."

Silas tilted his head. "And what is she to you?"

"I aim to make her my wife."

Silas chuckled. "A woman like that, you pay for a ride, not buy the whole pony."

"For her, you wish you were a better man," said Jerrod.

Silas rolled his eyes and said, "Well, if you go to church now, you'll walk into one of Rook's secret meetings. Preacher's at The Mare anyhow. Come on, we'll toast your bride."

Inside the brothel, Jerrod spotted the pastor on a stool chatting with the old barkeep. The latter followed Silas's saunter from entrance to long mahogany counter before sighting beady eyes on Jerrod. He probably thought two Kelly brothers doubled the likelihood for trouble. It had been true enough before, but he still served them.

Jerrod said, "Rook's meeting, is it a mutiny?"

"He's disbanding the gang, hiring their guns to safeguard progress in Prospect."

"Creating a buffer between himself and Malloy," said Jerrod.

"He's got the men convinced I'm the Judas steer. And the politicians and mine owners convinced he's protecting their interests."

"How do you know all this?"

Silas grinned. "His investors go to the same watering holes and cat houses that I do. And whores talk. Rook would know if he ever had need of one." His grin faded and he said, "Our brother intends to have me killed."

"Horse feathers," said Jerrod.

"You know Rook. If he can't control a factor, he'll eliminate it." Silas said, "There are only two men who could match me."

"Did you think that's why I was here?"

"Rook would convince you it was a matter of honor," said Silas. "To Wyland, he'll offer something unattainable."

Jerrod knew Silas meant Aimee. He wondered if his brother was fishing for information regarding her and Josiah's whereabouts. He said, "What will you do?"

"Maybe I ought to follow your example." Silas looked at something over his shoulder. Jerrod turned to see a woman, obviously a prostitute, though her looks and costume reflected an elegance well-above The Mare's standards.

"She looks familiar," said Jerrod.

"Evelyn Deveraux, formerly of The Treasure Room," said Silas. "If Rook were really clever, he'd put a derringer in the hands of a desperate whore and let me find my own end. But I can be clever too." He raised his glass. "To each his own?"

As Jerrod watched Silas sift through the crowd toward Evelyn Deveraux, he reckoned it was farewell. He approached the pastor and offered to buy him a drink.

***

"A penny for your thoughts?" Josiah's gaze drifted to take in the rippling meadow all about them and the pure blue sky above, but Aimee's soft inquiry drew him back to her. They had removed their shoes to wade through the sandy shallows between river banks before stretching out in the long grasses mixed with wildflowers across from the farm. They lay facing one another, Aimee's bare feet resting on the tops of his.

Josiah said, "Seems I must have stole a day from another man's life to be here with you."

"It's your life," she said.

He settled a hand on her waist and swept his thumb downward. He asked if she was certain there was a baby inside her. She said that she was but he could undress her and make them both certain. Though Aimee blushed at her own suggestion, she watched him with an earnest glint in her eyes. Josiah stared at her a moment, dipped his head to conceal a smile, and was surprised when she raised her fingers to trace its curve.

He took her hand and kissed the scar on her thumb. When he closed his mouth around it, she gasped to feel his tongue against her skin. Josiah took his time, undressing her slowly, noting every subtle way she responded to his touch—how her eyes went to fog, her quietest sigh, how each reaction built upon those previous so that when long fingers at last slipped between pale thighs, he found her ready.

When he undressed, Aimee did the touching. Delicate fingers explored ridges of lean muscle, jutting bone, and every rough scar. She catalogued his responses as well, was fascinated with the bowed shape of his cock and the way it bobbed beneath her touch. When her hand closed around him, she watched his eyes go to blue flame.

For the first time in his life, Josiah Wyland made love to a woman. Aimee opened for him, took him into her, and never once looked away.

After, she dozed above him, her cheek to his chest and sun-heated hair spilling over his shoulder. Through his eyelids, Josiah saw sunflowers—dark orbs swaying against a brilliant orange backdrop.

Aimee awoke to Josiah's fingers stroking her ankle and Holly calling her name from across the Gila. She cuddled atop him, her knees bracketing his hips. His shirt draped over her back, a shield against sunburn, and sweat pooled between their bodies. They were still, already, joined. "It's our wedding day," she said.

***

Josiah and Aimee were married at sunset standing on the porch, with Holly and Jerrod beside them, and Tyler and Beth as witnesses. Meanwhile, Trace arrived in Phoenix.

He stopped first at the telegraph office where a message from the governor had been recorded for him that day. It read: *False report raid Canyon Diablo Kelly gang outbound Prospect opportune time claim office.* Trace left a request for additional news to be sent to his hotel. He stabled the weary pinto, got supper, and went to bed with plans to leave again at dawn.

It was still dark when he was awakened by knocking at his door. He stumbled out of bed, cursing when he tripped over his boots, and groped for the knob. In the hall stood an errand boy, looking as bedraggled and bleary-eyed as Trace. The youth held a candle in one hand and a telegram in the other. Squinting against the flame, Trace blinked the words into focus. They read: *Inbound Prospect pursuit Josiah Wyland Silas Kelly wanted dead backup.* Trace thanked the lad and when he was gone, stood in the dark room, rubbing a hand over the stubble on his face. Then he lunged for the bedside table, once more stumbling over his boots. He struck a match and searched the second telegram for the sender's name. It was from Del Cooper.

Seconds stretched into minutes as Trace struggled to decide which city—Phoenix or Tucson—was closer to Prospect. He reckoned the zealous old lawman would already be underway. Trace left as soon as he could dress and saddle his horse.

28

Two men, Malloy from the north and Cooper from the south, converged on Prospect as the clock struck noon. They rode into town as the first chime rang out, and as the last clang of the bell echoed from the tower, both heard gunshots. A wave of people fled the scene, cuing each man as to the epicenter of the violence.

Josiah Wyland came from the west, riding into the glare of the sun—now raised to its highest and most impartial position above the world, where it gave favor to no man whether righteous or wicked. He left his horse out behind the jailhouse and approached Main Street from between buildings. Opposite him, on the eastern boardwalk, stood a woman.

Evelyn Deveraux would be cited as a witness in Trace Malloy's report. She waited on Silas Kelly who was inside with his brother the sheriff.

Rook had received word earlier that morning that the men he hired out of the Kelly gang had all left town, drawn away by report of a raid planned on the bandit haven of Canyon Diablo, gone to save their stockpiles of loot. It hadn't taken Rook long to determine the false news forwarded from Flagstaff had originated in Prospect. From his desk, he studied its author leaning against the jail's front wall where wooden slats ended at the doorway, open to let in the light. Silas too was leaving. Rook said, "You lost me the one thing I wanted."

"Their loyalty is to themselves, but you had to have known that to exploit it. I only sped along the inevitable." Though Silas's posture was lackadaisical, Rook figured his hand was on his gun, between his body and the wall, where Rook couldn't see it. He gazed out across the street. "Your star was lost regardless," said Silas, knowing Rook would only see it that way, knowing men clung to what they couldn't keep, oblivious to the freedom exchanged.

"And now you'll abandon me," said Rook.

Silas finally looked at him then, his expression rueful. "I don't pretend to be any different than the rest of them."

"You're my brother," said Rook.

Silas straightened up from the wall and stepped even with the doorway. He said, "I already killed three people for you." He turned and walked out.

Rook got up from his desk and followed.

Josiah came around the corner as the two men moved into the street. Silas glanced over him then around at Rook, watching his brother take in the same critical detail: Wyland was without his guns.

In her account of the incident, Evelyn would say she saw Rook Kelly raise his revolver and aim at the back of his older brother as he crossed the street toward her. She screamed a warning, but Rook got off two shots in the time it took Silas to skin his six-shooter and face about. Rook's other bullets went wide as

Silas returned fire, shooting Rook through the knee and grazing his neck as they both fell. From the ground, Silas emptied his gun into his brother's torso. But there was one detail Evelyn had missed: after his first two shots, Rook's barrel swung toward Josiah.

Josiah approached as Silas's blood pooled in the dust. He reckoned by the way the fallen man was twisted at the waist with his hip in the air and his back to the street, a bullet had found his spine. Silas's hat lay between him and the woman rooted in shock. Only his finger through the trigger guard kept his pistol in hand. Josiah came to stand at the edge of the crimson puddle, the stub of his midday shadow shading the other man's face.

"Wyland." Silas wheezed wetly, drawing air into a punctured lung. "Is my brother dead?" Josiah looked from one Kelly to the other. Rook lay flat out. His white shirt was red below his ribcage. His chest still rose and fell. Josiah shook his head. Silas said, "I don't want him to suffer." He fumbled to draw a cartridge from its loop, giving up when his fingers wouldn't cooperate. "We were pals once, you and I," he said.

Josiah crouched down and plucked the cartridge from Silas's belt. He picked up the revolver. He emptied it as he walked, letting the shells fall.

Rook listened to the trudging gait accented by ringing spurs. Squinting against the glare and the pain, he watched Wyland chamber the round and lower the weapon to his side. The gunslinger drew back the hammer and said, "Your brother don't want you to suffer."

Rook lifted his head and looked back where Silas lay. He met dispassionate blue eyes and smiled. "Then I'll see you in hell."

Josiah shifted his arm and shot Rook through the head.

***

"Wyland!" Josiah whirled and brought the revolver up, thumbing the hammer as he aligned the barrel with his challenger who stood with pistol already pointed. It was a habitual series of motions ingrained over the years, once life-preserving but now made futile by the conscious thought that chased it—no other chambers were loaded. His finger squeezed the trigger out of reflex. He knew it would click empty. It already had countless times in his dream.

Del Cooper fired. Even as the air cracked with the explosion, Josiah felt the bullet impact his middle. It hit with no more force than a stone from a slingshot, but the searing heat spreading through his stomach brought him to his knees. He tossed the six-gun away, and Trace Malloy scooped it up.

Trace had left his horse, wanting to avoid trampling anyone in the crowd, and raced down the street afoot. He arrived in time to see Wyland crumple. He continued toward the gunfighter though Del barked at him to halt.

Wyland braced himself with one hand in the dirt, his head bowed, clutching his belly with his other hand. When Trace crouched beside him, Josiah looked askance at him and he saw the man's eyes were bright with pain, only a fraction of it physical. Trace opened the loading gate and shook the single spent cartridge out into the palm of his hand. Del approached and Trace held it out for him to see.

"Reload it," the old lawman said. When Josiah shook his head, Del said, "I'll have justice for my boy."

"Not without a trial," said Trace. Del gave him a disapproving look.

"We'll call it mercy then." He cocked his revolver.

Another man might beg for what Del offered—he'd faced men that had—but Josiah said, "I'd rather you saved your bullet, Cooper."

"That's a mortal wound, Wyland."

Josiah said, "Then you've got your justice." To Trace, he said, "I promised Aimee."

Trace nodded and stood. He held out his hand for the old judge's gun. Del handed it over and Trace went to get Wyland's horse. Del watched Josiah dig in the pocket of his jacket and pull out a battered tin box. He didn't open it but merely ran his thumb over the top before replacing it. Del said, "I wouldn't have thought you a man for honoring promises."

Josiah said, "I know what you think of me, Cooper."

As Trace led the black stallion toward them, Del watched the wounded man bring one foot beneath him and push to his feet. He heard Wyland tell Trace, "It'll keep." Del decided if any man could survive a gut-shot, it would be Wyland. There'd be no satisfaction for him if the devil lived. He said as much. Blue eyes turned toward him. Wyland said, "Tell you what, Cooper. If I'm alive tomorrow, I'll surrender to Malloy. But I want something from you." Wyland mounted his horse while Del waited to hear what the bastard had the gall to request.

Josiah said, "I didn't kill your son because of bad blood between you and me. Don't blame mine for the things I done."

***

287

Trace retrieved the sheriff's badge from Rook's body. Silas was dead. Tucked inside his hat, Trace found a tattered photograph, several years old, of Silas and Josiah. One was on the verge of a smirk, a look of boyish mischief in his eyes, his revolver held carelessly in his hand. The other had a shiny new pair of Peacemakers on his hips, fewer scars but guarded eyes. Trace confiscated the portrait, thinking Aimee might like to have it.

A newspaper man arrived on the scene. Trace told him he'd have to wait his turn to interview the witness. He led Miss Deveraux to the jailhouse and ensured she was comfortably seated. He left the bodies to await the coroner and Del Cooper to whatever ruminations accompany vengeance served. Walking beside the stallion, Trace escorted Josiah Wyland to the outskirts of Prospect as folk looked on and whispered.

****

Josiah made much of the journey slumped in the saddle, trusting the black stallion to remember the way. The spots before his eyes reminded him of the sunflowers in the meadow where he'd made love to Aimee.

When he caught their scent and felt the long grasses brush the hand hanging down near the belly of his horse, Josiah knew he was close to the river. When Aimee awoke the next morning, she'd find the tin in the window sill, a little dented, a little scratched, and on her pillow, a clutch of wildflowers, a little smooshed, a little wilted.

Sunset was fading to dusk and Josiah was conscious when he came within sight of the farmhouse. He knew Aimee was awaiting his return and that he'd kept his promise. He saw a speck of white in the corral and had a few moments of twilight to picture his wife barefoot with a halo of golden hair and to wonder about their unborn child.

Maybe he'll have his daddy's blue eyes…

THE END

MORGAN LEE WYLIE lives in Idaho with her husband, daughter, dogs, and horses. She and her husband are expecting their second child New Year's Day 2021.

To learn more about Morgan, her writing process, and current projects, please follow her on Instagram @morganleewylie.

To receive an email when Morgan's next book is released, please join her mailing list at https://morganleewylie.com/signup.

Special thanks to my husband for his unwavering support, to my mom for reading this story first, to family and friends who have been waiting to read it.

Did you enjoy this book?

Please leave a review.

ALSO BY MORGAN LEE WYLIE

Wanted

(A Standalone Sequel to Unscrupulous)

A lawman. A lady outlaw.
She keeps bringing him to a line he's sworn not to cross.